THE IMMIGRANT

A Young Man's Work Skills Spark His
Love Affair with America's Economy

PAUL BARLIN

iUniverse, Inc.
Bloomington

The Immigrant
A Young Man's Work Skills Spark His Love
Affair with America's Economy

Certain characters in this work are historical figures, and certain events portrayed
did take place. However, this is a work of fiction. All of the other characters, names,
and events as well as all places, incidents, organizations, and dialogue in this novel
are either the products of the author's imagination or are used fictitiously.

iUniverse books may be ordered through booksellers or by contacting:

iUniverse
1663 Liberty Drive
Bloomington, IN 47403
www.iuniverse.com
1-800-Authors (1-800-288-4677)

Because of the dynamic nature of the Internet, any Web addresses or links contained in this book
may have changed since publication and may no longer be valid. The views expressed in this work
are solely those of the author and do not necessarily reflect the views of the publisher, and the
publisher hereby disclaims any responsibility for them.

ISBN: 978-1-4502-7098-4 (pbk)
ISBN: 978-1-4502-7099-1 (cloth)
ISBN: 978-1-4502-7100-4 (ebk)

Library of Congress Control Number: 2010916052

Printed in the United States of America

iUniverse rev. date: 12/18/10

CHAPTER 1

1903

Hovering between sleep and wakefulness, fifteen-year-old Yussel Reinerman lay face down on his bare mattress in the steerage bowels of the ocean liner, *Voyager*. He thought he was still fighting for his life against Igor and Vanya, as of the night before when they discovered he was a Jew. It made his body twitch wildly and he kicked furiously at his would-be killers. He fought his way out of the house to run the icy streets and to hide between buildings whenever he saw the Czar's horse police. When he passed the turnoff to his father's hut guilt wracked him because there was no time to take the two other family survivors, his brother Moish and father Duvvid out of Russia with him. Yussel beat a fist on the bare mattress in time with the growls of the ship's loud motor. "Moish, Papa," he mumbled in Yiddish, "I'll send this *golem* (savior) for you. I will ... I will ... " The blows of his fist on the mattress grew weaker. Exhausted, he slept.

Uprooted from all he knew, the skinny kid Yussel headed for the unknown world of America without money or a change of clothing. Sometime during the night the turbulence of his escape woke him as he tried to remember whom he was supposed to contact when he arrived in America. Back in Riga, in the windswept warehouse of the Office of Hebrew Charities, the woman wrapped in the fur coat sitting at the interview table told him to look for the ... the ... Society ... the Hebrew Immigrant Aid Society when he landed. Mumbling the name repeatedly he relaxed down to his mattress, the turmoil of his last hours in Russia still clawing at him. *If I hadn't fought like a crazy one, I would have burned alive in Yarinevitch's house.* Slipping on the icy streets, exhausted, frozen, he had made it to the OHC's warehouse and finally the ship . . .

In steerage's crowded family section, adjacent to the single men's area, the sobs and wails of crying children threatened to unglue the pains and fears of the adults, which they repressed to maintain sanity. Day one of fleeing all that was familiar ruptured their eating routines. Inadequate bathroom facilities impeded their ability to wash properly, and painfully delayed their relieving themselves. By days three and four the steerage occupants had been depressed into a sense of being more concerned with animal functions than human.

During day three the inevitable seasickness grabbed Yussel's gut. After that he rarely had the strength to get up and sit at the long wooden table bolted to the floor in his section of steerage and eat some of the food that was served. The waiters, knowing that there would be no tips from steerage travelers, did little more than put a dish of food on the table and remove it when the passenger had had enough and left the table for his bunk, less work for the waiter if seasickness kept many from the table. Yussel forced himself to sit at the table occasionally because he knew that he had to stay alive. Spending the time mostly on his bunk, the light display coming through the porthole, morning bright and fading into night told him of days passing.

By the 14th day, when a view of the Statue of Liberty was rumored, those who were still able, grabbed what few garments they had available for warmth, and hurried out into the cold to look, to see, to try to believe the promise that their lives would finally be different.

Yussel Reinerman, still unable to keep food down, weak, thinner than usual, and stinking from recurrent seasickness, lay on his bunk and ignored the excitement that was erupting around him as the ship hove into sight of the statue on Bedloe's Island in New York harbor. If he had had the strength to listen, he would have heard the electricity the event sparked in the voices of passengers in steerage. Word of the renowned icon raced down the Voyager from first class, to second, to third, to the Russian-Jewish escapees in steerage. Many on all the decks were sea sick, but the news excited most enough to overcome weakness and dare the cold outside. The ambulatory steerage passengers jammed the exits to the deck and crowded against the ship's rails to get their inaugural look at the fabled statue, its promise of a reincarnated life, evidence that they had really left their fears behind. It also signaled the end of the fourteen-day pitch and toss of the ship, the incessant day and night rumbling of the engines, and the icy winds that had imprisoned them indoors in a stench-gagging captivity.

During the two-week voyage, they felt hung in a powerless limbo that dragged them to the cliff edge of hysteria.

Yussel and a scattered few remained in their bunks in the bowels of the ship. The squealing, groaning floor timbers under the steel plate that covered the steerage floor for easy hosing off, had been their musical accompaniment for 14 days. Even when the others in steerage returned from viewing the statue to collect their belongings, so carefully chosen to carry into the new life, Yussel lay there hoping to gather strength for whatever would come.

A new, louder rumbling disturbed him. After the ship passed the Statue of Liberty and approached the Hudson River harbor, the Captain reversed the engines to slow the Voyager's speed. The noise and tremors built to a frightening intensity as the reversed propeller screws churned the water to slow the huge ship's tonnage. Then suddenly, the engines were cut. Silence. Even the floor timbers were quiet. Gently the Voyager nudged the dock pilings of the New York port. The crew threw ropes to dock hands who moored the Voyager securely to capstans on the dock at the bow and stern. The rattle of chains and banging of lowered gangplanks told Yussel no matter how he felt, he had to get up and find someone to tell him what to do, where to go. He knew only that the woman in the Office of Hebrew Charities had said that when he landed to look for … who …? Lost again in nowhere he knew, he felt rudderless and panic grabbed his gut.

Crewmembers roamed each deck telling everyone in four languages to disembark. People, bundled with their belongings and their children, flowed down the gangplanks and were moved along to the far end of the dock, where ferries waited to take them across for the short trip to Ellis Island. The ferries were motorized barges without walls to keep out the cold, only a railing to prevent their falling overboard. Yussel was glad for the standing immigrants packed around him, because they provided partial protection from the wind, and reminded him of the relief he felt as he left the warehouse in Riga standing in the wagon, and being taken to the Baltic seaport outside the city, where, finally, the Czar's police could no longer touch him. The barge to Ellis Island, yet another step further removing him from the Russian horrors, gave him the strength to stand with the others.

On the short trip to Ellis Island Yussel huddled down as far as the crush of people permitted. Shivering, weakened from malnutrition, he felt glad again to be surrounded by people and their bundles protecting him from the worst of the weather.

At the Ellis Island dock, he moved mechanically with the crowd into the large receiving hall. Those who knew where they were going and expected friends or relatives to receive them queued at the health inspection stations. Yussel and others who had no contacts in America, waited in the crowded hall. He fought the fog in his head to remember the rushed instructions he'd received in the Riga warehouse . . . Somebody . . . the Hebrew . . . Society . . .? He desperately questioned his fatigued brain but his fractured memory could make little sense of the scattered pieces.

Hardly able to stand, Yussel looked around for somewhere to sit, but there were no benches. He thought of moving over to the side and sliding his back down a supporting wall to rest his weakened body on the floor but he feared being trampled by the emotional crowd.

A large banner on the wall caught his eye, HEBREW IMMIGRANT AID SOCIETY. *Yes, yes,* he thought, *that's it.* Suddenly he felt that someone was there to help him. He was no longer alone, no longer lost. His feeling of being reconnected stirred enough adrenalin for him to work his way through the churning crowd toward the sign.

Directly under the sign, stood a tall man with earlocks, a wide-brimmed black hat and black coat. He stretched one arm high to wave white papers above the heads milling around him and called in Yiddish, "HIAS, HIAS, Hebrew Immigrant Aid Society, over here."

So good to see the black hat and earlocks, Yussel thought gratefully. In Russia, when he had to masquerade as a Christian to be accepted as an apprentice shoemaker, he had cut off his earlocks, isolated himself from his family for two years, negated his culture, his God, in order to learn his trade. His guise discovered, his life threatened, he'd been on the run all night until the ship sailed in the late morning. Now, the black hat and earlocks of the Orthodox Jew told Yussel he was no longer alone. *A Fromme Yid* (a religious Jew) *in America calls me. There are Believing Jews in America and I won't have to hide. I won't have to hide* tumbled repeatedly through his excited mind.

He even tried to imagine how different his life would be in America. HIAS, his safety net called and reached out for him. He could now say without fear that he was a Jew. It gladdened him so to be restored to his own.

For his beacon, Yussel's eyes latched on to the face in the trim black beard and earlocks under the stiff, black hat as he worked his way through the laughing, crying crowd. As he drew closer to his immediate savior he panted, "Reinerman, Yussel Reinerman, Reinerman, Yussel Reinerman."

Gladly he touched the man's arm, held it to support his weakened frame and also to again feel connected to his own.

It seemed impossible for Yussel to comprehend that only fourteen days ago, his Christian masquerade was exposed, his interrupted apprenticeship ended in madly fighting off death and fleeing in a desperate run for safety. He felt he hadn't stopped running until he lay on his steerage bunk, with all his pains and fears bottled inside him when the ship's engines suddenly growled to life under him. Now, only at this moment, holding the arm of an Orthodox man in America, did he finally feel removed from the Russian madness.

The man saw Yussel's condition and let his arm be used for support while he searched his list. "Yes," he affirmed, "Yussel." He turned and called out in Yiddish above the noise to another man in the traditional black hat and earlocks. "Yockov, this is Reinerman. Take him to the others."

Yockov worked his way to Yussel's side, took his arm and brought him to a long line of men being checked for health. At the front of the line, a man in a wool cap, with a HIAS tag hanging from his thick cloth jacket, was helping the customs agent by translating his questions into Yiddish, and the answers of the immigrants into English.

"Name?"

"Yussel Reinerman."

"From where?'

"Tchernivakh."

The HIAS interpreter grimaced, questioning. He had never heard of it. "What city is it near?" he asked Yussel.

"Riga." Answered Yussel.

"Russia," said the HIAS man to the customs agent.

"You have relatives here?"

Yussel felt a spasm of fear. He had no one here but then he remembered. He pointed to the tag hanging on the man's coat.

The man spoke for Yussel. "He's under the HIAS arrangement."

Yussel might have been the one hundred thousandth Jew to immigrate under the HIAS' care. HIAS was known to the customs force.

Finally through customs, Yussel and as many men who could fit into the wondrous electric trolley rode off to the Turkish baths. When the escapees had washed the Czarist Empire out of their hair and from their bodies, they were given a change of clothes, and assigned to a room subsidized by HIAS for a month.

Yussel's room was with the Zofia Wolansky family on Manhattan's Lower East Side. When he arrived, Mrs.Wolansky saw his condition and she fed him before letting him collapse on the bed in his room.

CHAPTER 2

Like all European Jews, the young girl Zofia Pietarski lived through the anti-Semitic horrors of Christian Europe. In 1890 during a Polish pogrom, her father, Thador was killed. As soon as it was safe to come out of hiding, his widow Carola, daughter Zofia, 13, and her sister Gretya, 11, scrambled to find the Office of Hebrew Charities to join the stream of Jews fleeing to Baltic ports to emigrate to America. On the fourth day of the crossing in the almost airless, stinking steerage, Zofia's mother developed pneumonia and died, leaving the orphaned sisters to be sheltered in the hands of the International Red Cross.

When they landed at Ellis Island, the girls were turned over to HIAS. HIAS volunteer women took them through customs, steam bathed the girls, clothed and boarded them in an overcrowded tenement. Five adolescent girls shared one room. In the summer heat, Zofia felt she was back in steerage, and not everyone on her floor of the tenement was careful when they used the one toilet.

Under the care of HIAS, orphans Zofia and Gretya also attended the Columbia Religious and Industrial School for Jewish Girls where they were taught and/or reminded to observe Jewish holidays the year round. They were also taught machine sewing and tailoring in the hope that they would eventually support themselves. When schooling was completed each girl made her own graduation dress.

Attending the Jewish school also protected the girls from the Catholic missionaries who were ever on the lookout for orphan girls in the area to win as converts. Both the church and the synagogue had their own reasons to care for needy girls other than providing for their humanitarian needs.

Zofia managed to finish high school. Her graduation diploma in her hands fired an ambition to apply herself to some promising project, something more rewarding than just being a housewife.

At the highly supervised social dances that HIAS provided, Zofia met handsome Jokob Wolansky. She thought that his grocery store might be just the project for her and he was good looking, too.

In Poland, secondary school, college, professions and industrial trades denied to Jews, they had to be resourceful to find a way to make a living. But seventeen-year-old Jokob Wolansky's full-time interest in the pleasures of adolescence had done little toward promoting his abilities to support himself and eventually, a family. What little money he earned for a day's work he spent at the local bar with his friends. He continued to live at his parents' house and seldom expressed any concern that his life would ever be different. His mother worried that her son Jokob was well on the road to nowhere.

She expressed her concern to her brother Wochak Yurins, a successful businessman, who was about to make an exploratory trip to America with the thought of living there. Like all Jews, Wochak resented being forced to live in a ghetto in Poland. He had a weak heart and had decided to never marry. To help his nephew develop a career Wochak felt could be his legacy to his family.

Uncle Wochak offered to take Jokob with him to New York City. Wochak promised his sister that he would set her son's feet on a useful path. "I will make him my junior partner in a business and put him on a strict budget. He will learn to enjoy it and take pride in supporting himself."

Seventeen-year-old Jokob, well aware that anything had to be better than living under the suffocating anti-Semitic restrictions of Polish law, and having all expenses paid by his generous uncle agreed to go.

When they arrived in New York on Manhattan's Lower East Side, Uncle Wochak consulted with Dershinsky's Real Estate.

Hearing that Wochak and Jokob were interested in making their home in America, Dershinsky agreed to give them a tour of the entire Jewish quarter. He invited Yurins and Jokob to join him in his horse and buggy.

The close-packed stores of the large Jewish area of Manhattan's Lower East Side seemed festooned with Yiddish and English signs in their windows. The noisy bustle of people on the sidewalks and streets impressed the would-be immigrants. The apparent freedom the Jews had to enjoy their own cultural, religious and industrial life captivated the would-be settlers. The busy bustling of the people over such a large area excited Jokob to burst out, "Like a whole city of Jews."

Uncle Wochak smiled, glad for the effect it was having on his nephew.

However, they were appalled by the poorer sections of the quarter where dark, elemental, wooden buildings were stuffed to bursting with 75 to 80 adults and children. They were without indoor plumbing and dependent on two faucets in the dark, narrow alley for all cooking, washing and bathing chores. Most shocking to Wochak and Jokob were the poorly serviced outhouses for that many inhabitants. The city authorities seemed ignorant of the need for sanitation.

Wochak gestured toward the shocking scene and abominable smell. "Hasn't anybody in New York heard of Louis Pasteur? Pasteur discovered this is what causes diseases." Pasteur's research that showed the indisputable connection between microbes and disease had caused dramatic changes throughout the literate world, but apparently not here.

Embarrassed for his city, Dershinsky stammered. "Well ... it takes a little time ... to ... to catch up with the science. Pasteur made his discoveries only twenty or twenty-five years ago."

Dershinsky went on to say that these holdover buildings were scheduled to be torn down. He further explained that the Building Laws of 1860 and 1879 had been passed to update those unsavory tenement conditions, but builders had been reluctant to give up their substantial profits gleaned from building only the minimally necessary basic structure, and doing it as cheaply as they could get away with. Dershinsky suggested that they probably paid off the housing inspectors.

However, the deplorable conditions had caused enough outrage and outcries among the people living in and near these neighborhoods, so that the shamed city government put the necessary teeth into the new Building Law of 1901. The law mandated the higher building standards and detailed punishments to non-complying builders.

The tenements built since then were dramatically updated. Dershinsky showed Wochak and Jokob one of the newest six-story tenements that included indoor flush toilets, one in the hall on each floor for two apartments, hot and cold running water in every kitchen and bathroom, and one window in every room available to sunlight and outside ventilation. On the street level the builder had constructed the space for retail stores. The three sided tenement was built around a courtyard which provided an area for wash lines and sunlight for the now-required window in every room of the inside apartments. Rooms of the outside apartments automatically had their windows available to sunlight and ventilation.

After his wide search of the Lower East Side, the improvements in one of the newest buildings impressed Wochak, and he thought that the street level store immediately underneath had real economic possibilities for him and Jokob. The many families living in the six stories should find the store convenient shopping.

Wochak bought the grocery store stocked as is and put a large deposit on a first floor front apartment directly above it; monthly rent for the apartment, fifteen dollars, and for the store, twelve dollars. He was doubly pleased that his weak heart would only have to carry him one flight from his store to his home.

Wochak and his nephew settled into their first- floor apartment. Having purchased the functioning grocery store below as is, three-quarters of the items he wanted to stock were already in place. While they were opening boxes of additional items, Wochak reminded his nephew, "All this will be yours when I'm gone, Jokob."

Jokob realized that he could amass a sizeable nest egg. It gave him a new incentive to apply himself to the success of the store.

Having read about Pasteur's invaluable medical discoveries, Wochak remembered that it included the benefits of pasteurized milk. Wochak wanted to make it available to his customers. He had a large icebox built against one wall with an upper steel shelf that held up to six twenty-five pound blocks of ice. The icebox could refrigerate two 15-gallon cans of milk and about a dozen wheels of a variety of cheeses.

One week before Wochak felt they were ready to open the door, he began to train Jokob to the inventory. After walking Jokob through an item-by-item tour of the store's inventory, Wochak stood behind the counter and called out the item, requiring Jokob to fetch it. The simple memory challenges had them both laughing when Jokob started in one direction, but then stopped and reversed himself. Clever Wochak had further excited his nephew's interest and cooperation through a game.

Under the large painted sign, "Yurins' Grocery" across the top of the store window, a streamer sign below announced the opening date. A separate, permanent sign printed on the plate glass front emphasized "Fresh Pasteurized Milk Daily." Wochak's innovations and attention to detail created interest throughout the neighborhood and the store opened successfully.

Jokob felt good that he too, held up his part well. Before closing for the day, Jokob opened a bottle of schnappes. He took the first swig, a long one.

Uncle Wochak was surprised at the ease with which his nephew drank so much.

After his two large mouthfuls Jokob raised the bottle in celebration. "To our store." He wiped it off with his apron and offered it to his uncle.

Wochak smiled and held up the bottle. "To our store," and swallowed a short one.

CHAPTER 3

Uncle Wochak's weak heart lasted only three more years. After the funeral, Jokob, almost twenty-one, realized that not only was he the sole owner of the store, but there was no longer an adult who questioned his actions or what he did with his leisure time. Jokob no longer had to answer to "Are you thinking seriously about the girl you're dating?" Or "What happened to the two bottles of schnappes from the kitchen cabinet?"

Jokob enjoyed his sudden freedom.

At the next HIAS Social Dance Jokob saw Zofia Pietarski for the second time. At a previous dance the perky, bubbling Zofia had come late with her group of girls and there was too little time to get to know her. This time he asked her to dance early in the evening. She accepted.

Knowing something about clothing materials Zofia thought Wochak wore an expensive suit. She probed to find out what he did for a living and learned that he owned a grocery store.

"You have a partner in the store?" Zofia asked.

"No," he answered, "I just have a clerk, Grigor"

While they danced, holding the energetic Zofia excited Jokob. He knew he didn't want to wait a month for the next dance before seeing her again. He invited her to have dinner with him. She agreed and they left the dance early.

After dinner at Sam Haas' restaurant Jokob suggested a tour of his grocery store. They boarded a trolley and got off at Essex Street. On the corner, on the large glass front of the store Jokob had had it newly repainted in Yiddish and English as "Wolansky's Grocery." Inside the store, Jocob was especially proud of his large icebox from which he sold pasteurized milk. From the store, it was only one flight up to show her his apartment.

Zofia knew what he had in mind and she decided on a strategy; half way only, and she firmly stayed with it.

On their following dates, despite Jokob's eagerness for on-the-spot lovemaking, Zofia held out until he finally agreed to give her the ring. The accoutrements of marriage followed.

Once wed, Zofia delighted in implanting herself into the routines of the store. Strong-minded, she unleashed her business sense and perhaps made Jokob feel somewhat unnecessary. She seemed to be giving the orders. Jokob felt that he was working for Zofia rather than the other way round.

Perhaps it was Jokob's lesser role that aggravated his alcohol habit. No longer a secret from Zofia, he kept an opened bottle handy in the store. Already pregnant, Zofia worried about Jokob handling the store alone when she had to deliver the baby.

But problems happened much earlier. In her fourth month she stained. Zofia worried that she could lose the baby. But she continued to carry on in the store. Her bleeding increased.

Dr. Smilowitz ordered her to bed.

Zofia explained that she couldn't leave her husband alone in the store.

Smilowitz shook his head sympathetically. He spoke gently. "Zofia, only you can decide. Save the baby or save the store."

Zofia chose to save the baby and went to bed. She tried to forget that Jokob was drinking, probably insulting the customers and forgetting to handle the necessary details; to open promptly at six a.m. so tenants could run down and buy their breakfast specialties, checking item inventories, reordering the fast-moving ones, and paying the bills on time.

During Zofia's difficult pregnancy, Jokob stubbornly argued that he was able to handle the work alone. Despite her arguments with him he hired no one. Dissatisfied customers shopped elsewhere and the store fell into serious debt.

When Zofia's agonies were over, she had a baby boy, a tenement apartment two months behind in the rent, a divorce, and the store was sold away at auction. Zofia's anxious face and tearful eyes looked ahead and saw herself living alone and supporting herself and the baby.

Zofia decided she had had enough with her adolescent urgencies of marriage, sex, and babies. Her flint-and-steel realism penetrated what remained of her lowered hormonal fog to look at her most immediate possibilities for making a living. She contacted HIAS and offered the extra three tiny bedrooms in her large apartment for immigrant boarders for the minimum monthly fee.

HIAS, always needing more space for their immigrants flooding to America gladly signed her up for her increased services.

Zofia sighed in relief. She had achieved an arrangement for her survival. *And who knows*, she thought, *maybe one of the greenhorns will be worth a second look.*

Ambitious, she wondered how she could expand her arrangement with her boarders. Under the HIAS contract she was responsible for the boarder's room and breakfast for their first month in America. But who can live on one meal a day? For another small charge her boarders could have lunch and/or supper in her kitchen.

By added nickels and dimes Mrs. Wolansky built up her income. And since she was also a milliner, she could either do the same stitching over and over for ten hours in a factory or she could find individual customers who could afford a dress, a suit or a coat styled especially for them. When her son, Shmuel grew old enough to guide immigrants around the area, HIAS agreed to pay her extra for her boy's services.

CHAPTER 4

When Yussel woke two days later in his new country, he was safely among Jews, and his Yiddish tongue was the lingua franca for that part of America, that part of New York City. It would be a familiar world to Yussel, but so much bigger than the enclosed Jewish ghetto in Riga. "Like a whole Jewish city," he would say repeatedly as he was being shown how to find his way.

His landlady, Mrs. Wolansky, was from Szcezcin, a western region of Poland. On first hearing her speak, her dialect of Yiddish confused Yussel. He worried. *Is it another language?* Her tight-lipped Polish dialect of Yiddish, spoken in bursts, reverberated in Yussel's Russian ears as intermittent squeals. Added to that, her short thin body was apparently equipped with more cylinders than others, which powered her to think and move in sudden spurts like a hungry bird darting for a breakfast before another got it.

But, adept at adapting, as poor people are, Yussel soon understood that breakfast would be at six-thirty, that the toilet in the hall was for the two families on the floor, and would he please be careful when he used it.

Neither stipulation was a problem. The toilet even flushed when Yussel pulled the wooden handle of the hanging chain, like Uncle Herschel's in Riga. Any flush toilet was a luxury to Yussel. For his first thirteen years he had shared an outhouse with the four other members of his family on a quarter-acre farm outside Tchernivakh.

Dressed and breakfast eaten, Mrs. Wolansky handed him a slip of paper. "This is my address on Essex Street. Put it in your pocket and keep it safe. If you get lost, show it to someone. They'll tell you how to get home. And here's five nickels, that's twenty-five cents. She held up a single coin as she explained. If you have to take the trolley later, it costs five cents, one nickel. Put the money in your pocket and don't lose it." She broke off suddenly, raised her head and called, "SHMU-EL!" And again to Yussel, "My son Shmuel will walk you to the local HIAS office on Eldridge Street."

Ten-year old Shmuel was Yussel's tour guide as they set out on Essex Street toward Delancey. The drone of sounds ahead grew louder and more insistent. Looking, Yussel thought he was seeing tables with goods spread on them. "Is this market day?" he asked Shmuel.

Shmuel laughed. "It's always market day." He added, " Every day is market day on Delancey and Allen. You can buy anything you want any time."

The 'tables' turned into pushcarts as they approached, some standing on two wheels and two sticks, some on four wheels for easier rolling. Those that sold produce or clothing had a tall frame built on the cart to support an oiled cloth cover that shielded the goods from the rain and hot sun.

Shmuel led the way through the lines of shoppers to the intersection where Essex crossed Delancey. Pushcarts on both sides of the street were packed solid on all four corners. Peddlers hawked their wares of food, pots, clothes, tools, anything a shopper might need. On some uprights, panties and brassieres, shirts and long johns swung in the breeze and cooking pots dangled from hooks.

Shmuel turned right on Delancey to pick their way past people going every which way in a steady clamor of noise and movement. "This happens every day?" asked Yussel.

"Every day," affirmed Shmuel, "except *Shabbas* (Sabbath) is not so busy."

Understanding about the holy day of the week, Yussel nodded.

Their progress was slowed by Yussel trying to take in everything with his eyes and his silent marveling at so many things, *so many things*. He couldn't help comparing it with the one-day-a-week market in Tchernivakh, where he and his mother, may she rest in peace, sold the cabbages he had grown for her.

They crossed Ludlow Street. Approaching Alan Street, the noises were louder and steadier. In the middle of the intersection of Delancey and Allen, Yussel stopped and looked to the north, which was teeming with pushcarts on both sides, and people milling between them as far as he could see. He turned and looked toward the south. Solid again, and an equal hubbub rising.

Staying in the center of the street, they walked with those going their way, crossed the intersection and left Allen Street behind. Yussel shook his head in disbelief at the size of it. He stopped to turn and look again, to see the crowds and pushcarts in every direction. *Like a whole Jewish city, a whole city of Jews.* He hurried after Shmuel to Eldridge Street, where they turned right.

After a moment Shmuel stopped and looked up.

Yussel looked up. They were standing under a flagpole from which hung a large white cloth printed in bright blue letters that read, HEBREW IMMIGRANT AID SOCIETY. Shmuel pulled the street-level door open and motioned Yussel in.

Immediately on Yussel's right, a low babble of voices drew him in to a large lighted room. Men and women, some holding babies, dressed in clothing that looked 'just off the boat', sat on a double row of chairs around the edges leaving a small oval space in the center of the room for people to step forward to the large desk in an alcove that faced the door. On the wall immediately left of the alcove, a large sign above a smaller desk, in Russian, German, Yiddish, and English read PLEASE REGISTER HERE.

Shmuel motioned Yussel to stand in the line leading to the desk. Yussel walked slowly forward to make the seventh person in the queue. A baby's sudden cry spiked through the hum of voices, followed by the mother's embarrassed, "*Shah, kindt, shah.*" The close air smelled of unwashed clothes and salami and pickles, which reminded Yussel he had no idea where he would eat lunch, or if Shmuel would still wait for him. He wondered too, how will I get home? He reached in his jacket pocket for the comforting feel of the piece of paper on which Mrs. Wolansky had written her address, and in his other pocket for the five nickels.

In Yiddish, the woman at the desk asked Yussel his name then located 'Reinerman' on the HIAS list. "What kind of work can you do?"

"I'm a shoemaker."

"You repair shoes?"

"Repair? No, I make the shoe. I measure the foot, cut the leather, stitch the upper--"

She raised her hand to stop him. "I understand, I understand." She checked her Workers Wanted list. "Lefkowitz and Son is looking for shoe workers," she said. On a short piece of HIAS letterhead paper, she wrote Lefkowitz's name and address and handed it to Yussel. "Give this to Lefkowitz so he'll know HIAS sent you."

Yussel took the paper and tried to understand it, but he had no idea if it was next door or five miles away. He frowned over it.

The woman saw his confusion. "You're at Mrs. Wolansky's?"

"Yes."

"Shmuel will take you on the trolley."

"Trolley?"

"Did Shmuel bring you here?"

"Yes."

"He'll show you the trolley." She pointed to the paper Yussel was holding. "Don't lose that. It's Lefkowitz's address. You'll take the Eldridge Street trolley to Canal Street. Shmuel will show you."

Yussel tried to digest, 'trolley'. At Ellis Island he'd been too worn to remember his first ride on one.

Shmuel was sitting in one of the chairs waiting. Yussel handed him the paper with Lefkowitz's address.

The elder Lefkowitz himself opened the door. He was a tall man. His height carried his bulk well. A blue shop apron from neck to knees helped further to make a simple monolith of his mounds of flesh. The small, circular piece of shiny black satin pinned atop his brown bushy curls floated like a child's toy on a wild ocean. But it was enough of a head covering to satisfy Lefkowitz's Orthodox obedience to God. He had surprising blue eyes and small fat features of a cherub's face, but not the good humor to go with it.

Behind Lefkowitz, Yussel heard the short drones and sudden stops of stitching machines. With each stop he imagined the operator turning the pieces of leather sharply to follow the designed angle. He discounted the dust in the air of the shop to relish the smell of tanned leather that enveloped him. He was in his world again.

Lefkowitz took the HIAS letterhead paper that Yussel handed him. "Can you stitch the vamp?"

"I can draw the pattern, cut the leather, stitch the vamp, nail the sole-"

"I only stitch the vamp. I'm not a shoemaker. I'm a sub-contractor for stitching leather."

"I can do it."

"Piece work only. When there's enough work we all make a living. When there's not enough work you stay home. Right now I've got plenty of work." He pointed to Shmuel who had remained just inside the door. "That's your brother?"

"No, a friend. He showed me how to come here."

"You just came over?"

"Three days," Yussel said, smiling, expecting another HIAS welcome by a fellow Orthodox immigrant.

Instead Lefkowitz took a finished sample of the day out of his apron pocket and showed it to Yussel. "Can you stitch this?"

Yussel quickly estimated that it would take four runs of the machine to stitch one vamp. "Sure."

"This order is for three-hundred and fifty pair. Ten cents a pair, left and right, four pair an hour, next week you'll be a wealthy man."

Confused by the sarcasm Lefkowitz loaded into his dissertation of Yussel's instant wealth in the *Goldene Medina* (Golden homeland) Yussel's lips parted in an uncertain smile. He was impatient to get to the machine to show what he could do.

"Can you start now? We work until six."

"Sure."

Yussel turned to Shmuel and explained that he was staying to work.

Shmuel reminded Yussel how to get to the trolley and left.

CHAPTER 5

1905

Yussel first become unhappy with Lefkowitz when he realized the boss was giving his son Marcus the easier work and Yussel the harder work, and still paying Yussel only ten cents a pair. Yussel set a time limit for how long he would work for Lefkowitz. His deadline would be when he felt that he had learned enough to set up a shop of his own. Secretly Yussel developed a list of shoe manufacturer's who gave work to Lefkowitz during their rush seasons so he could contact them later on.

Compiling the list, Yussel became aware of the different nationalities in the industry. The companies that were giving vamp-stitching work to Lefkowitz were named for their Italian, Greek, Jewish and Irish manufacturers.

Strongly as Yussel felt that he wanted his own shop it made him uneasy to think of going out into that mixed world to get his own orders, as he knew he would have to do when he left Lefkowitz. So far he was comfortable only when talking Yiddish. He dreaded having to put his thoughts into English. That's why he loved living on Manhattan's Lower East Side. He would often think in self-assurance, *it's like a whole city of Jews.*

Riding home from work on the trolley that evening he already imagined telling Mrs. Wolansky at supper about his plans.

After the meal Mrs. Wolansky and Yussel stirred sugar into their tea. Yussel spoke in Yiddish to Mrs. Wolansky, the way they usually conversed. "I'm thinking of leaving Lekowitz."

Zofia stopped stirring. "You're leaving Lefkowitz?"

Her son, twelve-year-old Samuel was on a kick to get the Yiddish accent out of his speech so he would stop feeling strange with the gentile boys and girls of Manhattan Elementary School. He wanted his mother to speak English to him and to use his English name and not call him *Schmuel.*

Since he knew his mother and Yussel would talk in Yiddish and he hadn't developed the tea-drinking habit, Sam left the table to wander the pantry area of the kitchen to look for cookies or leftover cake. Seeing nothing to his liking he went to the icebox and opened it.

"Take en epple, Semuel," Zofia called to him in her accented English.

"Yeah, Ma." He chose one and went to his room.

Mrs. Wolansky and Yussel relaxed into their conversational Yiddish.

"You're thinking of leaving Lefkowitz?" Mrs. Wolansky repeated.

Yussel nodded vigorously. "Yes, I think I can do better on my own."

Zofia nodded and smiled approvingly at Yussel's ambition. But she was skeptical. She remembered what it took to run the grocery store with her ex-husband, which failed because he didn't pay attention to the many details. But about Yussel she thought, *Yes he's different, ambitious, but so young. Will he know how to go about it? Running a business is not simple.* Zofia spoke gently to the eighteen-year-old youngster. "Who will send you work—?"

"My work is good," Yussel interrupted heatedly. "I'll show them samples like they've never seen."

Yet when he thought of talking to the factory owners, his inadequacy with English language skills humbled him. "The only thing is," he said more quietly, "I don't talk American that good."

"Maybe you should go to night school. The Henry Street Settlement, and the Neighborhood Settlement have classes every evening."

Looking down at his glass of tea Yussel shook his head. "Who has time?"

"You want to learn English, Yussel? You make time."

He looked up at Mrs. Wolansky with mixed feelings. He liked her telling him what to do, and then he didn't. After a moment he said, "You think--"

Her nod interrupted him. "How else will you learn?"

Yussel's fifteen years under the Czar's anti-Semitic terror had hardened a layer of fear in him that would never leave. Yussel needed the comforting familiarity of things Jewish. The thought of taking a class in English made him fearful that he would be leaving what he knew. His "Who has time?" had more in it than not enough hours in the day.

Mrs. Wolansky startled Yussel by saying, "I did it."

He looked at her. "You did what? You took the classes?"

She nodded. "When Shmuel—I mean Samuel--said he wanted me to talk American to him … " She shrugged, gestured with her hands and finished in English. "I t'ought, v'at cen it hoit?"

Yussel, still undecided about leaving his Yiddish, and hesitant about turning his thoughts and his feelings over to another language, yet he tried joining Mrs. Wolansky in English. "Maybe," he said. "I'll t'ink about it."

On the trolley the next day after work Yussel looked forward to sitting at the table with Mrs. Wolansky and Sam. *A kid brother, like sitting at the table with Moish and Avram.* It was as close to feeling like a family as Yussel might have found in his new country. In this warm friendship with Mrs. Wolansky of three years Yussel had slowly shed his terrors of Russia's Holy Host and the Black Hundred. Yet he was unaware of how much Mrs. Wolansky's ambience had enfolded him.

Yussel's appearance changed. His regular eating schedule filled out his skinny frame. And he never turned down an extra *nosh* (sweet) that his landlady offered him. His Jewish surroundings relaxed him from much of his Russian angst. He was beginning to look settled and mature beyond his eighteen years.

Spending some part of every day with Yussel for three years had affected Mrs. Wolansky as well. Wanting to plan tasty meals for him she grew to know his favorites and she enjoyed surprising him. She had begun to look forward to his asking questions about her experiences in the ghetto outside the Polish city of Szcezcin and in America. Even as Yussel shared his Russian experiences with her, Mrs. Wolansky told of her life in Europe. Talking with Yussel became something she looked forward to every day; she even answered his questions about her marriage and why it had failed. Without realizing it, she had gotten used to having this man around her house. Relaxation slowed her rhythm. She too, put on weight, but luckily, it filled out her lean frame to make her a more attractive woman.

When work at Lefkowitz's slowed again, Yussel worked only part-time. On one of his days off he took the trolley to Canal Street where there were plenty of empty storefronts. Any one of them was big enough for the two worktables he needed to start a shop. He chose one and wrote down the name and address of the owner and went to see him. The rent would be ten dollars a month, as is. Yussel would have to do his own cleaning and fixing up to get started. Yussel paid him the first month's rent.

Yussel hired Mrs. Wolansky and Samuel to clear out the broken boxes and other trash, clean the dust from every corner of the store and wash the dirt from the large plate glass window that fronted on Canal Street. "Make it shine," he told them, "so people will stop and look."

Mrs. Wolansky told Yussel about the sign painter, Mr. Darchenko, who did the signs on most of the stores in their neighborhood. Yussel struck a price with Darchenko to letter on the cleaned plate-glass front the sign, **Reinerman, Leather Stitching,** in Yiddish and English.

Yussel searched the second-hand furniture shops for two solidly built tables and four stools and had them moved into his store. In a used tool and equipment outlet he found two heavy-duty stitching machines.

When his little shop on Canal Street was ready for him Yussel was faced with the big decision; should he leave Lefkowitz now and spend his time contacting the shoe manufacturers for work, or stay part-time with Lefkowitz and work part-time for his own shop?

Even with the difficult work at Lefkowitz's, Yussel's skill was such that he could still make his four to five dollars a day. That would pay for rent and other expenses for starting up his contracting business. Yussel decided to work at both jobs, until he made enough money as his own contractor.

To prove his skills with leather and show manufacturers what he could do, he made three pair of complexly designed uppers, yet different from each other, and put them in a brown paper bag to keep them clean. Now Yussel felt that he was ready to be his own salesman.

He lingered after breakfast the next morning to bring Mrs. Wolansky up to date on his plans.

She was impressed. She smiled at him in silence for a moment then shook her head admiringly. "Only nineteen and ready to become a businessman." Silently she wished Yussel were ten years older. When she spoke it was with more than an advisory interest in the ambitious young man with a solid trade. She gestured to his worn work shirt and spoke deprecatingly, "Like this you're going to talk to customers?"

Yussel looked down at his clothing then questioned his landlady. "No?"

After a short, definitive shake of her head, she said, "No, at least a jacket. Maybe also a white shirt and tie."

Machine operator Yussel Reinerman, used to dressing in work clothes for Lefkowitz's dirt encrusted, hole-in-the-wall of a factory looked up at Mrs. Wolansky's face and suddenly felt inadequate. After living in her apartment for four years Mrs. Wolansky had become something of a parent and perhaps more subtly, an attractive woman. His morning prayers were enough to remind Yussel that Jewish boys and girls don't touch if they're not married. But the day was longer than the morning and peak hormones of a nineteen-year-old sent strong signals all day and all night and Mrs. Wolansky was noticeably a woman.

Yussel swallowed and struggled with his words. "You … you think I should buy a jacket?"

"And pants, a suit. You have the money?"

"A … yes, yes, I have the money."

"Good. I'll take you to Schvenker's Clothing and you'll come out of his store looking like a prince!"

Sunday, at Schvenker's Clothing Mrs. Wolansky said much to direct Yussel's choice to a dark suit with a pin stripe and had him add a white shirt and a dark and light blue striped tie. On the trolley going home they sat like a couple out for the day in their holiday best. On the seat beside Yussel was a paper bag marked Schvenker's Clothing, which held his every day shirt and pants.

In Mrs. Wolansky's kitchen Yussel stood in his new suit, white shirt and blue striped tie waiting yet again for her approval.

Mrs. Wolansky held her hands together and waggled her head in wonderment. Not only was Yussel's transformation something to behold but before her stood a young man with a solid trade.

"Now you could be a business man, Yussel," she said.

Sam came in to join them for supper and also noticed. "Fancy, Yussel, fancy."

Yussel, embarrassed to be the center of so much attention, smiled shyly then left to leave his jacket and tie in his room.

Zofia checked the brisket of beef that she had left on a low oven and asked Sam, "You're ready fa' school tomorrow, boychik?"

"I'll finish after supper, Ma."

"So sit und eat. Ve're ready."

Yussel came to the kitchen in his new pants and shirt, collar open. He sat in his usual place, opposite Mrs. Wolansky.

She felt the pleasant ambience of the three of them around the supper table. Smiling sadly, she thought, *now why didn't I pick one like him? But,* she thought, even more sadly, drawing her final line in the sand, *he is ten years—no-- twelve years too young.*

CHAPTER 6

1907

Four years after Yussel Reinerman fled for his life from Russia, he finally made enough money in his shoe contractor's shop to pay third-class passage for his younger brother, Moish and his father, Duvvid. He could have had them come sooner as charity cases of HIAS, but he didn't want them to experience the hell of steerage. In third class, Papa and Moish had a small private stateroom and their own bathroom.

After he secured their passage, the following Sunday morning, when he didn't have to rush to open his shop for Bagelli and Alcinio, his two machine stitchers, Yussel sat after having breakfast with Mrs. Wolansky. Samuel had no school and continued sleeping in his room.

While Mrs. Wolansky cleared the dishes, Yussel suddenly found it difficult to tell her that he was leaving. He sat quietly while she soaked the dishes in soapy water. She left them and came toward the table wiping her hands with her apron. "You're not going to the shop, Yussel?"

She sat opposite him and waited.

"Uh ... yes, yes, I am." He stopped and waited for the sudden tumult in his chest and in his head to quiet and let him speak.

She saw his upset. "Something's the matter, Yussel?"

"Yes," he blurted. "In a few days ... the end of the month ... I'm moving."

It was Zofia's turn to feel a stab of pain. "You ... are moving, Yussel?"

Afraid he would cry if he spoke, he nodded vigorously.

For all of her line in the sand, which she thought had prepared her to sail through this, she sat stunned. She felt tears in her eyes. She blinked hard. She heard him affirm it. "Yes, Mrs. Wolansky."

"Where?" she asked.

"I rented an apartment so … so I … we could be like a family again." But there was no longer a woman in his family. Suddenly Yussel felt the loss of his mother as if she had just died. Tears welled in his eyes and he wanted to reach out to Mrs. Wolansky to have her hold him. But, Orthodoxy's injunction strong in him kept him seated.

Mrs. Wolansky got up. "I … I'm sorry you're leaving, Yussel." Resisting her desire to rush to him, she turned to the sink, picked up a glass and drank a quick swallow of water.

Yussel stood up.

She held up the glass. "Would you like some?"

"Y … yes. Thank you."

She partly filled the glass and walked it toward him.

Yussel started to reach a hand for it, but she quickly put it on the table and threw her arms around him.

Yussel responded instantly. He held a woman in his arms and hugged his body to hers for the first time. Holding her close the passions that thundered through him lifted him to another world, one he had not ever known.

Mrs. Wolansky felt his arousal hard against her. She whispered, "Love is good, Yussel, Love is good."

Yussel had a vision of Rabbi Bronstein at his pulpit. He pulled back and looked at Mrs. Wolansky.

Her face was flushed. Already she imagined being with him in her room.

Yussel whispered, "What … are you saying?"

"I'm saying," she whispered back, "that love is good."

"That … that kind of love?"

"Yes, that kind of love."

"But we're not married."

"So I was married and we didn't have love." She put her lips on his and taught her eager pupil to kiss.

Mixed in with his charging hormonal tumult, were remembered Riga images of Igor with his arm around Sonya at the Corner Spot bar. He tried to think, *but this … this isn't like with Sonya. Mrs. Wolansky is not a woman like Sonya,* and he kissed Mrs. Wolansky hard. His hands found the wonderful softness of her body.

When Mrs. Wolansky saw that Yussel's panting excitement had left his Orthodox prohibitions behind, she walked him to her room and closed the door.

Some time later Yussel woke. Slowly he realized what had happened and felt a sudden urgency to get to his room without being seen by Sam. Mrs. Wolansky was asleep. He carefully extricated himself from her and started to gather up his scattered clothes unaware that she had awakened, and smiling, watched him. He felt a strong connection to her and he didn't want to leave without saying something to her. But he had no idea what to say. His feelings in a turmoil, he opened the door and listened for Sam. He heard nothing and he slipped out, got into his room, closed the door and felt great relief that no one had seen nor would know about what had just happened.

Yussel never got to his shop that Sunday. Instead, he sat on his bed and remembered Rabbi Wallenberg's lecture on the Bible to the boys' class in Tchernivakh preparing them for Bar-Mitzvah. "There are three ways a man can commit himself to be married," Rabbi Wallenberg reminded his students, "the giving of a ring or coin, signing a contract, or sexual intercourse, but" he emphasized, "only the first two should be used. Yet in any one of the three cases, the promised marriage ceremony has to be performed in one year."

Unwilling to enlighten the boys about their third option, the rabbi concentrated entirely on the first two. That God's word even made it available to young men was always a shocking puzzlement to the rabbi. *How could it be,* he thought, *when God's word also said, "Men and women are not to touch before marriage?" Or is one of the conflicting ideas not from the Bible but from the Mishnah, which compiled the many, later, rabbinical interpretations of the Bible's laws?* In any case Rabbi Wallenberg decided that the boys were too young to be discussing such matters.

Yussel also thought that with Papa and Moish coming, there was so much to do to get them settled, and to get Moish started on making a living that it was difficult for Yussel to think of even considering his religious obligation to marry Mrs. Wolansky after one year. And he was only nineteen. There was time yet for him to find a wife.

CHAPTER 7

Yussel moved out of Mrs. Wolansky's furnished room where he paid four dollars a month, and moved into a whole apartment in a new tenement with three little bedrooms for $15 a month. Spending so much money for his brother and father assuaged some of the guilt that still prickled him because he'd left them behind when he fled the Russian anti-Semitic terror.

The new tenement had been updated according to the more stringent Building Law of 1901. Moish and Duvvid were properly impressed with the luxuries of hot and cold running waters in the kitchen and bathroom, a plumbed bathtub in the bathroom where it belonged instead of a portable washtub placed near the stove, which heated the buckets of water. Only the toilet was still in the hall to be shared with the other apartment on the floor. But a flush toilet was also a luxury compared to the outhouse they had known in Tchernivakh.

After his family was settled, Yussel brought Duvvid to the synagogue and introduced him to Rabbi Bronstein and he brought Moish to his storefront shop on Canal Street.

Moish had no interest in the synagogue, felt no obligation to the family's belief in the Jewish Almighty. "If there is a God," back in Tchernivakh Moish had argued with Yussel, "Why would he let his Chosen People be whipped, beaten, and killed in every country in Europe? For this we were chosen?"

What did impress brother Moish, and Papa Duvvid, was that on the Lower East Side in America's Manhattan, Yiddish was spoken everywhere and the sign in every store window advertised its product in Yiddish and English. The Jewish area of New York City's Manhattan seemed as big as the city of Riga, like a whole city of Jews.

Yussel sat Moish down in his storefront shop on Canal Street and showed him how to stitch the upper part of a lady's shoe. Yussel felt good that he was doing Moish such a big favor. What could be better for a greenhorn, than to walk into a shop in America, sit down at a machine and make a living?

Yussel started by showing his brother the finished sample stitched from three pre-cut pieces of leather. "This is what it should look like when it's done." With a scissors Yussel cut replicas of the leather pieces from a brown paper bag. "You'll practice this morning on paper Moish. I shouldn't lose the sixty-eight cents for a pair. "Now," he continued, "you take two pieces and line up the edges exactly, slide the pieces under the needle and, turn the wheel with your hand to bring the needle down to hold them. Then you start the machine and sew them."

Step by step, Yussel spent the morning with Moish. After lunch, Yussel started him on the leather. By six o'clock, Moish had sweated through two-and-a-half pairs of uppers. He figured that he had grossed $1.70 for the day.

Moish's figures puzzled Yussel. "How?" he asked.

Moish explained, "Two-and-a-half pair by sixty-eight cents."

"Sixty-eight cents is what my shop gets for a pair. The operator gets twenty-two cents a pair.

Moish made a face like his day was a total loss.

Yussel rushed to explain. "The shop has to pay rent, lights, and heat to keep your *tukhus* (ass) warm in the winter."

Moish smiled sourly. "So I made fifty-five cents all day?"

"Don't rush it Moish. I worked two years to learn. Remember? As a Christian yet." With a hand Yussel indicated the other side of his storefront shop where Bagelli and Alcinio were working at stitching machines. I have enough work now to hire two Taliainishers (Italians)."

Dubious about his future as an operator, Moish shook his head.

Seeing his brother's reluctance irritated Yussel. "By you, Moish, everything's got to be quick. Don't give up on the first day. Tomorrow you'll double it, and the next day again. It's a good trade, Moish. I was able to rent a whole apartment for you and Papa. I've got capital in the bank for the slow time."

Two weeks later, Yussel went over to see how his brother was doing.

Moish stopped his machine and jumped up. "I can't do this Yussel."

Yussel stared like he didn't hear right. "You can't do this? You're doing it."

"I can't sit at a machine day after day . . ."

Yussel couldn't understand Moish's frustration about sitting in one place from sunup to sundown. Yussel didn't understand Moish's need to be out there exploring his new world of New York City and wrestling with its challenges to find his place in it.

Yussel's desired niche for his life was smaller, and he already had it. He didn't have to know much more about where he was than that he was making a living and he was without fears.

But part of the excitement for Moish in Russia happened when he joined the Socialist Workers Party to make it better for the Jews. They sent him on political errands to different parts of the Kurland province. Moish met gentiles who were also suffering under the rule of the czar, peasants who rarely had enough food to last through the winter and factory workers whose wages only bought enough food to keep them alive. And, most unusual, the Socialist Party people accepted Jews as members.

"Moish," Yussel continued, "it's only two weeks for you here. I've been doing it five years."

"This is not for me, Yussel. Being tied to a machine from seven in the morning till six at night is slavery."

"Slavery?" Yussel shook his head as if he couldn't believe it. "Moish, still with the big mouth." Yussel's next spoken thought was one that had always confounded him. Looking at Moish he said, "From the same parents two brothers, like a horse and a cat." When Yussel said 'horse' he had the image of Mishka, the huge dray who performed endless tasks in Tchernivakh for their family and was so much a part of their lives. The cat caught mice but couldn't be expected to do anything else that was useful.

Moish longed to be outside checking out his opportunities all around New York. He countered his brother's argument with a plan. "Yussel, instead of you running around collecting orders, dragging bundles of leather on the trolley to the shop, and dragging them back again, let me do the lugging and getting the orders. You give me a small salary as an errand boy and a commission on the orders I get. You can stay in the shop and see that the work gets out."

Twenty-year old Yussel, already running his own shop for two years, listened to Moish skeptically, but thought his kid brother might have something. Yussel hated leaving the shop to pick up and deliver, losing hours from his stitching machine which made the money. But he had never thought to trust an errand boy to carry the finished work. What if he burned spots on the leather with a careless cigarette? What if he met a girl and was late getting the finished uppers to *Kelly Bros?* Would Moish drop a bundle in the snow? Or leave one on the trolley? Could Moish really get orders?

"I'll think about it, Moish," Yussel said. "In the meantime, make the upper."

At a time when he had enough work on hand to keep Bagelli, Alcinio, and himself busy for two weeks, Yussel reluctantly started to put on his coat to make the delivery of finished uppers to *Salvini Shoes*. He thought about what Moish had proposed and decided to stay at his machine, help get the work out and bring the money in. He rehung his coat on the nail, went to Moish sweating over his work, tapped him on the shoulder and said, "Moish, you're the errand boy. Take the bundle to *Salvini Shoes*."

Moish bounced up with a whoop and clapped his brother on the arm. "We're going to be big business, Yussel."

Moish delivered the uppers.

With the first week's wages Yussel paid him, Moish bought a light blue suit, started Night School For Immigrants at the Henry Street Settlement House to quicken his learning of English, and legally changed his name to Moe. Cigarettes he smoked already, so with the change from the suit, he bought three cigars. With the blue suit, red hair, moustache and grimacing funny faces to more clearly articulate the words of his new language, Moish looked like an animated Jack-in-the-box. But when he made a delivery to *Ladies Footwear* or to *Salvini Shoes*, his charm made him eligible to hang around the buyer's office with the salesmen and listen to them talk about the trade; about samples time, rush season, dead time, and other economic concerns of the ladies shoes industry.

Moish brought in more orders from the accounts Yussel already had. Immediately they wrangled about Moish's commission. The agreement had been vague, and each defined it in his favor.

Yussel flared. "Already taking money from me? I can't trust even a brother."

"Look how much time I'm saving you and I'm running my feet off."

"You *pisher* (baby in diapers)! I took you in six weeks ago and already you want to make as much money as me. I've been here five years working my fingers off."

Yussel lapsed into his poor English and exaggerated his language difficulties by facial grimaces with his words to mock Moish's night school efforts to get rid of his accent. "You t'ink de menufecturers are buying you fency voids? NO!" Yussel hit his chest bone with a hard thumb. "Dey're buying my good uppers. And don' you fa'get it, Moish. Hahd voik is no good fa you on de machine? You don' like doity de hends? Who do you t'ink opened dese accounts, you, running from police in Tchernivakh?"

Reminded of his brash failures in Russia, which indirectly caused the death of their mother and their youngest brother Avram, Moish shrank.

Yussel piled it on. "V'ile you vas shooting off da mout' mit politics in Russia, I vas here getting orders, and I should pay you for accounts I got?"

Moish backed off.

Even though he made his points and withered Moish, Yussel felt no victory. He hated arguing with his brother. Every argument with Moish shattered his feeling of we-are-family, a feeling he needed. Through the worst of the Russian anti-Jewish terrors, each member of the Reinermans strove to stay connected to the others. Arguing with Moish left Yussel feeling alone and as lonely as when he lived as a Christian and had to cut himself off from his people.

Now again, Yussel's argument with Moish left him feeling alone. For the moment that the brothers exploded and hurled words at each other it relieved Yussel, but minutes later he was confounded by the tumult he stirred up within himself yet again. He plumped himself down at his machine to relieve his turmoil with the hands-on satisfaction of his work. To further ease his upset, he justified his angry outburst by remembering his years of hardship in Russia and in America before he could bring Moish and his father over . . .

Reverend Vilitsin had explained to Yussel that Jesus, the Lord God of the Christians was born a Jew, who became a Rabbi and a Jewish prophet! Yussel spent months as a student of Reverend Vilitsin in Riga to understand all about the Christian deity, so that no one would see through his Christian masquerade. He learned to cross himself and say Hail Marys instead of *Shemas* ...

Marveling how he had managed to live as a Christian, Yussel shook his head in wonderment. Would Moish have had the patience to study how to be a Christian in order to learn his trade? Then live as a Christian for three years?

In the grip again of his Russian memories Yussel struggled with his fears. He stopped his machine. After a few minutes he shook his head and gestured angrily with his hand as if wiping Russia away. Ending the painful moments Yussel blessed America again for giving him his life, to live it without fear. In America he had only to worry about continuing to obey his Judaic Laws.

Would those terrible memories ever leave? "*Pisher*," he mumbled scornfully of his younger brother, "I start him at the top so he won't have to go through what I went through, but he doesn't like to get his hands dirty."

Reminding himself yet again how grateful he was to America, suddenly he was in the darkened room, in bed with Mrs. Wolansky and his sensations overwhelmed him. He put his twenty years of Orthodoxy on trial again for daring to argue its case against the greatest physical pleasures an adolescent with ravenous hormones could know. It was the sublime relief of satisfying his hormones for which men will go to any woman, someone like Sonya in Riga, for instance, who was any-slut-will-do. But at the other end of Yussel's new spectrum, who fulfilled his needs for lovemaking and for love, Mrs Wolansky was a different woman; a housemate of four years who also filled the roles of advisor, mother, companion, and most wondrous of all, lover. She had put before him the simple truth, "Love is good," to justify taking him to bed. "Without love," Mrs. Wolansky said, "marriage is a vacant, cold apartment that keeps you shivering all your life, no matter how much furniture you put in it." Mrs. Wolansky knew whereof she spoke. Marriage without love had left her alone, a baby to care for, and without means.

Now, reliving his life-changing encounter with Mrs. Wolansky, Yussel ignored his machine and the two leather pieces in his hand. He stared out the plate glass window, awestruck by his experience with her, relishing the wonder of it. *Is this love, the "Love is good," she spoke of?* A sudden thought flashed him back to his Bible classes in *Yeshiva* (religious secondary school); *the three ways a Jewish woman is engaged to a man is by accepting his ring, or his signed document saying that they will marry, or by having sexual intercourse with him.* Yussel stared out the plate glass at the gathering darkness and asked himself, *are we … engaged? If we follow Biblical Law we are required to marry in a year. Is this enough to marry?*

He knew the answer to his next question but he asked it anyway. *What would God say?* He pictured Rabbi Bronstein officiating under the wedding canopy, the bride walking under it with a veil covering her face to symbolize that the groom had never seen her. It suddenly struck Yussel why that was important. *If I have never seen her we could not have ever touched! This is what Orthodoxy says God wants. But … yet in the Bible …*

Mesmerized by the memory his mouth had fallen open while his mind and heart fought on both sides of his war. His throat was uncomfortably dry. He coughed and swallowed to restore his saliva flow and realized he had been holding two pieces of leather in his hand for a long time. He turned to work his machine again when he remembered that something had happened in the street outside his window. He looked again. The day was noticeably darker. He worried that the setting sun signified that the Friday night Sabbath had begun. But the glare of the large bare bulb over his machine was still in his eyes. With a groan he heaved his body off his bench. Automatically brushing thread ends and leather fuzz from his clothes, he walked the few steps to the dirty plate-glass expanse and squinted. *Yes, darker.* The Sabbath had begun. Yussel had mixed feelings; sorry he missed the prayers, but relieved that the time for them was over and his obligation had passed.

Yussel took out a watch from his vest pocket and snapped open the case. "A quarter after five," he muttered in Yiddish, "It's dark early, we're not out of winter yet," though he didn't hear himself above the intermittent, high-pitched drones of the two other machines.

Bagelli and Alcinio were scheduled to work until six. Every pair in this order of ladies' shoe uppers that the Italians stitched netted Yussel thirty-four cents. He rationalized to excuse his disobedience to God. *How can I send them home early because I have to attend Sabbath Evening prayers?*

Yussel remembered that Lefkowitz worked late on Friday night and decided he would do like his former boss. Yussel muttered, "He wears his *yarmulke* (head covering) like a *fromme Yid* (religious Jew), but he works after the Sabbath sundown.." Yussel felt the *yarmulke* on his head. "God understands," he rationalized, "sometimes it's hard for a Jew to obey His laws. And this is a different country."

Yussel had given up the daily evening prayer service in the synagogue when he first hired Bagelli, because Yussel couldn't leave a stranger alone in the shop. But he had continued to say the most important of the evening prayers, the *Shemas*, at his machine.

It was more troubling to him not to be in the synagogue for the Sabbath Eve prayers on Friday night. Remembering the compromise that he had worked out with God while posing as a Christian troubled him yet more. His memories of Riga made Yussel smile bitterly. While he worked for Shoe Master Yarinevitch he had said his Hail Marys but only permitted himself to *think* his Jewish prayers. He didn't dare let his lips move. To compensate for those two years when he lived as a Christian, he made a pact with God that if the Almighty would protect him in his disguise, and help him become a shoemaker, there would be no more pious Jew than Yussel Reinerman.

This Friday night, he sat down again, said a prayer, and pressed his thigh against the power bar. In the start-and-stop stitching of three precision-cut pieces of leather into a shoe upper, he recalled, yet again, his sins against God during his Christian apprenticeship. He had attended church, not synagogue, eaten non-Kosher food, even pig. He did not put on phylacteries for morning prayers, and he had to laugh with apprentice Vanya when he spat his filthy anti-Jewish slurs. Yussel's disguise was uncovered. Yussel felt again his pounding fear and relived the desperation of fighting for his life. Thrown to the floor, Yussel kicked at Vanya in a frenzy. Vanya fell backward over the lamp and set the attic ablaze. Yussel bounced up and sprang past the heavier Igor--

Fear that night that he would not see morning had branded Yussel. While he could always recall his terror, his desperate fighting had also vaccinated him. Yussel would never again give into his disease of fear. Fighting for his life that night he knew that as long as he breathed he would fight to go on …

"But dis is America." Yussel interrupted himself, muttering in English, reminding himself yet again that he no longer had to be plunged into the terrors and pain of terrible memories. "Dis is America, and dis is my shop," he repeated into the thrumming of the machines. The noise was music to him. The spoken word, "America …" He savored it--no he felt love well up in him when he said the word. America gave him the freedom to utilize his skills with leather and achieve a financial success. It rid him of fears that wracked him when memories dragged him back into the bondage of Russian life. Freedom to work in America had become his ladder to climb out of his inner Russian cesspool.

Like a horse freed of restraining harness and released into open pasture, his shop was a field all his own, where he could spend every minute of his time. Working was his way of running free. *America gave me that,* he thought gratefully.

Thoughts of pleasure whisked him back to Mrs. Wolansky. For him America had meant even that kind of freedom. But his guilt argued with the waves of pleasure that rolled through him. *Was this also one of God's gifts? But not yet,* he thought as he argued for God's case, *I'm-- we're not married.*

He returned his thoughts to his work, his dream of making the whole shoe in America. Two years of apprenticeship in Russia and five years in America, Yussel could figure out any problem that had to do with making a shoe. He felt equipped to take on the challenge of being successful in the American lady's shoe business.

But his expanding work time continued to butt heads with mandatory religious observances. *And I promised Him,* Yussel recalled, *I promised Him.* Yussel had thought he had a solution when he brought his brother and father over. Because Moish observed no religious rituals Yussel had figured that his brother wouldn't mind working until six o'clock in the winter so Yussel could leave for synagogue at five, or whenever the sun began its descent. Moish would take charge until six and close up.

Suddenly Mrs. Wolansky again intruded in his thoughts. *Of course.* He had promised in his daily prayers to obey the laws of Orthodoxy but he had failed God again. Yussel, the man, had chosen licentiousness rather than wait for the blessings of marriage. A sudden thought unsettled him. *Should ... should I ... marry her?*

He felt that that would ... might ... make it all right. Could he live with her? For the rest of his life? A woman who was 12 years older than he? Yussel shook his head. *No, no, it's not right.* Yet he felt so comfortable with her. Thinking of the four years, sitting with her at their early breakfast together, and supper. Riding home on the trolley after a day's work, how he looked forward to talking with her as they ate, his reluctance to put an end to their day, say good night so she could go to her room and he to his. Yussel sat and wondered what was it that had happened to him and to her?

It would take him a long time before he could fathom his sexual encounter with Mrs. Wolansky, if ever. It might become dimmer as the years passed, but not any better understood. The stern rules of his Orthodoxy continued to attach further complexity to his human complexities.

Each year it was something he brought up with God during the ten days of atonement between Rosh Hashonah and Yom Kippur, the time for the Jew to confess his/her sins of the past year and to promise to do better in the coming year.

CHAPTER 8

Two weeks after their big argument Moe had more ideas. Released from the mental prison that Russia had been for him, America set his mind free to explore. *What's out there? Who's out there? How do they make a living?* Sitting in his brother's shop all day at one machine had made Moe feel encircled by barbed wire.

Moe figured it would be fair for him to get a commission on new accounts that he opened. But before he approached his brother, he waited for a day when work was slow.

When he returned from the one delivery of the day, Yussel was checking Bagelli and Alcinio's finished work. They had run out of uppers and left early. Moe approached his brother. "Joe, why don't you let me be a regular salesman?"

" 'Joe'? What kind of a name is Joe? I'm Yussel."

"You're in America," Moe insisted. Give yourself an American name, like I did . . . Hey, Moe and Joe. That's a great name for a vaudeville act." Moe laughed. "Like Weber and Fields. We're a team."

Yussel had never taken time to attend any of the many theaters on Second Ave where the audience of immigrant Jews relived their European sufferings in a good cry at the tragedy playing out on the stage. Or they could go to the theater next door for belly laughs at the comedy antics of vaudeville acts.

The many theaters on Second Avenue suckled their most heartbreaking tragedies and their comic vaudeville acts at the warm breast of their *Mammalushen*, their Yiddish language. Moe struck a pose of the Sholem Aleichem character from the play, Mendel, Incorporated. Mendel, the inventor, suddenly hits it big, and shouts to the world that he has arrived. The play is a tribute to the Jew who makes good in America, lifting the immigrant audience's hopes for themselves.

Yussel stared at Moe's theatrics. "Mishugganer (crazy) Moish."

Yussel remembered Moe's original request and grew cautious. "Good accounts I got already, Moe. Who needs a salesman?"

"You do, Joe. You're the best damn fitter around. I hear the salesmen from *Kelly Brothers* and *Taranti's Shoes*, and the others talking. They all agree about your good work, but you need someone out there to tell the big boys about you."

Yussel was flattered. He never felt comfortable seeing himself keeping up with the plushy put-on of the big boys ...

When he had gone from factory to factory to show his samples to get work Yussel only asked to talk to the shop foreman who could look at the samples and give him a yes or no in a minute. Instead he lost further time from his shop by the receptionist saying, " Please have a seat, Mr. Reinerman and I'll see if Mr. Matalini can see you," and with some magical equipment around her head, she talked into a small spittoon in front of her mouth to ask the foreman behind the factory door if he could see Yussel Reinerman.

"Mit' samples," Yussel would tell her, still standing at her desk holding the brown paper bag.

"With samples, Mr. Matalini," she added.

Her head came up to tell Yussel with a smile, "He says for you to wait, Mr. Reinerman." She gestured toward the couch, club chair and coffee table that took up the rest of the space in the small reception room.

So Yussel sat on a fancy couch looking at fake flowers on the little table, or watched the dolled up secretary writing letters on a typewriter with that funny telephone equipment around her head, and he thought, sarcastically, *The shop foreman is so busy that he can't take one minute to look at my samples and give me a yes or no?* At least there was an ashtray on the table. Yussel smoked a Murad, the strongest Turkish tobacco available while he lost time from his machine.

When the factory owner finally emerged Yussel had been uncomfortable in the presence of the owners' fashionable clothes and his own stumbling around the English language for words to explain the worthiness of his samples. Yussel was surprised to hear that they praised his work, let alone that they even thought about him. Yussel looked at his kid brother. "They think I do good work, Moish?"

"Yes."

Yussel thought that was nice but not comfortable in the spotlight, he decided he'd rather stay in the shop and let someone else make with the fancy manners. As long as his shop had work, and produced it well, he didn't have to worry what the industry big shots 'out there' thought. He was especially relieved not to have to deal with an Italian, Irish, or German manufacturer, be forced to leave the solid shore of his Yiddish and sail on his rickety English to navigate an important deal.

Yussel smiled shyly at Moe's compliments, and dragged on his Murad. He looked at his kid brother in the bright blue suit, lavender shirt, and shades of orange tie.

Under Yussel's scrutiny and waiting for his brother's answer, Moe manipulated his cigar with lips and teeth so that it rolled from one side of his mouth to the other and back again, a Look-Ma-no-hands trick he'd seen a salesman do. Moe thought it made him look like he was debating an important decision.

Yussel knew he couldn't talk to buyers like Moe the Mouth could. For certain, he knew he couldn't dress like Moe. He envied Moe's looking like an American in such a short time, while he was content to stay with the dull garments of the Jews on Manhattan's Lower East Side. But he liked living in a Jewish city that had all the things a religious Jew could want. *What could be better*, he often thought, *to be in America where I'm free to make a living, and still be surrounded by my own people?* Yussel, sure of his economic abilities smiled wryly at Moe, thinking, *you may look like a big shot, but, without my shop, would you know how to make a living?*

But Moe is right, Yussel had to admit to himself. *If I want to get bigger I need someone out there finding more customers.* "Chutzpah, you got plenty, Moe," Yussel said, not sure whether he was giving Moe credit or criticizing him. Yussel accepted himself as the inside man who does need an outside man. Yussel yearned to get back to making the whole shoe, not just a piece of it. But he couldn't run the bigger shop and be out there selling his work too. Every manufacturer had salesmen out there getting orders. *But,* questioned Joe, *is Moe the right one?*

"Let me think about it Moe, " Joe said.

Monday and Tuesday of the following week, only Yussel was in the shop, because he'd rather be there than anywhere else. But no work came in until Wednesday, when Moe brought in enough at least for the morning for the two operators. Moe also brought with him an impatience for the answer to his proposal. "Nu, Joe, have you thought about me being your salesman?"

"Yeah … Yeah, Moe, I've thought about it." Yussel had tentatively decided in the affirmative. But he could always drop back to *if he doesn't sell, I'll put him back on the machine.* Yussel spoke next in his poor English to attempt to join Moe in his new, stepped up direction.

"Nu, salesman, so vat you vanna do?"

A wild look came over Moe's face and he grabbed the cigar from his mouth. "You mean it, Joe?"

"Yeah, yeah."

"I'll get Liebman Shoes!"

Stunned at Moe's daring Yussel snorted embarrassed yet mocking laughter. "You're crazy. Liebman'll take my work?"

"Of course he will. He'd be crazy if he didn't."

Pleased by Moe's chutzpah and Moe's compliment of his work, yet still unwilling to accept it, Joe backed away from it it as if he would not share such wild thinking. His hands went up as if to say, *Moe, you're talking nonsense so leave me out of it.*

But after another moment, when he finally spoke, he said, with a shy smile, "All right, Moe," go ahead."

"How much will you give me for each pair?"

Yussel stiffened. But the sudden recurring heat of their last argument cooled quickly. Yussel thought it a fair question. "Eight cents a pair."

"Make it ten."

"*Chutzpah, chutzpah,* Yussel thought, but he was smiling, enjoying the wild ride of his thoughts on which Moe was taking him. He did a quick calculation; *ten for Moe, twenty-four for the operator, and for me and the shop, thirty-one.* He added it up. "If it's seventy-five cent work, Moish, I'll give you ten."

Moe was already paying himself out loud. "A hundred pair, that's ten dollars in one deal." He held out his hand. When Joe offered his, Moe grabbed it and slapped his other hand on Joe's and sealed the verbal contract in English, "Agreed!"

Yussel was thrown by the sudden change in language. By the time he understood, Moe was at the door ready to leave to take the trolley home and put on his suit.

"Pisher," Joe called, stopping Moe whose hand was already on the knob, "Where are you going?"

"I'm going to get my suit on and start selling."

"With what? Your mouth?"

"Yes."

"You're a talker, but who has seen what you're selling?"

"The buyers know your work. I've been hanging around them when I deliver the uppers."

"You're a kid, Moish. You think Liebman will give you a hundred pair bundle because you tell him?"

Moe let go the knob, drew himself up as if readying to announce to all in the shop. He double-clapped his hands to command attention. Yussel, facing Moe, jumped. The sudden sound startled Bagelli and Alcinio who stopped their machines and turned to look. "Ladies and gentlemen," Moe said in his Yiddish-accented English, as if he were a barker for the circus sideshow, "I'm here to tell you about vun of New York's vunders. You'll be glad that you chose to visit our t'riving metropolis, because vee hev' in dis city, the shop of vun of the finest ladies' shoe contractors, Joe Reinerman." Moe swung an extended arm so that his stretched finger pointed to his brother, who stood with his mouth open.

His face hot, Yussel giggled, as delighted as embarrassed. "You crazy," he said in English, then fell back on the more comfortable Yiddish. "*Mishugganer Moish*, talk for you is easy but *tukhus offen tish* (facts on the table), what are you selling? You need samples to show what Reinerman can do."

No longer able to follow the fun, Bagelli and Alcinio restarted their machines.

"So make me samples," Moe said.

"I don't have to make them. I got."

"You have samples?"

"Of course. How do you think I got my accounts?"

On the open shelf near the nails for hanging coats, among the odd scraps of leather, Yussel searched out the dust-covered, brown paper bag. He shook and blew off the dust and took out three finished uppers. Lying on the palm of his hand, he moved them closer to Moe.

Moe picked one up and examined it, fingered the other two. Each a different work of artistry, the designs were intricate, the stitching difficult. "You did these, Yussel?"

"Who else?" He put them back in the bag and offered it to Moe. "Here. Now you have something to talk about."

"Yeah . . . oh yeah," said Moe smiling.

He was on his way toward the door when Joe called and stopped him again. "Salesman! Take some cards," Joe said as he dug into his vest pocket for a few of the cards he'd had printed at Shnitzler's. "Give Liebman a card so he knows where to call to place an order."

"Oh, yeah." Moe responded. He turned, took the cards from Joe and slipped them into his pocket.

"You'll learn, salesman, you'll learn."

Moe was at the door again his hand on the knob, but his excitement about leaping onto a new plateau caused him such tumult he needed a moment for his head to clear. "Yah," he barked suddenly and was gone.

Yussel's conflicted feelings exploded into English and mixed with the noise of the two machines. "Goddemmit! No vun makes a betta uppa den Joe Reinerman." He sat down to congratulate himself with the affirming thunder of his machine.

CHAPTER 9

Jerry Cohen, foreman at *Liebman Shoes*, entered the reception room and closed the door to the factory behind him. He walked toward Moe standing at the receptionist's desk. Moe immediately pulled a cellophane-wrapped cigar from his breast pocket and offered it with a grin. "One of the best."

Cohen waved it away. "You have samples, kid?"

Moe's hands dove into the side pockets of his jacket and pulled out the results of Joe's work and offered them to Cohen.

Cohen took one and while he was inspecting it closely, the underside of the stitching as well as the topside, Moe was aware of the steady rumble of many machines working behind the closed factory door. The noise permeated the reception room. Moe ached for Joe's machines to be part of that rumble.

Cohen handed the one back and continued holding his hand out, silently asking for the others.

After more moments of similar inspection he asked, "Where did you get these?"

"Joe Reinerman, contractor.

Cohen handed them back. "Related to you?"

"Brother."

"I've heard about him. That's nice work."

"He does great work and gets it back on time."

"So I've heard."

Moe couldn't contain himself. He jumped in. "You've heard about him?"

"Yeah. I don't have anything now--"

Moe hung on. "A sample order, ten pair ... five pair?"

Good to have him available, Cohen thought. *The rush season could be a bitch.* "Wait here." Cohen went into the factory and closed the door.

Moe stood there chewing on the hairs of his first attempt to grow a moustache. He didn't know what Cohen had decided, or if he had decided. He wondered if he should leave. But he remembered that Cohen said for him to wait. Moe looked at the secretary behind the desk, typing. *No, she wouldn't know. Maybe,* he thought jokingly, *I should offer her a cigar.* Moe the salesman thought of greasing everyone he thought could do him some good.

The factory door opened. A tall lanky man in a blue shop apron came into the reception room carrying a large brown paper bag. He asked Moe, "Reinerman?"

"Yeah, yeah."

He offered Moe the bag. "Jerry wants them by the end of the week."

Moe said assuringly, "Yeah, yeah, by the end of the week. Sure. Thanks. Thanks."

Moe bounced into Joe's shop and slammed the door.

Joe stopped his machine and looked up just as Moe held the brown paper bag in front of Joe's face. "I got him," he said triumphantly.

"You got who?"

"Liebman. I got Liebman."

Joe's eyes widened. "Liebman? How many?"

"I don't know. I didn't look."

"You didn't look? So open it."

Moe opened the bag and looked in. At the bottom lay some leather pieces under a stitched sample. Disappointed, he looked at Joe.

"What," Joe asked, "it's empty?"

"No, but it's not much."

"Gimme." Joe took it and put his hand in, gathered all the pieces and looked at what he had in his hand. "A sample. Three pieces. Nu, a beginning."

"He wants them by Friday."

"You'll wait. You'll take them back today."

"Today?"

"Of course. Five minutes work," Joe demeaned. He looked at Moe and said sarcastically. "He had nothing easier?"

Moe shrugged his shoulders to silently bow out of it. "I'll wait," he said.

Joe put aside his other work and stitched up the samples one, two, three. He dropped them into the bag and handed it to Moe. "Here, say hello to Liebman for me."

Moe suddenly remembered. "Joe, I didn't ask him a price."

"For samples you don't ask a price. Samples you do for nothing."

"Oh."

"You have the cards?"

"Cards?"

"With the telephone number."

"Oh, yeah." Moe slapped the breast pocket of his jacket. "Here."

"Good." After a moment, "So what are you standing? Salesman, go."

"Right. I'll be back." He was out the door.

The receptionist phoned Jerry Cohen to say Moe Reinerman was here to see him.

Cohen came into the reception room and saw Moe holding the paper bag. "Something wrong with what Dave gave you?"

"No, nothing wrong, Sir. They're done."

"Done?"

"Yeah, Joe stitched them, finished them."

Cohen relaxed, smiled wryly. "What took him so long?" He retrieved the three samples and looked at them. "Fine. Tell your brother I'll be calling him."

"Great. Thanks."

"You have a card with the number?"

"Oh, sure." Moe's hand went to his pocket and offered one.

"Fine," Cohen said and turned toward the factory.

Moe didn't bother to pull the cord of the elevator. He bounced down the stairs and out into the street to catch a trolley back to Joe with the news.

Moe dropped by Liebman's every other day as he did with the other shops. Two weeks after he gave Cohen the card, Moe got Liebman's first order. Dave, the lanky boy in the blue apron carried the brown paper bundle into the reception room where Moe was waiting.

Cohen came out with Dave to talk price with Moe. "Seventy-eight cents a pair for these, a new design. If your brother wants to talk about it or has any trouble with them tell him to call me.

Excited, Moe said, "Right." He put the large bundle under one arm and was on his way back to tell Joe.

In the next two months, with his charm, hard talk and showing Joe's samples, Moe picked up two more new accounts. Moe smiled in self-satisfaction. There would be no argument about him getting his full commission. But on the trolley with the brown paper bundle on his lap Moe felt that it was a waste of his time to be carting the bundles back and forth. His mind was racing ahead to their having a bigger shop. He began to think of spending his time more profitably by learning about the busy season for ladies shoe manufacturing and how he and Joe could increase their volume.

But Moe realized there was a limit to being a sub-contractor. The amount of work in Joe's shop was dependent on the shoe manufacturers being so burdened for production that they had to seek secondary help to get orders out on time. Joe's shop was getting only a small piece of the action. As a result Moe saw clearly that he had to be in touch with many shops to keep Joe and his operators busy.

The next morning Moe brought in 17-year-old Henry Olshansky.

Joe looked up from his machine and wondered what was going on.

"This is Henry our new errand boy, Joe. You won't have to worry about him. I'll tell him what to do."

CHAPTER 10

1912

"This is good soup, Papa."

"A hard worker needs a good soup."

"Onions, celery, cabbage, carrots; where did you get vegetables in the middle of winter?"

"Zvi Lebenhauser."

"From his pushcart? He stands in the winter cold and sells?"

"No, not from his pushcart. Would you believe, he has a large room, all windows, where he grows them, in the middle of winter, at the end of Division Street. I couldn't believe it. I had to see it. You know, Joe, I was foreman for Levidov's orchards. I know something about growing so I wanted to know how he grows in the middle of winter."

"He grows vegetables in the winter?" Joe was suddenly in Tchernivakh standing beside his mother's garden. He had just finished spreading rotted manure from the pile outside their barn, checked the gray sky, felt the chill on his body and knew he couldn't plant seeds yet for three weeks. Joe looked at his father. "How does he grow in winter?"

"At Levidov's, being orchard foreman didn't mean anything in winter. Once we spread the manure, the trees slept so I worked in his lumber mill. The Count himself couldn't make fruit trees grow in the cold."

"I remember," Joe agreed.

"I couldn't believe Lebenhauser could grow in winter, so he took me."

"He took you?"

"Yes, I saw it. He uses the electric inside to keep it warm. Inside you don't even need a coat. Electric doesn't stink like gas and the wind can't blow it out like gas."

Duvvid stopped talking and looked at his son, worrying how Joe would feel when he told him the bad news. While finishing his soup,

Duvvid struggled with how he would say it. He was glad that Joe still asked about Lebenhauser.

"His business doesn't sleep in the winter?"

"No, he grows, not as much as he likes, it's not the whole Division Street, but he doesn't sleep. He works with his vegetables in the winter.

"My business doesn't sleep either."

"Joe, you're a big success in America."

Joe smiled and nodded acknowledgement.

"Yussel and Moish," Duvvid said with a father's pride, "you're a good team." He chuckled. "Or like Moish says, 'Moe and Joe.'" He paused.

"Yes, it's going well, Pa. Moe is a good salesman." Joe smiled and shook his head. "With his crazy colors and his cigars and his red hair ... but they like him and he brings in the work. In the season we work steady, six days a week. He's making almost as much as I am."

"Good, good," Duvvid said, "You're both making enough to support families."

Joe smiled and nodded in agreement.

Duvvid hesitated then said, "Do you know where Moe is now?"

Joe was about to fill his spoon again with soup. Instead he stopped and looked up. "Except when he's in the shop, do I know where the *mishugganer* goes?" he dug his spoon into the soup again.

Duvvid waited a moment before speaking.

Moe had finally made a choice from among his many girlfriends and told his father that he was engaged to Lily. Things happened quickly for the Reinermans after Moe's announcement. That's what had spurred Duvvid to talk with Joe. Moe was eyeing the new apartments being built in the Bronx and which had room for Papa Duvvid as well. When they moved it meant that Joe would be living alone in his apartment.

Duvvid said to Joe, "Moe's in the Bronx, looking at the new apartments."

About to lift the full spoon, Joe stopped. He looked at his father. "Looking at ... why is Moe looking at new apartments? He has all the room he needs here." Joe had a sudden thought. "Is he getting married?"

"No, no, he's not getting married."

"I thought maybe he finally picked one. Sarah, Khannnah, Lily, Rachel, Bella; he's trying out the whole city before he picks one."

"He's younger than you, Joe. Don't rush him."

Duvvid's last point silently asked his oldest son what were his plans? Did Joe have any plans?

Duvvud asked his question aloud. "Joe, you haven't seen any girls that you like?"

In answer to his father's question he had a flash memory of his cousin Esther at his Bar-Mitzvah party in his Uncle Herschel's Reform Temple in Riga. She took his hands and pulled him onto the dance floor. In a few minutes of fumbling to follow her steps, he was doing a polka to the music. Nobody yelled *Shanda*! (Shame). Nobody complained that he was holding a girl's hands. Other boys and girls were dancing, and men with women too. Yussel learned that not all Jews are the same. Not all Jews are Orthodox.

Joe chewed and swallowed. "Hmmph," he grunted. "Who has time?" He lowered his spoon to fill it again, but instead, played with the vegetables while he chewed thoughtfully. *Who has time* repeated in his head to excuse his not knowing how to go about getting a wife. Bound by Orthodoxy's, '...a man doesn't touch a woman before they are married...' blocked him from even entering the starting gate. Certainly, there was no point in his attending the monthly HIAS dance where he would have to hold the girl. He had solved his problem of the awkwardness he felt at the thought of holding a girl. He excused himself from taking such a bold step because God didn't allow it.

Suddenly he was back in Riga again. He remembered that his urge to see Naomi Rabinowitz had made him bundle up against the winter and walk down the slippery road to Tchernivakh to visit her. Earlier, in August, when he had knocked on her door to sell her mother a cabbage from his mother's garden, he had fallen in love with Naomi. On his subsequent visits she had been very daring while they sat at the table in her mother's kitchen. Hidden behind the almost-to-the-floor-tablecloth that she spread on the table they moved their legs toward each other and touched shoes. Yussel remembered that they hardly drank any of their tea or eaten their bread slices. They seemed interested only in touching higher than the shoe to each other's leg. When he lay in his bed that night he wondered if God saw that he and Naomi had touched legs under the table.

For two years, with all his focus on staying alive and learning his trade, the few moments of dancing with his cousin Esther and those three short visits to Naomi had been his only experiences with a girl, until Mrs. Wolansky, in America, ... with whom he had done more than dance a polka, or touch legs.

Joe questioned his father. "If Moe is not getting married why would he move to the Bronx? He has to take two subway trains to get to the shop."

"He says these tenements are an old design. There's no privacy in the bedroom. He says he can't even talk to Lily or Sarah or Khannah or Rachel without you or me walking through to get to our rooms. A railroad flat, he says, built like a train. You have to walk through one room to get to another."

Joe, who didn't date didn't have the same need for privacy as Moe. He had wanted to treat Papa and Moish to the best. He argued for his tenement that he had been so proud of when he first rented it. "The landlord put in electricity, Papa, no more gas."

"The plumbing, Joe, the plumbing. In the Bronx apartments Moe won't have to share the toilet with God knows who?"

"Moe buys fancy suits, now he wants a fancy apartment."

"Why not, Joe. He has the money. You have the money--"

"There are Jews there?"

Duvvid grunted cynically, ""Hmph. We have been pushed all over. There are Jews everywhere."

"That's why I like it here, Papa. It's like a Jewish city." Joe had a sudden thought. "Are you going to move with Moe?"

Duvvid took a moment. "I would like a new apartment, too."

Joe wrestled with the feeling of being deserted by the two people closest to him. "I would have to take two trains on the subway to get to my shop."

"So you'll start work at eight in the morning instead of seven-thirty. Of course if you had a wife, you wouldn't mind that Moe and I are living in the Bronx and you are here."

Duvvid, while delighted that one of his sons had maintained their Orthodoxy, he understood Joe's dilemma. Whether it was Joe's shyness or the tenet of Orthodoxy that made Joe's courtship of a girl difficult, Duvvid made the logical suggestion. "Maybe you should talk to a *shadkhan* (marriage broker)."

Joe stopped eating, looked at his father and listened.

"She will tell you about the girls who live here and even suggest one who would be right for you."

"A religious girl?"

"Of course."

Joe thought about it. "You know a *shadkhan?*"

"At the synagogue I can find one for you."
"Joe nodded. "Find one."

Conversation with Papa Duvvid had put it on the table. Joe finally faced the possibility of his choosing a woman to live with as his wife. Successful adult in his world of business, but untried in the consideration of a love, Joe continued to lean on his Orthodoxy instead of apportioning some of his thinking time to ask and to answer the many questions about his feelings that he should grapple with. Rather, he continued to focus on the eventual establishment of his own factory and would wait for the *shadkhan*, a Mrs. Rosenberg, to come up with suggestions. It was his habitual way in such matters, the easy route in which he gave short shrift to matters other than work and business. Thus Joe avoided involvement in having to make a decision that required him to know his feelings.

CHAPTER 11

1913

Hannah Henneberg was born in a New York tenement to a Romanian immigrant family. She was their first American born. Two more siblings followed, Al and Arthur. Her older siblings, Lena and Sam, born in Europe, had a tough time learning the English language. In their European ghetto they had spoken Yiddish mixed with Romanian. Transplanted to America, they had the usual difficult time expressing their thoughts in English and would never get rid of their accents entirely. Hannah, born in America, easily avoided those problems.

When Hannah played children's games at school, her classmates chose the American-born child over the immigrant. Hannah felt good about being accepted as an American. She determined to never speak English with a Romanian or Yiddish accent. She spoke fluent Yiddish but she would keep that a secret for appropriate times.

The one ingredient that dominated immigrant life more than any other was money. For the men it was "Will I be able to find work? How to make enough money?" For the young women expecting to marry, like Hannah Henneberg, the caution was "Don't fall in love with a man who can't make a living."

Displaced into a new country, men who had a particular skill hooked up with the industry that could utilize them, as Yussel Reinerman did. With a few adjustments, like working on ladies' shoes only, and just the uppers of ladies' shoes, instead of the whole shoe for a man or a woman as he did in Russia, he immediately found his niche in the American shoe industry that had already become specialized to that degree.

Specialization was the key to the profitable expansion of American industry. In Riga Joseph had been responsible to produce a pair of shoes all by himself. But in America when he worked for Lefkowitz he stitched the upper only. In his own shop he continued to do just the one operation.

When Henry Ford decided to produce the whole car his thinking was no farther ahead than Yussel's had been in Riga. Ford assigned a group of skilled metal workers and ignition technicians to produce a finished car. When done, the group started to make another. However, Ford determined there must be a better, faster way. He found his cue in the assembly line production of Chicago's meatpacking houses. As hanging carcasses were carried past workers on a motorized endless belt they hacked off the same piece from each carcass during their ten-hour day.

Ford decided the assembly line was the answer. He worked five years perfecting his Model T assembly line, 1903 to 1908. The moving belt brought the work to each worker's station where he repeated the same operation all his working day, pointing the way to changing the character of American industry. Such manufacturing specialization led to higher output per worker and became universally sought to expand every industry of American Capitalism.

In America, Joe Reinerman was a success at his specialization. He stitched the uppers of ladies shoes for companies that manufactured the whole shoe. But he remembered his satisfaction when he, himself, made the whole pair of shoes from start to finish. He had started the process by penciling the outline on paper around the customer's stocking feet, which became the pattern for the size and width of the left and right shoes. He then went on to cut, stitch and nail the leather into a finished left and right shoe.

In his mind Joe ran through the specializations of labor that would be needed in his eventual factory. A designer would have to create a new style of shoe that Moe and he agreed was right for the market. The pattern maker would make the metal-edged patterns from sample size 4B to 10D. Joe would oversee the manufacturing process that started at the cutter's block, the pieces sent to the stitchers, then to the lasters, the heelers, inspectors, and finally, packed and shipped to the customer.

When Moe moves to the Bronx, thought Joe, marries and settles down, I'll talk to him … see what he thinks about setting up our own factory.

The *shadkhan*, Mrs. Rosenberg, knew of Joe's standing in the Orthodox synagogue as a result of his generous contributions, which had been announced from the pulpit. When she heard that 19-year-old Hannah, also of an Orthodox family, was interested in making a match she knocked on the Henneberg's apartment and offered to talk with them about the fine young men who would make Hannah a good husband.

Hannah listened to Mrs. Rosenberg talk about each of the four likely men who had paid her an exploratory fee. Hearing that Joe Reinerman was already a business success, most of Hannah's questions were about him.

"He's been here nine years?" Hannah asked.

"Almost a native," joked Mrs. Rosenberg.

"But he still speaks English with an accent?"

Rosenberg hesitated. "Well," she hedged, "You can tell he's from Russia."

Hannah didn't like that he still spoke with an accent, but that he had his own successful business aroused Hannah's strong interest. With a good businessman for a husband she would show her family and her brothers and sisters that she too knew how to make a success of her life. Hannah asked about Joe Reinerman's appearance.

He was five feet five inches, two inches taller than Hannah; not fat, but healthy looking.

Rosenberg explained that Joe was living alone because his brother Moe had just married and Moe and his father had moved to the Bronx.

Hannah sat quietly processing Rosenberg's information. Joe living alone had a positive side, an important selling point to Hannah. She'd had more than enough of sharing her daily space with four siblings and two parents. Alone, with a husband only, she could actually be running the household without having to worry about the needs or opinions of six other people.

All of Hannah's questions were about Joe's externals. Since they were both Orthodox it was silently accepted that both were virgins and had no experience in making love. After the proper wedding, with God's help, the bliss of marriage would bless them both.

Of the four young women Mrs. Rosenberg described to Joe, he chose to think seriously about Hannah Henneberg. Orthodox too, he expected that she would keep a kosher house and do what Joe needed her to do, shop, cook, clean and run the house. Because of his early turbulent life, he had never courted a woman. His need to apprentice to learn his trade had to be his focus under the difficult conditions of pretending he was Christian. Joe had inadvertently avoided the time when a young man and woman experiment being with each other. Courtship could have taken Joe steps further in the maturing process had he at least talked with a young woman, spent time often enough and long enough to know whether he did or did not like to be with her.

Joe had gladly avoided such confusing complexities of emotional decision-making. With Naomi in Tchernivakh he had just begun to put a first foot into the courtship process when the threatening wave of new attacks on Jews alerted his Uncle Herschel. Herschel prepared Joe and sent him to Reverend Vilitsin's house in Riga to learn how to don his Christian masquerade to start his three-year-apprenticeship to learn a trade.

In Russia, whether it was Tchernivakh or Riga, Yussel was always on guard, automatically questioning, *"Am I safe here?"* When he met someone, his first concern was, *"Will I be safe with him?"*

In America, where he no longer had to fear being assaulted brought him such immense relief yet it would take him a long time to relax and take it for granted. Little wonder that he felt comfortable only when he was snuggled into the Jewish culture and religion of Manhattan's Lower East Side. That was the reason that Moe's moving to the 'outside', unknown world of the Bronx stunned Joe. He couldn't imagine himself moving away from his *Mammalushen,* his Yiddish language. He had felt awkward in the early days of his contracting shop when he had to speak in his heavily accented English when asking for orders. It was a great relief for Joe to find out that his brother Moe was such a good salesman and handled their business with that 'other world' so well.

Mrs. Rosenberg had Joe Reinerman and Hannah Henneberg meet in her small office. She arranged the chairs so that her two applicants sat facing each other.

Hannah had pulled back her coal black hair from her face and gathered it into a bun high on the back of her head, colored her lips and nails a light red. She determined that she would not shave her head and wear the *scheitel* (wig) of the traditional married Orthodox woman. But she decided not to mention it unless and until they agreed to marry.

Joe saw that she was an attractive young woman. Knowing that she and her family were Orthodox answered all his other questions. He would provide the money for running the family. She would do all the rest. He didn't know what else to ask her. Joe decided yes but he didn't say so. He thought he would ask that they meet again before accepting Hannah.

Hannah had come prepared to say yes based on his successful business, but she waited for him to talk, maybe ask questions. He was a little fatter than she was told but he seemed healthy.

Joe asked, "Can we meet again and decide?"

Mrs. Rosenberg looked at Hannah.

Hannah nodded and said, "Yes."

A week later they sat facing each other, nodded, smiled to each other, said yes, they agreed to marry.

"I will keep my hair," said Hannah.

About to offer them a paper to sign, Mrs. Rosenberg stopped and looked at Joe.

Joe frowned, puzzled at the possible obstacle.

"I will be a good Jewish wife," Hannah said, "but I will not shave my hair and wear a wig."

Joe sat and thought.

The two others held their breaths and waited.

Joe shrugged, nodded. He offered a puzzled smile to Hannah. "All right," he said to her.

Hannah and Mrs. Rosenberg breathed again.

Mrs. Rosenberg had them both sign the paper that guaranteed her fee.

Joe and Hannah married for the wrong reasons. Each had left too much of the relationship in God's hands. Joe didn't know what Hannah wanted in life.

He would find out.

CHAPTER 12

1914

The high roundness of the middle of the braided bread seemed to be pushing upward against its white linen covering. It made her wonder which of Joe's crude efforts at lovemaking had made her pregnant. She had taken for granted that they both had waited until after the wedding to learn about making love. Yet after almost a year, it never seemed to change. Hannah had thought to ask her older sister Lena, who seemed happy in her marriage to Harold, but at the last minute Hannah felt too shy. *Anyway,* she decided, *who can talk about such things?*

Hannah did count her blessings. *At least,* she mused, *there is always enough money. Joe is a good provider. But a man who works as hard as he does should have a better place to live, newer, with a private toilet in the bathroom. Here on the Lower East Side it is concrete sidewalks, asphalt streets and old, smelly buildings, buildings, buildings, so crowded it feels we're on top of each other.*

Her advancing pregnancy was pushing Hannah toward having her first argumentative encounter with Joe about moving to a better place. She knew she didn't want to have her first child in this tenement, or any tenement. One of her strongest reasons for accepting marriage with Joe was that he was an established businessman who, she thought, would want to live in as nice a place as he could afford.

After reading a large sign advertising new, modern apartments in Brooklyn, Hannah asked Lena to go with her to check out the new apartment building in the Reid-Stuyvesant area of Brooklyn.

The sisters came up out of the subway onto De Kalb Avenue, the noisy business district. In the gutter, commercial horse-and-wagons dominated the few automobile-trucks. Streams of people crowded the sidewalks to shop the unbroken line of small stores on each side of De Kalb Avenue for everyday needs. They spilled over into the street, causing the passing trolley car's motorman to clang his gong constantly to clear the tracks of people. A street cleaner dressed in white and white helmet, wheeling a trash can, shovel and broom, dodged his way among them to clean up the occasional horse droppings and trash that people left behind.

The noisy hurry and flurry reminded the sisters of the crowds and yelling in Manhattan's pushcart area of Delancey and Allen Streets. But pushcarts were not allowed here. Stores, one after another under the apartments on both sides of the street carried everything from furniture to food, whatever the local residents needed.

Hannah and Lena walked the half-block to Kosciusko Street and turned right toward Reid Avenue. After crossing Reid they felt they were entering a jungle. The sidewalk slate slabs were bordered tightly on one side by the fence of each small house that was built right up to the sidewalk, and on the other side by the fat trunks of maple trees that hung their leafy canopy just above the sidewalk all along its length. The leaves, darting in the breeze played a game of twinkling lights and shadows over the walk.

The slabs-of-slate sidewalk was uneven. The tree roots had grown large over the years and lifted the sidewalk slabs in an uneven pattern of ups and downs, causing the sisters to carefully plan their steps. Bent over and cramped in between the fences and the trees reminded Lena of the narrow streets of the crowded *shtetl* (hut) in the Bisnivinya ghetto in Romania where she had lived for her first nine years.

Halfway down the block the jungle suddenly released them to sunlight, blue sky, and a wide expanse of level ground. The owner-builder had chosen Kosciusko Street full of single-family cottages, as the place to drop his two-storied, eight-unit apartment building, smack dab in the middle of the block between Reid and Stuyvesant Avenues. There seemed to be an equal number of cottages lined up on either side of the new structure.

Hannah and Lena looked at the new building. High on the thick, clear glass above the entrance door they read the address in ornate gold numbers, 555 - 57. The builder had apparently bought two lots for his outsized structure. The building stretched its sides to utilize every inch of the land. The cottage resident fences on either side shared the same lot lines with the new building, with no mandated legal space between them. The two-storied structure towered over the cottages on either side like the commander's bridge of a ship.

The unique feature of the new building's entrance was that it had no yard like each of the small, single-family houses all along the block. Instead, the twenty feet of setback space in front had been combined with the ten feet of the city sidewalk and the entire open area of 50 feet wide by 30 feet deep was cemented flat.

Hannah and Lena, daughters of Manhattan's Lower East Side crowds and crowded tenements stood on the open area feeling the sun's warmth and seeing blue sky as they turned to all sides enjoying their expanded sense of open space. Lena looked across the street above the parked horse-and-wagons to the seemingly distant brownstone houses on the other side of the street. "So ... so open," she said.

"And the trees smell so good," Hannah added. Anxious to see what the new apartments looked like, she turned to read the sign hung on the inside of the glass front of the storm door;

Apartments for rent.
See Manager in 1A.

Conflicted, Lena stood quivering like a stalk resisting a strong wind. What a treat it would be to see a new apartment. But she knew her husband Harry, an upholsterer for Signello's Furniture Co., couldn't afford anything more expensive than the tenement apartment they were in for $16 a month. *And these new ones in Brooklyn? Who knows how much the rent is?*

Holding back, Lena looked at her younger sister's excited face. *Sure,* Lena thought, sad with envy, *Hannah's ready to move in. Of course, her Joe makes good money and she doesn't even have her first baby yet.* But Lena realized again the difference between them. Hannah was born in America. She didn't know what it was to be a frightened Jew jammed into the Bisnivinya ghetto. Lena smiled wryly.

Knowing that Hannah was pregnant with her first, Lena moved ahead of her sister to mount the two, wide concrete steps and pull open the heavy glass door framed in solid steel and painted black. They entered a square storm vestibule, 10 feet by 12 feet, its floor made of hundreds of tiny, white ceramic tiles. Lena pulled open the second heavy glass door and followed Hannah into the hallway where the entire floor was laid with thousands of the white tiles. No furnishings, every sound echoed off the tiles, steel and stone in the empty space. Ahead of them was a marble-stepped staircase to the second floor. On their left was the door to an apartment, but it was not the manager's. Close to the entrance on the right wall was a gleaming brass square of letterboxes. Hannah stopped to look at the nameplates. One was marked Greene, Mgr. Four nameplates were labeled Sopolsky, Brodsky, Cohen and Sokolov. Four were empty.

Hannah and Lena walked to the back of the floor and found the manager's door under the staircase. Hannah rang the bell.

A woman opened the door and continued wiping her hands on her apron. "Yes?" she asked.

Hannah said, Mrs. Greene?"

"Yes, with an E at the end."

Hannah nodded. "I'd like to see one of your empty apartments."

"The front ones are taken already. The back ones are still empty."

"I'd like to see them," Hannah said.

"Sure. I'll get the keys."

Waiting, the sisters felt the newness of the building. There was even a faint smell of fresh paint.

Mrs. Greene led them up the stairs that felt so solid to the sisters of the tenements, and the white marble of each step was attractively grained in wispy curving lines of pink and gray. *Pretty*, thought Hannah as she climbed with her baby up the flight, *even the stairs are pretty*. The dark, grained wood of the banister she held on to attracted her eye as well

On the landing, the manager walked a few steps and opened the door to the apartment. The sisters stepped into a flood of sunlight that made them gasp. Walking the length of the apartment they discovered two bedrooms, a living room, a complete bathroom of sink, toilet and a white porcelain bathtub on a floor of gleaming white tiles, and a complete kitchen, all of it a joy to Hannah. She had no trouble reveling, imagining living in it. Out the back window was a yard with poles that supported wash lines.

Again Lena felt sad knowing she could not afford it. Without money so much was beyond her reach.

Hannah had no such barrier. She swung open the gate of her restricted tenement life and let her imagination run wild. She pictured furnishings in the children's room, her bedroom, but most of all the living room. Suddenly she was remembering the furniture ads in the newspapers, the different styles. She turned so suddenly and with such energy, she startled her sister. "What do you think Lena," Hannah exploded gleefully, "what do you think?"

Lena smiled wispily. "It's beautiful." She turned away from Hannah and spoke to the sunlight quietly. "It's beautiful."

Hannah said, "Let's go down and find out how much it is."

Lena nodded without saying anything.

Hannah knocked on Mrs. Greene's door.

The door opened and the manager smiled pleasantly. "Yes, ladies?"

Hannah said, "It's lovely. How much is the rent?"

"The rent is forty-five dollars a month."

Lena rolled her eyes and turned away.

"Thank you," said Hannah.

Mrs. Greene reached into her apron pocket and came up with a card, which she offered to Hannah. "Here. Call me whichever way you decide."

"Yes. Thanks, I will."

As they left the building Hannah said, "Lena, did you notice the names on the letterboxes?"

"Yes."

"Sopolsky, Brodsky, and maybe Reinerman. The building sounds like Palestine surrounded by the Arabs." Hannah was remembering the Hadassah women. One of them talked about the Jewish National Fund that continued to buy land for new Jewish settlements in Palestine.

CHAPTER 13

On Friday afternoon Joe wondered whether Moe would come back to the shop.

But Moe didn't show up.

Friday is a dead day for salesmen. Moe had a contact call to make at two o'clock and then he spent the rest of the afternoon schmoozing with the other salesmen at Glickstein's Kosher Café. Since he didn't come in on Sunday like Joe did, it gave him an early start on a relaxing weekend with Lily.

The two Italian fitters turned off their lights, said goodnight to Joe and left. Only the one bulb over Joe's machine lit the darkness in the small shop. Joe got up to use the toilet at the far corner of the store and came out lighting a Murad cigarette. The shop was quiet. He drew the smoke in deeply and let it out like a long sigh; the end of the day; the end of the week; a good week. A sudden strong gust of March wind rattled the plate glass window. Joe had a sudden spasm of fear remembering the Russian Christians breaking Jewish windows on All Hallows Eve. But here in New York the wind passed on without doing any damage. Joe continued to look out. The street was darkening quickly. Thin lines of people hurried homeward wrapped in coats, scarves and hats.

Joe saw the small pile of uppers lying in the corner, his big mistake. Thirty-two pairs stitched wrong. Thank God it was not the whole order of 245 pairs. The new brown leather and the thin pale linings no longer reflected the light, so thickly were they covered with dust. "Why do I leave them there to aggravate myself?" He muttered. "Monday morning I'll throw them in the ash can."

He reached up and took the worn whiskbroom from off its rusty nail over the dirty cast-iron sink that smelled foully of soap scum. He brushed at his vest and bulging waist. The thread ends and the leather nap reluctantly dropped from him. He brushed his thighs to his knees but couldn't bend further to brush his lower legs. His face reddened uncomfortably and he unhappily gave it up. He stomped his feet hoping it would do what he couldn't.

Straightening and exhaling his constrained breath he stood for a moment and felt the peace of his silent shop. He also felt the heat of his cigarette's burning end on his fingers. He threw the butt into the sink, put on his scarf, coat and hat and locked up.

On the clanging, clattering, cross-town trolley that would take him to his tenement he felt hunger gnawing inside him. He smiled wryly as he remembered his meager menu days in Russia. He sniffed cheerily as if he were already inside the flat having *Erev Shabbas* (Sabbath Eve). *Hannah will have lit the candles. The kitchen will smell sweet from the fresh-baked khallah. There will be hot soup, browned chicken and tsimmis.* He smiled, but it barely moved his lips. His plump face remained sad, puzzled, thinking of his two lives.

*   *   *

Hannah Reinerman lifted the cooled khallah, the large, braided Sabbath bread from the stove. She placed it in the center of the starched white tablecloth, and covered it with a large, white linen napkin. One end pointed to Joe's setting and the other end toward hers. From the shelf near the stove she took the two candles in their brass holders and stood them in front of the bread. She struck a match on the side of the matchbox and lit them. For a moment she watched the small flames waver as they grew to full size and flared steadily. She lifted the clean white kitchen towel from her shoulders and spread it on her head so that the hanging ends guided the heat of the flames to her face in God's caress.

In response Hannah whispered the Hebrew prayer. "Blessed art thou O Lord our God, King of the universe, who commands us to light the Sabbath candles."

After the prayer, in silence, she moved her hands continuously to gather more heat to her face. Thankful for the warmth, she smiled. She lifted the brass holders and placed them behind the bread so that the light would continue to bless the meal.

Joe had bought the large kitchen table in preparation for Moe and Papa Duvvid coming to live with him. The surface was sheet steel covered in durable white porcelain that could be cleaned quickly with a damp cloth. Placed against the wall it could still seat four people comfortably. For the Sabbath, its utilitarian simplicity was elevated by the starched white tablecloth and sacred holiday items.

The sweet smell of the fresh baked bread mingled with that of the browned chicken and the sweet potatoes, carrots, and prunes of the cooked *tsimmis*. Hannah felt that she had created something good for the Sabbath. Despite the ugly smells of the tenement outside her door, at least in her kitchen all was clean, white, and with the good smells of plenty as God asked for on His Sabbath.

Joe pushed his plate from him and wiped his mouth, chin and hands with the white linen napkin reserved for Friday nights. "Ach, Hannah, that was very, very good." He had eaten until he felt stuffed. *What a good feeling.* "Where's my paper?"

"It's on the dining room table."

Usually she brought it to him when he finished eating, but Hannah remained at the sink scraping bones from the plates into a brown paper bag and running the warm water over the large rectangle of soap imprinted with the word *Kosher* in blue for dish suds.

Matching the agitated work rhythms of her hands and fingers was Hannah's active mental review of the synagogue meeting two days ago of the Women's Auxiliary. A committee from Hadassah, the Women's International Medical Committee, spoke to them about Hadassah's activities. One was in charge of finding homes for orphans, not only in Palestine, but right here in New York. One woman was in charge of raising money for a new hospital in Jerusalem. Another woman was in charge of finding and sending medical supplies to people in Africa. One worked with the Jewish National Fund that continued to raise money for new settlements in Palestine. The Hadassah women offered their audience of Orthodox women the chance to support and help with the international work of Hadassah, not only for Jews but for people of the world who were in need.

It was not only extraordinary for Hannah to hear about women connecting with other places and people beyond their homes but to think that their lives were more than being only concerned about whether the *khallah*, chicken and *tsimmis* were cooked just right for the Sabbath meal. The Hadassah women had broken through religious restraints not only in their thinking to actively help other people as well as Jews, but in their stylish dress they differed from the standard, dull dress of Orthodox women.

Hannah, American-born into a vortex of Jewish immigrant Orthodoxy, had always felt her difference. The Hadassah women fulfilled the American Woman image for her. Their modern appearance in the latest dress and hairstyles opened Hannah's heart and mind to what they were saying. Hannah realized that these were the modern American women she yearned to emulate. Seeing and hearing them helped her to understand why she had always wanted to get beyond the Lower East Side of Manhattan. She thought sadly she would have done better with Joe's brother, Moe, who was already living in a new apartment in the Bronx. *Oh well,* Hannah thought resignedly, *this is my marriage, but I'll make it work.*

Their dining room was next to the kitchen. It had been just another room in the railroad flat until Hannah convinced Joe they should buy the mahogany dining set, a small table and four upholstered, straight-backed chairs. It had been expensive but she convinced him that they had to have something besides a kitchen table when relatives came to visit.

Unhappy as he had been about the prospect of spending so much money, when he sat on the straight-backed chair to try it out, he quickly agreed with Hannah. He was too short and heavy for the soft upholstered chair or couch, and had a terrible time trying to get up out of them. His arms waved wildly as if he were drowning as he tried to throw his weight forward to stand up.

But tonight the cold and dark of the unlit dining room surprised and disappointed Joe. Before sundown on Friday, Hannah usually snapped on the light of the overhead chandelier because that's where Joe liked to read his paper. Not being lit, he returned to the kitchen, for on Sabbath eve a pious Jew may not kindle or extinguish a light.

"How come you didn't light the dining room?" he asked her.

"Oh, I forgot." Hannah plunged into an apologetic fabrication. "I had so much to do today. I couldn't get a chicken at Davidson's so I went over to Rosenbaum's . . . " She continued with more excuses but Joe had dropped into his chair at the table and was straightening out the creases of his newspaper.

Hannah came over to the table with a straight butter knife and a plate to scrape the breadcrumbs from the tablecloth. The sweet warm smell of her as she worked briskly, stirred him. He looked at her active breasts and enjoyed the pleasure of knowing that she would satisfy him tonight. *Later, later,* he thought happily. He turned a page of the newspaper. He wondered vaguely how much her pregnancy would interfere with his pleasure in the coming months.

It didn't occur to Joe that Hannah's continuing to work was not normal. It had been a long and exhausting day of shopping, cooking, baking and she would have been happy to sit at the table and chat with him and think pleasurably of going to bed with him. But angered agitation stirred a hidden energy in her as if she had just risen in the morning to her first tasks of the day.

Finally the dishes were done. As she wiped down the cracked cement drain she wondered how she should say it to him. To guess what Joe's reaction might be Hannah rehearsed a sentence silently, It's a shame for such a pretty dining room set to stand in such a room. She felt that it set a non-argumentative tone. She decided to start by saying it from the sink. "It's a shame, Joe, for such a pretty dining room set to stand in such a room."

Joe looked up from his paper and grunted, asking her to repeat it.

Hannah said it more loudly. "It's a shame for such a pretty dining room set to stand in such a room." Relieved that what she said was without hostility, she thought it a good beginning.

Puzzled, Joe said, "It looks nice in the dining room."

Hannah spoke more pointedly. "It's such a beautiful set, it should be in a more beautiful room."

"Where else could we put it?" Joe asked. "In the bedroom?" He laughed at his unexpected joke.

Hannah smiled a weak appreciation and carried on. "It needs a new flat, a new apartment."

Joe put the newspaper down and turned his head toward her.

Hannah saw his blank look and she waited nervously.

"A new flat?" he questioned.

Hannah nodded, and added, "Yes, a new flat."

Joe's horizon was limited to Lower East Side tenements. "Why should we get a new flat? This is one of the best."

But her older siblings' stories about trees and fresh air in the old country filled Hannah's head. During the day in Bisnivinya, when her sister Lena and her brother Sam had been allowed out of the ghetto, they spent hours wandering in the woods outside Bisnivinya. The air was so sweet and the birds sang to them.

Joe thought of another argument. "A new flat for four chairs?"

"No. Not just for four chairs. We're going to have a baby and I won't let a baby be born into such a house."

Joe stared, not comprehending. "Why not? There must be a hundred children in this house."

"That's just what I mean. It's a pigsty, a noisy pigsty. I wouldn't raise a child in this house."

Joe had picked out this latest of tenements with loving care for his brother Moe and Papa Duvvid. He could not see it with Hannah's eyes, nor remember how many years it was since he first rented the apartment. And she had raised her voice at him as if he had made some terrible mistake. But she had been happy to marry him and live in his house. What happened?

"We have what we need," Joe said, wondering where and what the problem was. "And it's clean--"

"Yes, I work my arms off keeping it clean. But I can't clean what's outside our door. And I don't want to use a toilet that everybody else uses. Doesn't that bother you?"

Hannah waited to see if she was having an effect.

Joe was stumped. He had to agree with her. He didn't like the shared toilet either. He looked at Hannah. "So?"

"So," she mimicked and put her agenda on his table. "Would you move to Brooklyn?"

"Brooklyn?" *Yenner velt*, (another planet). Joe had gotten so used to his tight little Kosher world of Manhattan's Lower East Side that he had never thought beyond it. "Brooklyn," he repeated, "why Brooklyn?"

"Because that's where they have new apartments and trees and it's sunny and it's clean and new and the toilet is private for us."

Joe wondered how she got all this information. Then he realized. "You saw it?"

"Yes. Lena and I went to see it when her Clara and Milton were in school."

Hannah, his wife, did something so important without telling him? He realized that he didn't even know she was unhappy here. "How ... how did you know about it?"

"There's a large sign over the bank on Hester Street."

"You took the subway?"

"Of course. That's the only way to cross the bridge."

Joe had thought of his wife as being in the house; never thought that there might not be enough to keep her busy and interested to stay in the house all day. Still surprised about this new thought, he said, "So you and Lena made a trip?"

"Yes, it was nice to get out."

Joe picked up his Yiddish newspaper, *Der Tag*.

"Joe, I want to move from here. I've had enough of the noise, the dirt and the garbage in the streets--"

Joe held up the spread fingers of one hand and shook his head. "It can't happen one-two-three. Let me think about it." He picked up his paper again.

"What's to think about, Joe. I'm not going to have your baby here."

"So you'll have it at the hospital."

"I'm not going to bring a child home to this."

"This is so terrible?"

Hannah knew where Joe was going. She cut him off. "And don't talk to me about Russia. You don't live in Russia anymore. This is America and you've got a good business. We don't have to live like poor people anymore."

Joe put the paper up in front of his face because he wanted Hannah to stop. He had to think. *We've got everything I need right here. She wants to change my whole life.*

CHAPTER 14

1914

Moe brought in an order of 220 uppers to be stitched and he proudly dropped the large brown paper package on the floor at Joe's machine. With a grin he rolled his cigar to the other side of his mouth and stood waiting for Joe's compliment for his successful trip to *Tartini's Shoes*. Joe raised his voice to be heard above the noise of Bagelli's and Alcinio's machines and said instead, "Moe, what do you think we make the whole shoe?"

Moe took a moment to switch gears. "The whole shoe?" He raised his hands to indicate the space they were in. "Where? Here?"

"No. We'll find a bigger place."

Moe hadn't thought that Joe would have the courage to take on that kind of project. And what a project! Moe looked critically at Joe. "Do you know what you're saying, Joe?"

"Of course I know what I'm saying. You're out there. See if you can find an empty building, at least empty floor space."

Moe stared at Joe. Questions were tumbling through Moe's head. "Are you ready to compete against the big boys?"

"Yes. Why not?"

"Why not? It's going to take some investment. Do you have enough capital?"

"I have enough. You'll be my head salesman. You're going to sell our shoes to the stores this time, not just subcontract with the manufacturers for ladies' uppers."

"Have you told Irv?"

"No, not yet."

Irv Grodsky, a first cousin to Moe whom he had recommended for Joe's accountant. Irv did Joe's books once a month and had become something of a financial advisor to Joe. Business trends fascinated Irv. Whenever Joe had time to listen, Irv would tell him when to expect his slow or his overtime work seasons. Irv continued his studies at City College to become a Certified Public Accountant.

Moe shook his head. "I think you should talk to Irv. Maybe this is not the right time."

"It's not going to happen tomorrow. I'll talk to him the next time he comes in to do the books. In the meantime while you're running around look for a space."

Moe suddenly had a vision that excited him. "Yeah, I will, Joe," Moe said. "I'll look." Moe saw himself not only as head salesman, but a full partner in the new business. "Yeah, Joe," he said again and sailed out the door.

* * *

Hannah determined that when her baby was born she would be living in the Brooklyn apartment. Even if, God forbid, Joe decides against it. If she had to do this on her own she would need money. Without Joe how could she find enough to put down a deposit, or may be the whole first month's rent? She had some arithmetic to figure out, a wife's secret mathematics, unless Joe changes his mind.

The baby was due in just under two months. Could she get together enough in that time to put a deposit, a healthy deposit on the first month's rent? Could the apartment be theirs and waiting if she could find a way to pay the first month's rent? Would Mrs. Greene accept a deposit and hold it for her?

Hannah struggled with her homework. Joe gave her an allowance of $15 a week to run the house and for all her personal needs. Joe paid the monthly doctor bill and, although he had fussed about it, a midwife bill. Lena had urged Hannah to be checked by the nurse, the older and very experienced Mrs. Olstein who would be there on the spot when the baby was born. Hannah agreed and argued with Joe to pay for the nurse's midwife services.

All this was new territory to Joe. Inexperienced in anything other than his work he couldn't give it the attention he gave to his shop. *Hannah insisted she needed the midwife?* Joe reluctantly agreed to pay for Mrs. Olstein's monthly visits.

Hannah continued to mentally put dollars together to come up with a possible solution in case ... in case ... if she could save $5 a week from her allowance, it would take nine weeks to have a month's rent. But someone might rent it in the meantime. What if she promised to give Mrs. Greene a $15 deposit to hold it for the extra month until she had all forty-five dollars. In the meantime she'd have Joe look at the apartment. She would have to convince Mrs. Greene that she really would move into it even if Joe decided No. *If Joe decides no,* thought Hannah, *what then?*

Hannah dialed Lena's number. "Lena, can you go with me again tomorrow to see Mrs. Greene?"

"At the apartment?"

"Yes."

"Why, what happened?"

"I'll explain on the subway."

"Call her to make sure she will be there."

"Oh, yeah, I will."

"All right, after nine when I get the kids off to school."

On the train Hannah explained to Lena the different possibilities she had thought of.

Lena listened to all of it then was silent. After a moment she said, "It all depends on Mrs. Greene. Stop upsetting yourself. Wait till we get there."

The walk from the De Kalb Avenue station to the house was slower than before because of the heaviness of Hannah's seven-month pregnancy. Especially difficult for her were the uneven slate slabs of the sidewalk.

Finally the sisters were relieved to get to the level area in front of the building. Lena pulled open the heavy glass door of the storm vestibule and then the second door. They walked to the end of the hallway and rang Mrs. Greene's bell. Hannah was noticeably panting by this time and Mrs. Greene immediately invited them in to sit down and rest while they talked.

As Hannah added dollars and subtracted dollars from the different possibilities she had thought about, Ms. Greene's face frowned and she looked puzzled. She interrupted Hannah to say, "Mr. Densky, the landlord, requires that you sign a year's lease and pay a month's rent in advance, before you move in."

Lena looked at her sister. Hannah sat speechless, her mouth open. There was no way this could happen without Joe agreeing to move. Hannah knew well how much Joe wanted to stay where he was. It brought Hannah smack up against the question, "Is the marriage only for Joe, or is it for Hannah also?" It frightened her to think of the argument that faced her.

Depressed, she spoke quietly to the manager. "Well, thank you, Mrs. Greene. I'll talk to my husband."

In the subway they put their nickels in the slots and went through the turnstiles. On the station, Hannah looked for the occasional bench to sit on and rest while they waited for the train. But there was none. She was on the verge of tears.

Lena put her arm around Hannah not only in sisterly sympathy, but in wifely understanding. Her Harold wasn't such a big shot. He was much easier to deal with. Hannah's Joe was the boss in charge. It was hard for him to consider Hannah's need if it disagreed with his.

After supper, instead of bringing Joe his paper Hannah sat down in her usual seat opposite him. Joe said, "You didn't bring my paper."

"No. Can we talk?"

"Talk?"

"Yes. It's only five weeks before the baby will be born."

"So?"

"I want him to start off in a nice house--"

"This is not good enough for you?"

"Is it good enough for you?"

"It's close to my work--"

"So you'll take the subway. Lena and I did it twice already. And," she continued pointedly, "you're not pregnant."

Not comprehending, Joe's eyes widened questioningly for a moment. Then for the first time Joe glimpsed that the pregnancy was difficult for Hannah. He'd hardly had to give it a thought. It was in her body, she was taking care of it. Like a ray of light that pierced his self-centeredness, he saw that his wife had a problem that maybe he too, should wrestle with. But uncomfortable with this rare acceding to her needs he stalled, said, "So?"

"So," Hannah mimicked, "I'd like you to go look at the apartment in Brooklyn this Sunday." Her voice was impatient with him, almost angry.

Joe didn't know why he felt uncomfortable at her giving him no choice. His lips worked silently until he found his voice. "All right, I'll go. Get me my paper."

Hannah let out her held breath in relief. She struggled her large belly upward to get his paper.

Sunday was a psychic revolution for Joe Reinerman. Walking to the subway with his wife he wasn't hurrying to the trolley to get to his shop, the center of his life. He paced himself according to the needs of his wife, to slow down when she was out of breath, or to stop altogether after she climbed the stairs from the subway to land once more on De Kalb Avenue. Of course he could have made the grand leap to maturity had he thought to call a cab for the ride across the bridge to Brooklyn and back because Hannah's condition asked for maximum consideration. But perhaps his hidden anger at turning control of his day over to Hannah sabotaged his being even more considerate of her than adjusting his pace to her needs as they walked.

It may have crossed Hannah's mind too, that it would have been nice not to expend so much extra effort walking, but perhaps she thought she had won enough concessions from Joe for the day. And now that he had agreed to look, their move may even happen! And in time!

Hannah rang Mrs. Greene's bell. She introduced Joe and accepted the keys. As Joe and Hannah approached the stairs Hannah asked Joe to hold the keys saying that she had to hold on to the banister.

Joe opened the door and followed Hannah into the short hallway. The smell of brand newness and the brightness were indeed *yenner velt* (another world) from the tenements. The difference startled, yet pleased Joe. The sensible layout and larger rooms had him ignoring the need that he hugged to his chest, to live primarily among things Jewish. The thought of living on this new level threw open even Joe's closed doors, his tenement environment that surrounded his daily living.

After a thorough tour he stood and kept nodding in agreement with Hannah's praises of the apartment. Yes, he thought, this is how a successful businessman should live. He smiled to Hannah and nodded vigorously.

Hannah reached over her belly and managed to embrace him, difficult but she had to express her love for him for his decision.

Joe held Hannah carefully. It was a rare moment for him too. He had done something for his wife and had won her warm reward. Their embrace mutually expressed love for the other, indeed a rare moment.

"Thank you, Joe."

Joe felt equally grateful for the unusual moment, but words didn't come as easily for him.

The movers were having scheduling troubles. Gasman, head of the Direct Move franchise, called to say that the truck slated for the Reinerman move was delayed in Albany by Mrs. Vonderhahn, who had postponed her move to a week later.

Hannah, now in her ninth month, panicked and called Lena but could hardly talk.

When Lena finally understood she said, "I'll call Mrs. Olstein and tell her she should look in on you every day in case something happens. I'll call Dr. Smilowitz and tell him it could happen any time."

At the end of his working day, just before Joe and Hannah sat down to supper, Smilowitz drove his Model T to their tenement. Hannah had two weeks yet for her full term. Smilowitz checked her. "So far, so good," he told Hannah and Joe. "If anything happens, God forbid, your water breaks," he turned to Joe, "You take her immediately to the hospital."

Joe nodded in agreement, but didn't know how he could do that unless Moe stayed in the shop all that day.

Gasman called and said the movers would be there in two days.

Hannah was in no condition to pack. She made a verbal arrangement with Gasman to have the movers pack everything and put everything in its place at the new apartment. She would be there to tell them where everything goes.

At dinner that night Hannah said, "Joe, I'll need seventy-five or eighty-five dollars in cash for the movers and for the cab."

"For the cab?"

"Yes, Mrs. Olstein and I need it to go to the apartment. I can't walk from the subway anymore."

When the movers were half through emptying their tenement apartment, Hannah called Mrs. Olstein. "You'll call the Model T Cab Company. You get in and come over here to pick me up and we'll drive to the new apartment in Brooklyn."

"Yes. Are you all right?"

"Yes, fine so far."

"Good. I'll be there."

"I'm excited."

"Don't get too excited, Hannah, you have a week yet."

"All right, all right."

Hannah could hardly manage the stairs to her new apartment. One hand on the banister, she held on to Mrs. Olstein with the other. Yet she tried to hurry to get out of the way of the movers.

Hannah finally made it to the apartment but there was no bed yet to lie down in. However, the kitchen table and chairs were in place. Mrs. Olstein helped Hannah to a seat in the kitchen so she could rest her arms and head on the table. Grateful, Hannah closed her eyes. Exhausted, she hoped she would sleep.

Despite the noises of the movers shouting directions to each other, their heavy footsteps and the thumping of the furniture, Hannah instantly went into never-never land. She dreamed she was again on the rare trip her family had taken to Coney Island to get away from the sweltering summer heat of their poorly ventilated tenement. Seated on the beach her bottom was warmed by the sun-heated sand. The cold, metal of the tabletop cooled her head and arms with ocean breezes, so delicious for the refugee from tenement land. Hannah felt things happening inside her. The ocean waves rose quickly and drenched the sand under her. The sudden wetness on her bottom startled her awake. "Oh," she exclaimed, sitting up. When she realized that her water had burst she repeated "Oh" in loud alarm and called out, "Mrs. Olstein."

Mrs. Olstein stopped directing the movers and hurried to the kitchen.

Hannah, dismayed at her helplessness, said, "My water broke."

Mrs. Olstein immediately thought to call Dr. Smilowitz but realized as quickly that there was no phone yet in the apartment. She held out a forbidding palm toward Hannah. "Wait. Don't move. Wait right there, Hannah. I'll call Dr. Smilowitz." She hurried down the stairs to Mrs. Greene's, explained and said she had to use the phone to call Dr. Smilowitz.

"Of course," said Mrs. Greene.

The doctor's secretary said he was out on a call but she would tell him as soon as he got back. Mrs. Olstein was sure to give the secretary the Reinerman's new address in Brooklyn.

Mrs. Olstein hurried upstairs and told the movers to put all the blankets and pillows they could find on the kitchen table.

Mrs. Greene came in carrying two of her largest pots. She filled them with hot water at the sink and put them on the stove to boil. Between the two of them they lifted Hannah to the thick layer of blankets on the tabletop that Mrs. Olstein had prepared.

Dr. Smilowitz arrived just in time to see the thin strands of dark hair on the baby's head poking out. He checked Hannah's heart, then added his voice to the other two urging Hannah to push.

After another hour of hard work on everybody's part, especially Hannah's, Seymour Reinerman was born on the family's kitchen table in the new apartment in Brooklyn.

CHAPTER 15

Irv Grodsky grinned to Joe. "The manufacturers who love you for helping them out with uppers are going to hate you when you set up a factory and compete with them, selling shoes."

Moe swung his hand with the unlit cigar. "Hey, that's business in America."

Joe said, "It's my turn to make the shoe." He opened his box of Murads and took out a cigarette.

Irv said, "Joe, please--"

"I'm not going to light it. I'm just going to hold it."

Irv was sensitive to tobacco smoke.

"Nu," said Joe to Moe, "you're not talking."

"I'm thinking," said Moe.

"What are you thinking, Moish?" Joe used his Yiddish name to remind Moe that he was the kid brother. They had pulled three workbenches into a circle in Joe's shop so they could talk. The three had chosen to meet on a Sunday to discuss the possibility of Joe setting up a factory to make the whole shoe.

Irv and Joe waited for Moe's response. In the quiet the shop seemed to hold its breath.

Joe repeated, "Nu, Moe?"

Irv said, "Well?"

Moe turned toward Joe and spoke slowly. "I'm thinking ... Joe ... we should be partners ... you and me ... equal partners in the new business." He jammed the unlit cigar into his mouth and held it in his yellowing teeth.

Joe stared at Moe.

Irv's eyes widened as his eyebrows went up and his jaw dropped. On their subway ride down from the Bronx to Manhattan he and Moe had talked of family matters. Moe's Lily was pregnant with her second child.

76

Bea, Irv's wife, was having difficulty getting pregnant. They worried that she might have some medical condition that had to be taken care of. But on the train Moe hadn't even hinted to Irv that he wanted to be an equal partner with Joe.

After Joe got through staring at Moe he shook his head. "Chutzpah, always chutzpah." He snickered cynically as he thought of Moe's *Chutzpadikeh* (nervy) reactions since the first day he took Moe into his shop. Yet Moe turned out to be an excellent salesman.

Moe took the cigar out of his mouth and grinned to both of them. "Chutzpah's the way to get ahead in America."

Irv recovered and climbed up to where Moe had taken them. "Whaddaya say, Joe," asked Irv, "to Moe being an equal partner?"

Thoughtful, Joe took the Murad out of his mouth and put it back in the box. "I say … I'll think about it."

Moe took the cigar out of his mouth and stood up. "I'll think about it too." He walked toward the door. "Ya' comin', Irv?"

"Wait," said Joe, "I can think while you're sitting."

Moe hesitated. "Okay." He strolled back and sat down again.

Joe looked at Irv. Joe was feeling uneasy. The shop's business was his alone, that he had built over six years, his way of life as much as his breathing. He worried, *Moe's gonna be able to tell me what to do in my shop?* Joe turned to Irv. "What does it mean, Irv, if Moe is an equal partner?"

Irv felt the tension. He cleared his throat. "Being partners means you both get the same salary, good times and slow times and you don't make any changes for the business unless you talk together and agree. As partners, you're both responsible for any debts you incur." Irv had a sudden thought. He looked from one to the other. "You guys are already a natural team. Moe gets the orders and Joe makes the goods, pulling together like a horse and wagon, together like ham and eggs."

Moe and Joe nodded slightly. Irv had described the obvious, but the unspoken question of money hung heavily in the air between Moe and Joe.

"And he'll get the same salary?" Joe said.

"If you're partners," Irv answered.

Moe looked at his brother. "No more salary plus commissions, Joe."

Joe grunted.

Yussel Reinerman had grown up in Russia constrained by fears for his life, had used his beliefs in Orthodoxy to deny himself courtships in adult life. He had evolved into an adult rigid in his self-protection. Still unable to open himself and let anyone in to share his emotional life or any part of it, his marriage had been all on his myopic terms until Hannah's crying needs forced him to take his courage in his hands and try something different. And it had worked! He had permitted Hannah to open his eyes to a better kind of life, Joe Reinerman no longer thought he could enjoy life only in the Jewish ghetto of Manhattan's Lower East Side. Certainly he learned what proper living quarters should be like.

Now his brother's attempt to share what had been Joe's alone, that he alone had built, made his cautions race back to enfold and protect him. Yet his six years of creating a successful business had taught him that he alone didn't always have all the answers. At least in dealing with his work he had learned to be open for new methods to solve problems.

The kid brother had turned out to be an excellent salesman. Joe knew well that he couldn't put up the front, the American front that Moe did. And if he didn't have Moe out there it would have to be some one else. *But who?* More uncertainty he didn't need. The realization hit him yet again that he couldn't run his shop alone … *but partners?*

It was Sunday. Instead of being with their families, Moe and Irv sat in Joe's shop being more than patient because they realized that for Joe it was such a life-changing decision. They knew that the shop was who Joe was. He had done everything necessary in Russia to learn his trade. The Czar's anti-Semitic laws had burned it into him. He doggedly stuck it out to get his place in life. Now his shop in America gave Joe his long-term lease. Secure in his new land, it gave him the courage to attempt something bigger, ten times bigger.

Yes, thought Joe, *Moe is good, better than any, but an equal partner?* Joe sat, hands together, pushing one hard thumb against the other while he thought it through.

He came back to the reality of his small shop, to Moe and Irv and he, sitting in a small circle on workbenches, talking. "Nu, Moish," Joe started, then finished in English and held out his hand. "Pahtners."

Moe let out a "Hey, Yussel!" With a wide swing of his arm he grabbed Joe's hand and shook it like he wouldn't ever let it go. "Partners," he said, "Moe and Joe Reinerman, partners!"

Moe found an empty second-story loft in a building amid a cluster of industrial buildings on the Brooklyn side of the Brooklyn Bridge. After his initial talk with the landlord, Sydney Oliphant, Moe brought Joe down to make sure it would work for what Joe had in mind. After Joe approved, they brought Irv to the final meeting with the landlord to make sure they had all the necessary papers and signing them would cover all their bases. Oliphant agreed to their putting up a large sign on the outside of the building if they would sign a five-year lease.

Moe and Irv automatically looked at Joe who would be running the shop.

Joe smiled. He would sign a ten … a twenty-year lease. When he looked ahead, a shop making shoes would always be in his life.

All agreed.

On the subway train back to Joe's shop, Moe silently tested different possibilities for the sign. Should it be M & J Reinerman or J & M Reinerman? Moe thought to ask Joe in English. Moe talked in English as much as possible to work more of his accent out of his speech and sound more American, especially now that he was going to be talking to buyers of Abraham & Strauss, Gimbels, Macy's and any others who would be listening to his good deals. But Joe's English response to Moe's wording of the sign would be so strongly accented that Moe couldn't be sure what Joe meant, and the loud noises reverberating through the speeding, rocking subway train discouraged conversation anyway. Moe decided to wait until they got back to the shop.

At the shop Moe decided to hold off on talking about the sign.

Irv's work for the move was done, but he said he would wait for Moe and Joe to agree on the details so he could ride back to the Bronx with Moe.

The brothers decided they would shop together for the ladies shoemaking machinery. It would help Moe the salesman to better understand how the shoes were made and give him the ammunition to talk more forcefully about them. Moe would call the movers when the equipment was purchased and ready to be shipped.

And now, Moe thought, *for more delicate matters.* "The sign, Joe, "he said, continuing in English.

Joe's head was full of machinery. He looked blank. "The sign? Vat sign?"

"The sign for the building, the factory."

"Oh … nu?" he asked, wondering what Moe had in mind.

Knowing that the shop was Joe's life, Moe decided to move quickly to something neither one could object to. "I was thinking J & M Reinerman, or M & J Reinerman, but maybe 'Reinerman Brothers' says it just right for two partners. What do you think, Joe?"

Joe was still adjusting himself to the idea that Moe was going to be an equal partner in his, Joe's, business. Joe was the one who knew how to make the shoe or there would be no business. "Reinerman Brudders?"

"Yeah."

Joe took a moment to think. "Nu ... so it's Reinerman Brudders." He didn't ask that the sign be printed in Yiddish as well as English, another sign that Joe dared to tiptoe out of his mental ghetto into the American world;

Reinerman Bros.
Hand Turned Ladies Shoes

painted in large red-brown letters on the blank white building did its bit to brighten the dusty industrial air near the Brooklyn Bridge for the next eighteen years.

CHAPTER 16

1916

Hannah was busy with one-year old baby Seymour and pregnant with her second. Husband Joe was busy with his new shop. Their days, their interests seemed very separated from each other except that Hannah had to worry about having dinner ready for Joe whether he came home at 6 o'clock or 8 o'clock. And there was always Shabbat, candles, *khallah*, soup, chicken and *tsimmis*. Joe had stopped attending the synagogue on DeKalb Avenue except on the high holidays, but he did manage to get home on Fridays to say the prayers and blessings that began the Sabbath meal. Hannah had begun to feel that she observed the Sabbath more for Joe than for herself.

While Hannah's day obligated her to think of Joe and what time he might be home for dinner, there was nothing during Joe's day or his week to make him aware of his wife and her concerns. For Joe, his shop that now made the whole shoe was his fragile baby until sales became stronger. It occupied him all day, seven days a week.

But Hannah went through her day wondering how she could be part of the work that the Hadassah women had talked about. That Hadassah meeting at the Manhattan synagogue had become a pivotal event in her life. Those women who addressed the audience were so American looking, such a refreshing contrast to the Orthodox women whom she had been among every day of her growing up. She knew she had to figure out a way to spend time with them, the kind of woman she wanted to be.

The birth of baby Seymour changed Hannah's life, as she had determined. She had freed herself of tenement life and she planned it to be onward and upward from there. She had Mrs. Olstein come in every day for the first two weeks after Seymour was born. With the images of the Hadassah women before her eyes she checked herself carefully in the long mirror above the dresser in her bedroom before leaving her apartment, even if it was only to buy some produce from the many vendors of fruits and vegetables who cruised the residential neighborhoods with their horse and wagons,

Her shopping on the busy De Kalb Avenue was restricted to Thursdays and Mondays. Thursday she bought a kosher chicken from Berkowitz's butcher shop for Friday night Sabbath dinner, and meat for Sunday dinner. Saturday, no cooking was allowed. Monday she bought meat for the other days of the week. Her icebox would keep the raw meat fresh for three days. She had the largest icebox available for residential use, one that could hold a 25-pound block of ice.

Although Hannah wanted to busy her self with improving the details of the apartment's furnishings, Seymour's hunger cries and demands for diaper change could not be denied. The final touches for the apartment had to wait, It will still be here, she thought, to fix and fuss with, thank God.

But she did make time for a phone call to Hadassah even though she couldn't go to any meetings for a while, a long while probably. When she put Seymour down for his afternoon nap Hannah thought to at least get member information. She found the number in the Manhattan phone book.

"This is the Hadassah Organization."

"Hello, I'm interested in finding out about Hadassah."

"Are you a nurse?"

"No. I just want--"

"Or training to be a nurse?"

"No."

"Are you interested in joining a support group?"

"Uh … yes. Could you send me some information about Hadassah?"

"Would you be interested in our newsletter?"

"Yes, yes, that would be fine."

Hannah gave her name and address, thanked the lady and hung up. She sat for a moment realizing that she felt pleasurably elated to have finally taken a step in the direction she had long wanted to move.

After the phone call, when she went to shop on De Kalb Avenue she searched out the women's dress shops first, to see the latest styles displayed in their windows and imagine how she would look wearing them. Would she look as well as the other women she had seen? She imagined sitting at a meeting with them, talking. Hannah suddenly felt nervous wondering what she would talk to them about. *Would they be interested in listening to Hannah Reinerman?*

Why did the woman on the phone ask me if I was a nurse, or studying to be one? The woman's inquiries made Hannah realize that she hadn't thought of training in anything to qualify her to help earn money for the family. The man she married would provide that. Oh, yes, Hannah had been sure of that before she stepped under the wedding canopy.

Hannah hadn't thought of achieving anything more than graduating high school before finding a husband and becoming a wife and a mother. After that her life would just 'settle down.' Hannah realized that settled down was about where she already was with one baby one-year old and pregnant five months with the next one, which caused her to wonder, *do those Hadassah women raise children, or did they choose instead to train to be nurses? Or did they do both?* Hannah shook her head. *How can a woman do both?*

When the Hadassah News arrived, Hannah eagerly skimmed the six printed pages. The large scope of Hadassah activities stunned her, made her feel again her lack of preparation to function in their class. How could Jewish women have time for all this? Hannah suddenly felt tied to the four rooms of the apartment and her weekly schedule of shopping, cleaning, cooking, and preparing for Shabbat and the holidays, raising a one-year old baby and five months pregnant with a second one. *Build hospitals in Palestine? Help support a hospital in Africa? Run health programs for the poor in America? Do those women I saw at the meeting in the Manhattan synagogue really do all this?*

On the second page of the paper a column headline, 'Lower East Side' drew an excited "Oh" from Hannah as an article she could relate to. From her safe distance of living in a brand new apartment in Brooklyn she was eager to read about the work Hadassah was doing in the Manhattan tenements that Hannah knew so well.

The Hadassah organization worked in conjunction with the Henry Street Settlement House and the Neighborhood Settlement House, which were also taking care of the impoverished sick. Aside from tending patients they handed out flyers in Russian, Yiddish, Italian and English that listed the things the tenants had to do to avoid getting the seasonal diseases.

Hannah enumerated her abilities defensively. *Well, I can speak Yiddish and English.*

She imagined the nurses in their long white uniforms climbing the rickety wooden stairs to tend the sick. She questioned whether she would be willing to do that. In defense of her entire focus being on her house and family and not feeling obligated to learn further she thought that those nurses couldn't be married with children and also work as nurses. Hannah couldn't imagine a woman who wouldn't want to be first of all, a wife and mother. She decided that for her, certainly, it was work enough.

Yet thinking of Hadassah women bold enough to go to college, train for a career then marry to take on those added responsibilities again made Hannah feel inadequate. She had congratulated herself when she graduated high school but had looked forward to nothing more than what her older sister Lena did, run a household and raise kids. And Lena hadn't even needed to finish high school to do that. But there was a difference. It was clear to Hannah that Lena hadn't looked beyond her tenement and raising Harold's children because she was an immigrant. Thinking about it now, Hannah had felt compelled to graduate high school because that was the goal that the HIAS community organizers set for American Jewish girls. Hannah had always felt different from the immigrant half of her family because she had been born in America. But now she felt challenged further by her mental embroilment with the women of Hadassah.

Hannah consoled herself. *Well, I did convince Joe to leave the tenement.* She smiled as she looked around at the brighter atmosphere of her apartment and compared it to her remembrance of their tenement. "Ugh, never again," she muttered. Suddenly she found her purpose. She would teach Joe how to spend the money his new business was making for them. What kind of apartment would be ideal? She wondered about her younger brother Al who had a business in ladies beauty supplies, and her older brother Sam who manufactured ladies fur coats. What kind of houses were they living in? She wondered what kind of apartments those Hadassah women lived in?

On the bottom of the last page of Hadassah News was a short statement about the history of the Hadassah organization. The Daughters of Zion had been a small study group interested in learning the historical chronology of Palestine, the Biblical homeland of the Jews. But aware of Jews living there in primitive conditions, in 1912, under the leadership of Henrietta Szold, DZ changed their focus to one of improving the health of the Jews in Palestine. They renamed their organization Hadassah to honor the Jewish queen of Persia who had saved her people from annihilation.

In the next monthly issue of the Hadassah Newsletter there was a notice that excited Hannah. The newly formed Brooklyn chapter would hold its second meeting at the home of Mrs. Janet Cohen. Members were advised to phone and reserve their place. Members were also encouraged to bring interested friends. It was scheduled for a Tuesday afternoon; date, phone number and address were listed.

In Brooklyn, a new chapter, Hannah thought with added excitement.. Hadassah was suddenly within her reach. She determined that she would go. But her second thought slowed her down. She put a hand on her five-month pregnancy and got out of her chair. She walked into the bedroom to look at herself in the large mirror that hung over the dresser. She turned to see her profile from both sides. No doubt, she was clearly showing already. Discouraged, she grimaced. She grunted negatively, "Hm," and thought aloud, "It's not going to get any smaller."

She had thought to call Mrs. Olstein and schedule her to stay with Seymour on the day of the Hadassah meeting. Hannah had also thought of asking Lena to go with her, but decided that Lena would not be comfortable there. And if they asked for donations, Lena would be embarrassed.

She thought of asking Bessie Grablowsky, the woman who had moved in under her on the ground floor. Hannah and Bessie had talked about the good works that Hadassah engaged in. But Hannah remembered that Bessie had started a training program to sell insurance. Bessie was taking care of her father, an Orthodox Jew with a long white beard who spoke only Yiddish. Every day he walked to the synagogue on DeKalb Avenue in time to be part of the *minyan* (prayer group) of ten to say early morning prayers. Bessie had chosen to be an insurance saleswoman so she would have a flexible schedule to take care of her father. She called him *Shver*, (aged and wise).

Despite having decided to wait until after the baby was born to attend Hadassah meetings, Hannah looked over her wardrobe. But she questioned whether anything there would still be stylish in six months. She decided she would buy something new at the time of the special occasion of going to her first meeting.

Next, she called the cab company to see how much the ride to the meeting and back would cost. Hannah decided that she could spare it from her budget. She decided not to tell Joe about her attending the Hadassah meeting nor ask him for extra for the cab fare. Of course he would agree that if it's good for the Jews it's worth doing, but she decided to avoid any further arguments about money. *The new business is not making a million yet.* Hannah looked at the Hadassah meeting as a worthwhile way for a Jewish woman to spend her time while her husband was working.

Having mentally settled her future entrance into Hadassah, Hannah went on to wonder why the Daughters of Zion, a study group devoted to learning the 4,000-year history of the Jews, changed to Hadassah interested in improving the health of the Jews in Palestine. She read the short statement of Hadassah's founding again. But it didn't give her anything further.

As if Hannah's third issue of the Hadassah Newsletter was sent in answer to her question, one of the columns outlined a short biography of Hadassah's founder, Henrietta Szold. After reading the first paragraph Hannah felt dizzy and ignorant of what she had read. She looked away from the print and took a breath. Hannah had never heard of a woman achieving so many accomplishments, and just in the first paragraph. She had thought only men led the American Zionist organization, founded the Jewish Publication Society, translated important French, German and Hebrew books into English

Hannah struggled through the first half of the article and into the second wondering when Henrietta Szold changed the name from Daughters of Zion to Hadassah. The article curtly explained that Szold visited Palestine in 1909 at age 49, where she was shocked to find that there were no medical services of any kind available to the Jews. She stayed for three years setting up clinics for the people, and supervising the training services for medical personnel for a hospital she founded.

Szold returned to America in 1912, explained to the Daughters of Zion the dire straits of the Jews in Palestine, and urged them to become an international health services organization. Knowing Jewish history well, Szold suggested they change their name to Hadassah, to honor the memory of the Jewish queen of the Persian Empire who saved her people from annihilation, the event that gave rise to the yearly Purim celebration.

Finishing the article, Hannah sat, not believing the words she had just read. "So much, so much," she murmured. "How could a woman do so much?" Hannah suddenly realized that there was no mention of Szold having children or even marrying. She quickly scanned the article again but came up with nothing further. Hannah questioned softly in wonderment. "She never married?" *Perhaps it is still a possibility for her.*

Hannah searched the article yet again to find Szold's birth date, 1860. Hannah calculated, "She's fifty-six." She shook her head sadly for Director Szold. "It's a little late for romance." Hannah remembered suddenly that her own mother had died at age forty-eight. Not comprehending the woman's extraordinary achievements Hannah sat stunned, puzzling, yet admiring of such a woman who did things that only men were known to do.

CHAPTER 17

1921

CPA Irv Grodsky sat up from bending over the Reinerman Brothers' books. Still holding the pen, he lifted his hands and waved them in time to his singing out a fanfare as if he were conducting an orchestra. "Da ra ra ra ra ra ra dum de da."

Joe looked up from studying the sample shoes on his desk, a half-smile of anticipation on his face and questioned his nephew-in-law. "It's good, Oiv, It's good?"

Irv continued as if he were the town crier declaring the message of great import to a crowd of waiting thousands. "The financial results for the first quarter of the year 1921 of the Reinerman Brothers Hand Turned Ladies Shoes enterprise have surpassed our expectations."

"Noo, Oiv, so tell me in English. How much?"

"The Reinerman Brothers--"

"I know, I know, Oiv. How much?"

Irv came down to earth abruptly. "14,874 dollars."

Stunned, Joe sat still, his jaw slack, his mouth open. "Fourteen t'ousand? You didn't make a mistake, Oiv?"

"Have I made a mistake in all the years I've worked for you?"

"You sure?"

"Does the sun rise in the east?"

Joe sat thinking, working to absorb Irv's figures. The many hard knocks in his life made him skeptical of good news. Questioning silently Joe did find the hole in Irv's prosperity report and worried that it could sink his ship. "How much is cash in the bank?"

Irv glanced at his final figures. "Eight thousand, round numbers."

Joe figured quickly. There was no celebration in his voice. "So six t'ousand, eight hundred dey owe?"

"Yeah, so?"

"Something could happen to those big shot accounts. And ve'll pay our bills mit vat?"

Joe's refusal to enjoy his success exasperated Irv. "Joe, for Chissake, you're not selling to you-don't-know-who from a pushcart on Essex Street. Dayton Department Stores, Kelly Brothers and the others are gonna be around for a long time. You want big accounts, you gotta handle them big."

Joe gave up the arguing. It wearied him. He shook his head." You handle them, Itz, (Irv's Yiddish name) it's too big for me."

Irv slapped his desk. "Joe, smile." Irv patted the ledger lovingly. "The books are good news this quarter."

"Nu," Joe said glumly, "so I'll laugh."

It was Irv's turn to shake his head at Joe's worried attitude.

Moe walked in as Irv patted the books again, saying, "You've got something to laugh about, Joe."

Moe went right to the ashtray on Joe's desk and tapped out the lighted end of his cigar because Irv couldn't stand smoke. Moe put the cigar back in his mouth to grip it with his teeth because it had become part of who he was. He talked through clenched teeth as he took off his light topcoat and walked it toward the wooden coat rack. "Sorry I'm late. I had to sit and have a drink with Resnitchek, the buyer. He knows a bootlegger." Moe continued talking as he added his fedora to the top of the coat rack. "He gave me an order. Could I turn him down?" Moe slid a chair under him and sat down between the two desks to catch up on the end-of-quarter results. "So Irv, what's the good news for the quarter?"

Irv smiled. He knew Moe would see the results differently than Joe. "Gross income, 14, 874 dollars."

Suddenly stunned to silence, Moe the salesman, always ready with words for any situation, sat like a fixed statue with his large mouth open. Finally he spoke. "Really?"

Pleased with the drama he'd created, Irv grinned and nodded.

Moe turned to his brother. "Did you hear that, Joe?"

"I hear."

"So laugh, Joe."

"I'm laughing. It's on paper."

"What's on paper?"

"Seven thousand dollars."

Moe turned toward Irv, silently questioning.

"Payable accounts, 6,874 dollars," said Irv.

"Oh." Moe turned toward Joe, his hands gestured his question. "So?"

"So," Joe repeated mockingly, "what if they don't pay?"

"What are we dealing with, robbers? These are respectable businessmen. For God's sakes, Joe, smile. It's something to celebrate. It gives us the money to expand to the Chicago market.

"Not again Chicago!"

"Why not Joe? People there will eat up our shoes like the people here. But you act like tomorrow is the end. What are you afraid of? This country has the greatest future in the world."

Moe suddenly thought of proof positive. "Joe, did you hear what the stock market is doing?"

"It's good?"

"It's great." Moe turned to Irv. "Are you up to date on our accounts, Irv?"

"Of course," Irv answered, "as of the closing bell yesterday," he added as he bent down for Moe and Joe's personal stock folders. He sat up and opened Moe's. "Six thousand and twenty-eight dollars as of three o'clock yesterday afternoon. Moe is ahead by $1,028. And, of course, Joe's is the same since we convinced him to invest his whole 5,000 and not just one thousand."

Moe turned to Joe. "Aren't you glad we convinced you, Joe? You made $1,028 without having to sell a single pair of shoes. You invested money and the stock market went to work for you."

"I'm glad, I'm glad," Joe said glumly, not daring to voice his worries in the face of such good news.

Moe carried on like a preacher who sees the light. "Did you ever see so much money in your life, Joe? Between shoe sales and stocks our capital gets bigger every day. All over the country people are buying Model-Ts and other cars like crazy. Do you remember when I had to carry my sample cases on the trains and trolleys until Irv and me finally convinced you we would save money if I drove to customers in a Model T? Now the whole country is driving. There's money outside of New York, too, lots of it. That's why I'm telling you we have to extend our territory to Chicago."

Crack salesman Moe spoke very emphatically. His lips and mouth seemed to be elastic stretching around the sounds of his words. It was a technique he developed to minimize his Yiddish accent. He was delighted that it made his speech sound very forceful. Just what a top salesman needed.

Joe steeled himself against Moe's pitch.

Moe continued his assault on Joe. "One big account like Marshal Field or Montgomery Ward and we've got 500% profit for every nickel we spend on the trip."

"Pui," mocked Joe, in English. "Marshal Field von't look on us."

"How do you know if you don't try?"

Joe stared at Moe. Could he believe him, his bigmouth brother? "Ach," Joe flung his hands up in frustration, "to them we're *pishers* (kids)."

"Only because they've never seen our shoes." Moe reached over and picked up a shoe from Joe's desk, a bright red, high-heeled evening shoe cut in a dramatic spiked design. "Do you think they would say that shoes like this are made by *pishers*?"

Joe blurted, "It's da best hand-lasted shoe in New York."

"Ya damn right it is. Isn't it worth $500 to show it to them?"

"If you go, it's a t'ousand." Joe laughed awkwardly to dull the sharp edge of his criticism. He hunched his shoulders and moved both hands out in front of him as if his whole person was trying to understand his brother. "Tell me, how many women can you use in one night?" He pushed out some more sounds that might sound like laughter.

Moe gestured angrily with his cigar, the remaining ashes flying. "Oh for Chrissakes, Joe, you don't take only the buyer out. He's got an assistant. A buyer like Montgomery Ward will probably bring three assistants. And it might take me a week."

"So Reinerman Brothers gotta feed da whole army?" Joe looked at Irv for support, but with mixed feelings. Irv had also argued with Joe that business in America could not be run without expense accounts for women, liquor and fancy restaurants.

Moe didn't let up on his brother. "That's business in America, Joe."

Expanding Reinerman Brothers to Chicago would be a feather in Moe's hat to parade in front of his wife's blow-mouth family. They never failed to remind Moe how well they were doing. His in-laws, in part, would motivate Moe to continue arguing for the Chicago connection. "How the hell do you think we came from that lousy hole-in-the-wall on Canal Street to this loft on Bridge Street?"

Joe fought for his role in the partnership. "Because I make da best demn shoe and ve sell it for da best demn price."

When they rented the loft, Joe had checked out each machine at the equipment exchange before buying it and sending it to the shop. He examined every inch of leather shipped in. He checked the product quality at each workstation. Every day he double-checked identification tags on the rolling racks to make sure orders were not being mixed. Joe was in his shop a half day Saturday and he sometimes ran in for an hour on Sunday even though it meant an argument with Hannah when he finally got home.

Joe mentally ran through his never-ending day in the shop again. He nodded. *Yup,* he decided, *Joe Reinerman is the one who makes the best shoe at the best price. Moe, with the big cigars, fancy suits and waxed mustache talks like he's the whole business.*

"You're right!" Moe barked in agreement to Joe's declaration of his importance to their excellent product. "But how do you think we've been convincing the eastern buyers to buy our shoes?" Moe took a turn to brag about his wise-ass technique. He laughed, "Heh heh, the cook book says the way to a man's heart is through his stomach. Well, the way to a buyer's order pad is through his putz, (penis) ha, ha, ha," and he laughed uproariously.

Joe and Irv had to smile. Moe, with his bulls---t, kept the flood of worries from drowning them.

Moe decided to quit while he was ahead. He swung his head from Irv to Joe and back again to make sure his allies were with him on this. "Right?"

Irv nodded slowly.

Joe released a great sigh and threw up his hands. It turned his worries over to his partner and his bookkeeper.

Moe wrapped it up. "We've got a month to decide. The Chicago Shoe Buyers' Convention is in May. The same Christmas samples we make up for our eastern buyers we can take to Chicago. Boy, will we knock their eyes out!"

Moe was not a trained statistical economist but he felt an intuitive excitement about America's sudden economic spurt. The new businesses Moe saw as he drove to the retail and industrial areas of New York City, Jersey and Connecticut made him feel that Reinerman Brothers could be part of something big.

The two-year recession that followed World War I was over. America came out of the post-war doldrums a lot faster than European countries. Europe's economies had been blasted almost out of existence. In contrast, the incessant shelling hadn't crossed the Atlantic to blow up America's buildings or America's turf. Its buildings and the where-with-all of the pre war economy still in place, America had only to convert to peacetime production. As the only remaining major economy that could rebuild its own and Europe's industries after the war, it was full speed ahead for American manufacturers.

American and European consumer excitement about new products also sparked the economic growth. The one product most responsible for revolutionizing America's thinking was Henry Ford's Model T automobile. America could now think of getting the bothersome and dangerous horse-and-wagons off the streets. Not only was the automobile a remarkable item for a horse-and-wagon society to see, but they could glimpse tomorrow's world that would be different from today's. Also different were Ford's unusual philosophies about raising the pay of his workers who made the car, and his cheapening the price of the T each year so more consumers could buy it. These were industrial incentives on both counts. It sparked interest in Ford, the man, as well as the many unquestioned advantages of his product.

After five years of experimentation, in 1909 Ford had finally straightened out the kinks in his assembly line production. He sold his first mass-produced Model T for $850. He soon saw that only the rich could afford such a price. He wanted more consumers to enjoy the advantages of his auto and pursued further production efficiencies to bring the price down. By 1912 you could have bought a Model T for $690, by 1915, $440, 1920, $290. To further spread the consumer base for his car, he jumped the pay of his workers from three dollars a day to five, to make it more possible for them to buy the product they helped to make.

The banks joined the buying revolution by offering loans to those with appropriate credit backgrounds, enabling more working people to purchase more goods. Banks standardized America's new thinking about borrowing money. It was okay to carry debt, as long as you could make the payments. Debt very quickly became the way of life for a majority of Americans. It led to a frenzy of spending in an upward spiral for the next ten years. Buying on debt became the consumer's parallel to buying the stock market on ten percent margin.

In the years when the price of the Model T was above $500, Moe Reinerman toted his large sample case on the subways and trolleys of the five boroughs of the city. But in 1913 when the price of the Model T dropped from $690 to $550, Moe sat down with Joe and Irv and made his case for the company to buy him a Model T. It didn't take an argument for Moe to make his points about the automobile saving time and money for Reinerman Brothers, compared to his enduring public transportation.

No waiting for trains and trolleys and driving directly to his destinations, Moe accomplished so much more in his workday. Driving, Moe felt the passion of America's economic boom and, flying high in the driver's seat as key salesman he took Reinerman Brothers with him.

Moe had the excitement of an immigrant who came from a country that denied his every ambition, even threatened his life. He landed in a country that said, "You like it? Go for it." Moe was more freed to go for it than his brother. Moe had never been religiously observant. In this new world he didn't feel that he was deserting his family's belief, nor the memory of his mother, if he spoke good American English.

Joe's dreams were smaller; he had his shop to go to every day where not only did he create the product he loved to create but it supported his family. Although he wasn't in the synagogue any more except on the high holidays, learning a trade to support his family ranked high in Jewish Sacred Literature and also in Joe's consciousness. Joe didn't care if his speech told everyone he was Jewish. His accent made him feel that he was only visiting the American language and he could continue to feel snuggled in the comfort of who he was, and he preferred not to leave it.

Fortunately for Joe's future as a businessman he was a pragmatist when it came to his work obsession. His ambition to make the whole shoe drove him away from his hole-in-the-wall shop nestled in the Orthodoxy of the Lower East Side, to accepting a loft in a booming industrial area where everyone was free to speak his version of American.

Moe, who did not have the satisfactions of creating and producing a product with his hands, was left with the words that his mouth formed to satisfy the goals of his dreams. The job of a salesman was to sell; influence people to buy, whether you told jokes or bull---t them, along with teaching them how to use the new product. Moe would tell you that economic America would go nowhere if the salesmen were not out there knocking on doors telling people about the products they had not yet seen or had not even thought of. For this period of 1920s America Moe figured it right.

After World War I America grieved for its loss of 117,000 soldiers, then endured a relatively short recession while the country changed over to peacetime endeavors. When the economy got under full sail again American families were dazzled by the array of offerings they were tendered, refrigerators, vacuums, stoves, new kitchen and bathroom plumbing.

Manufacturers were not shy about telling Americans about their new products. A publicity/marketing industry developed new media ways to tell the population about the wonderful products available to them.

Radio commercials dunned listeners day and night with statements, ditties, jingles and songs about products that would make their lives easier, taste wonderful---"Have you tried Wheaties, the best breakfast food in the land?" even cigarettes were touted "... Winston tastes good like a cigarette should, ..." or "Call-ing for - Phil-lip Mor-ris"... The deluge of ads told America, "Buy our product and get more out of life." They filled whole sections of newspaper with advertising, from full-page ads to classifieds. Elegant women were pictured languidly holding cigarettes, gesturing toward a refrigerator, or vacuuming a rug, and smiling, in the ads always smiling, as if saying, *If you had this product you'd be smiling too.*

To financially tempt and enable people to buy these new products, varied forms of consumer credit were created to permit them to "buy now and pay later." Consumers were surrounded by sounds and images to seduce them to accept debt in exchange for the wonderful things that could be theirs. Installment plan variations were also opportunities for the banks to charge additional fees and/or higher interest on loans. In essence, America was told that it was all right to go into debt in order to own the items that make for a better life. After all, we are Americans, the greatest nation on earth. We deserve to have it all. With European countries in a post-war shambles that would take them years to recover, it was no contest.

With all the credit, industrial and psychological assists in place to entice buyers, the manufacture of new products was off to a fast start in 1920. Moe Reinerman's overview of the American economy was quick to understand that this was the time for Reinerman Brothers, makers of the best ladies hand turned shoes, to go big.

Moe and Irv voted for Chicago. Joe shrugged, accepting the inevitable.

CHAPTER 18

When the first child born to a religious Jewish household is a son, it's as if God has favored that family with a Bible prophet, a Holy One. On the death of his father, the first-born male sees that his father is buried in hallowed ground. After that, the son recites the prayer for the dead over the grave periodically so that the father may continue to be in eternal peace in God's hands.

Also, the father gone, the first son carries on with the family's daily and weekly prayer rituals and weekly and annual holiday celebrations. On the legal side, the first-born male inherits the power of attorney and sees that the will of the father is carried out.

Their first male child, Seymour Reinerman was doubly welcomed by Joe and Hannah as the carrier of 4,000 years of Judaism. Hence they sang silent accolades to Seymour as the most important addition to their family. None would say aloud that the second child, even a second male child, is less important, but it often resulted in that. If the second one is female, well, that's a wholly different, (though among nice people, unspoken) concern. If it's a daughter, the mother, who has the daily responsibility of the children, is burdened with the worry that in too few years she will have to take steps to see that the daughter does not become prematurely pregnant. Of course, if the second is also a boy, Mother breathes a private sigh of relief and gives thanks to God, who, in His goodness, eliminated that concern.

Baby Seymour seemed to be a Bible scholar at birth. He instinctively knew the story of Cain and Abel and acted out the revered position of the first male child in a Jewish household. When he called to his mother his cries demanded that she immediately run to cater to his need. This lasted for the year-and-a-half while he was the only child. During that time, Seymour learned, "This is how the world works," and it spoiled him rotten, making it difficult for him to understand why things changed when his brother was born.

Of necessity, Hannah had to constantly hold and carry helpless baby Daniel, paying less attention to the already ambulating Seymour. But Seymour wasn't about to give up first place to his brother.

Hannah made Seymour even angrier when she stopped her occasional breast feedings for him and put him entirely on the bottle so she could have enough breast milk for Daniel. But the bottle didn't feel at all like the real thing, not even close. And Seymour didn't want to give up to his competitor that special seat while feeding, front row, center.

Hannah's response to baby Daniel's cry of helplessness was always immediate. Whenever Hannah was busy with Daniel, Seymour would raise some make-believe ruckus to have his mother come to him. But Hannah soon learned that Seymour's fussing was a put-on. After that, when Seymour suddenly cried out, Hannah chose not to interrupt her meal preparation, or house cleaning, or her breastfeeding Daniel, but threw her elder son a vague "I'll be there, Seymour." It increasingly angered her firstborn, to learn yet again that he had been removed from his position of directing the orchestra and he was now only playing second fiddle.

Two-year old Seymour's anger climaxed when six-month old Daniel was asleep in his crib. It was Friday, Hannah's busy day in the kitchen to prepare the many extras for the Sabbath Eve dinner and ritual. She carefully rolled the sleeping Daniel's crib to just outside the kitchen entrance to have him readily available should he need changing or more feeding. Well aware now of Seymour's anger, she positioned Seymour's toys well beyond in the living room. She sat his teddy bear in his wagon and instructed her older one, "Give your teddy bear a ride, Seymour," then left him and began her work in the kitchen.

Ma had her hands wrist deep in the huge bowl of flour and water that would provide the basic dough for the Sabbath bread, and for enough honey cake and cookies to last through the week when Seymour went into action. He sat teddy up in the wagon and swung his fist in a roundhouse swing. He knocked teddy to the floor where it landed nose down and Seymour waddle-walked over to the crib that he had previously owned for a year-and-a-half.

Out of the corner of her eye Hannah saw him coming. "Be nice to the baby, Seymour."

Seymour looked between the slats and saw his enemy sleeping peacefully.

His mother reminded him, "He's your brother, Seymour."

Seymour pushed. The crib moved a few inches but the wall stopped it.

Awakened from peaceful dreams, Daniel made noises.

"Seymour, don't bother the baby."

Frustrated that he couldn't roll his brother out of the house, Seymour grabbed the slats and pulled the crib towards him with the idea of turning it on its side and dumping him out. But he did not have the strength. Frustrated, he pressed his glaring eyes and red face between the slats and growled at his competitor.

The sounds coming from one eye and a nose between the slats frightened baby Daniel and he yowled.

"Seymour, leave the baby alone."

Seymour shook the crib with what strength he had.

Daniel panicked as if an earthquake had struck and aftershocks were continuing. He yelled uncontrollably for help.

"Seymour, go 'way from the baby."

'S' for smart, Seymour knew that by the time Ma could clean her hands and go after him, he could growl and shake the crib all he wanted. And he did.

Ma frantically tried to clear the sticky dough from her hands, but Daniel's uncontrolled howling told Hannah there wasn't time enough. She came out of the kitchen, doughy hands held shoulder-high, to avoid making contact.

Seymour looked up. He saw an angry face between two threatening clubs. Fearing the monster, Seymour froze.

Hannah's hands were more than occupied with doughy messes and she couldn't spank him but she stomped one shoe on the wooden floor and yelled a threatening, "Seymour!"

Seymour fled, swept up teddy on his way to his room, jumped into bed and hugged his partner to him.

Hannah turned and bent over her Daniel baby saying nice things, but his crying had gone to full-time hysteria and he was incapable of responding to words. Daniel's fear was such he didn't even hear her loving phrases.

Hannah rushed into the kitchen, washed her hands and hurried back drying them on her apron. Desperately mumbling "Baby, baby, baby, Mama will take care of you, " and other nice things, she picked Daniel up, held him close, tapped her hand on his back and hummed softly.

Seymour sat in his room with his teddy, planning their next move, the fratricidal mark of Cain clear in the cunning on his face.

Hannah held her hysterical baby close. She felt pity not only for his uncontrolled suffering, but for his being too young and incapable of understanding the cause of his fear. Suddenly, in empathy with the baby's ignorance, Hannah felt the blindness with which she had stepped into her marriage and into motherhood. As she walked her baby, Hannah hummed softly and rhythmically in time to her hand tapping his back, both her responses automatic. She picked up and shook his favorite rattle to capture his uncontrolled cries and to deflect him toward his burgeoning curiosity. Daniel suddenly interrupted his wailing to suck desperately for oxygen.

Hannah, inhaling as suddenly in empathy, recalled again her own ignorance of marriage and of motherhood, her inexperience in the harmony of passions that were required of her and of Joe. She knew now that she had been unprepared and she knew now that Joe didn't know any better than she. But who ever talked of those things? Orthodoxy turned those matters over to God, who promised, if each one prayed as per the many rituals, that the knowledge would become part of His blessings to the couple. Now, just the thought of saying something to Joe about what was happening sexually between them—and not happening, made Hannah feel uncomfortable, even queasy. *Who can talk about such a thing? The man is supposed to know what to do. If he does, "Mazeltov!" (congratulations). If not? Nu, another of life's disappointments.* No, she would have to put up with things as they were and hoped God would finally say something to her Joe.

Hannah wondered again about her high school friend, Stella Menkavitch. Both seniors, both Orthodox, both prohibited from experimenting in expressing their interest in boys, found solace in talking with each other about their conflicted feelings. The two girls were also drawn together by their upset about whether to go to synagogue on the high holidays and accept three 'unexcused absences' on their school records, or defy their families and attend school classes on Yom Kippur and Rosh Hashanah, their religion's High Holidays.

Both girls knew well the subtle and overt anti-Jewish prejudice of the New York schools and didn't dare ask the teacher's permission to take the Jewish High Holidays off. They simply accepted an 'unexcused absence' for each weekday they spent in the synagogue.

In the New York City schools the Christian religious holiday of Christmas had become an automatic American holiday, observed with a two-week closure of the schools until after New Year. Jewish and other non-Christian holidays were not observed. Jewish students, if they were Orthodox, simply did not, could not, show up on Yom Kippur and Rosh Hashanah. It was up to the teacher's sense of fairness whether to punish the student with a demerit (for unexcused absence) or not. Stella and Hannah were drawn closer by the conflict their families caused by their insistence that the girls observe those sacred holidays.

Stella was the first to question the rightness of Orthodoxy's rules. She told Hannah that she was thinking of attending HIAS' monthly dance. During one of their talk-your-heart-out-to-each-other sessions, Stella bent closer to Hannah and lowered her voice to a whisper to say that she was going to the next HIAS dance. It shocked Hannah. She had automatically closed out that possibility, knowing that her parents wouldn't allow it.

Their friendship survived Stella's attending the monthly dances, and even her reports of meeting and dancing with the good-looking Arnold, a college student and *Yeshiva bokhe*, (Orthodox School student). Arnold wouldn't allow himself to experiment further than holding Stella as a dance partner with proper space between them. Stella, in a rare moment, stunned Hanna by whispering that she would like to try for 'a more physical relationship' with Arnold.

Stella reported that during the next monthly dance she engineered their first embrace by pretending to trip, forcing Arnold to spontaneously grab her to support her. In that embrace she had whispered, "I love you, Arnold."

Obviously, she caused the greatest emotional flood that Arnold had ever experienced. His guilt for ignoring the Torah's teachings agitated his tumult even more, frightening him, causing him to step back and excuse himself from the moment. He left the dance immediately.

But as they continued to see each other, stirred by Stella, Arnold's hormones would eventually decide his direction. He learned from Stella how to put one foot forward, then the other, toward accepting their relationship. He eventually responded to her whispered love with, "I love you, too, Stella."

Stella and Arnold stopped waiting for the monthly dances to be with each other. Still keeping their relationship a secret from their religious parents, and despite imminent spring final exams for each of them, Arnold phoned Stella from a friend's house to arrange their date.

It was dark when Arnold walked Stella back to her house. As they eased out of their goodnight embrace Stella took Arnold's hand and put it on her breast. "Have you been thinking, Arnold--?"

"I have, I have," he interrupted her, "but, but, not … not before you graduate."

"I'm eighteen and three months, Arnold, of legal age--"

"I know--"

"I'm not talking of marriage, Love. That will … I hope it will happen, Arnold—"

"I know, I know," he said, feeling guilt and fear about his impetuous desires. "Let's wait until you graduate. I … I … will … will feel better about it then."

Stella stretched up and kissed him. Happy, bubbling joyously that it would finally happen, she breathed ecstatically, "Good, sweetheart, wonderful!"

But Stella and Hannah graduated and that was as much of Stella's story as Hannah heard. School had been their meeting place and their moments together stolen from the school day for Hannah to listen to Stella's love adventures dropped out of their lives.

Walking, soothing baby Daniel, Hannah couldn't help wondering again how the story of the courageous Stella had ended, or if it did end. Hannah stopped suddenly. *Courageous?* She wondered if she secretly admired Stella by thinking of her as 'courageous.' Painfully aware of Joe's failure and her failure as lovers, Hannah had to admit to her envy of Stella, whom she knew would dare to go ahead with Arnold, if he would. *Did he?* Wondered Hannah. *Did he finally turn as brave about consummating their love as Stella, as he had promised her?*

Hannah's key concern about Orthodoxy piqued her again, as always. Before her marriage she never thought to question the rules. But now, each time she thought about Stella's story it disturbed Hannah to wonder at other possibilities for her and Joe. *What if…?* But Hannah shook her head. No, both Orthodox, it had not been possible between her and Joe.

And Arnold? If he allowed them to consummate their love after Stella's graduation did they follow it up with marriage, or did they not? Hannah, so ruled by her religion, perhaps in envy, chose to judge Stella. She thought, if they didn't marry, after all that breaking of the rules, it was a *shanda*, (a shame) on the Jewish Community.

After high school, Hannah had looked ahead to her own possibilities. She was delighted when Mrs. Rosenberg, the *shadkhin*, came calling and moved the next steps of her life toward marriage. Even as Hannah stepped carefully within Orthodox guidelines toward her future she did breathlessly wonder whether her Orthodox girlfriend really dared to have an affair before marriage—but then Stella had already broken the rules by going to the dances, as did Arnold. *So, well, after that they could have dared to do anything.*

As she soothed Baby Daniel, Hannah thought of how the romance of Stella and Arnold had developed over the year. She knew that her own stepping into marriage had been nothing like that. Both she and Joe had had little experience in relating to the opposite sex. With Joe's ever intense focus to succeed at his work and Hannah's looking forward to creating a home for her husband, they had moved into marriage leaving thoughts of romance and understanding of its passions in God's hands.

Hannah wished that she could see Stella again, to get answers to her own burgeoning questions about love and marriage. Her childish view during adolescence had been "When I marry, it will take care of itself." But rerunning Stella's story while she cleaned house or prepared a meal, Hannah wondered about other ways to explore love, to enjoy marriage. Did Stella and Arnold, both Orthodox, really have sex first? Did God punish them? Did they marry?

Hannah and Stella did meet again, most unexpectedly.

CHAPTER 19

Moe had a daunting job in Chicago. He didn't know any of the buyers and the city's shoe buyers didn't know that Moe Reinerman existed. But when he got off the train the bustling pace of the people and the purposeful tenor of the noises excited him to be there. He had had the same feeling when Joe put him to work at a machine and he knew he wanted to be outside exploring his new land and finding ways to be part of it. Here was a new land to explore. Moe was immediately glad to be in Chicago and to attach himself to the noisy clamor around him.

He checked into a swank suite in the Bayard Hotel. He asked the desk clerk to send up with his baggage a copy of all the daily newspapers and a list of the radio's daily news reports. Moe settled in to a quick but thorough study of what was happening in Chicago.

Activities in the city were more varied than Moe could have imagined. Chicago represented what was happening nationally in America's urban centers. Since the end of World War I, manufacturing and retailing spurted ahead and a solid percentage of the innovative, industrial activity was centered in this Midwest hub, a railroad terminal that served as the nation's focal point for both east and west. Giddy with the manufactured wonders that would improve their living, Chicagoans were buying refrigerators to replace iceboxes, vacuum cleaners to simplify house cleaning, and since 1920, Ford's Model T had been selling for $290, way down from the original price of $850. Avid about moving up to the better life, people were willing to go into debt to live well. Stores arranged installment buying. Banks arranged interest rate loans.

Prohibition's 18th Amendment to the Constitution denied the wealthy cocktail connoisseurs their daily drinks and the day laborers their beer. Furious, the drinkers didn't let illegality stop them. They knocked on the doors of speakeasies hidden behind a pool hall, an eatery, bakery or tobacco shop, and found a nightclub equipped with everything needed for their pleasure and entertainment, liquor, hostesses, a jazz band, dance floor and food. Bootlegging of alcoholic beverages had become rampant throughout the country and criminal gangs arose as quickly to control the importing, concocting, and distribution of the illegal intoxicating drinks.

In Chicago, Al Capone's gang-controlled speakeasies fed him sixty million dollars a year from the sale of alcoholic drink and forty-five million from gambling, prostitution and other rackets. He paid off the police and public officials with seventy-five million during his four-year reign in Chicago. Capone made his money the law and the politics of the city. On election day his paid agents manned the voting booths to make sure that Capone's political stooges, who were well-greased to favor his activities, were elected.

After Moe was comfortable that he got the picture, his next job was to find out what special goodies were available to break down the resistance of the shoe buyers. Great food? The best liquor? Choice women? Moe learned quickly that all of that and more were available in the Capone's 10,000 speakeasies accessible throughout the city.

The gangs in charge of these illegal rackets threw money around like confetti. It had the psychological effect on the public to join in on the spending and enjoy the good life. So many new things to buy excited the public, even if they had to borrow the money at interest. The buying fever had struck. Money, real or borrowed became the god of the era.

With so much money being thrown around and the increased excitement over the new products, working for a pittance could no longer be acceptable. Ford had long since raised wages for his assembly line workers from three to five dollars a day. Other workers said, "Me, too,"and asked for a raise to live like the rest of the population. The buying frenzy prompted their cries to organize unions.

After getting the sense of what was happening in and around the city from the newspapers, Moe listened the radio's daily news reports of the economic excitement happening in the city and nationally. When he felt he understood and could talk in the tenor of the times he sat himself down with Bell Telephone's Business Directory and phoned the buyer of every shoe store in the City. He managed to insert into each conversation "Reinerman makes the best hand turned shoe in America."

Some didn't return his calls. Some said they had already placed their orders for the coming spring-summer season.

Moe knew that was mularkey because it was only late winter and shoe designers were still working feverishly to get their new numbers ready for the sample season.

Moe decided to do it right. With the hotel's help he hired a knowledgeable secretary to work with him for the two weeks that he felt he needed to make inroads, had her list the name and address of every shoe store in the city and noted whether it handled expensive, middle, or low cost merchandise.

In Reinerman's home market in the northeast, their hand turned ladies shoes sold for $11 a pair, an expensive shoe, discounted occasionally during slow sales to nine dollars. Moe reasoned that the ferment in Chicago that created an upward income spiral could make more shoppers available for his high-end product. He decided to start on the upper-end retailers, including the mail order giants, Montgomery Ward and Sears & Roebuck, and the department stores, Macy's and Gimbels.

But before setting out for the day, Moe opened his two large sample cases to confirm again that Benno Spolio, Reinerman's designer, had outdone himself in preparing samples for Moe's trip. Pleased with what he had, and with his perennial cigar between his fingers, Moe blew a grateful kiss to Spolio in New York, phoned for room service to carry his cases down and call a taxi.

Moe did understand the tenor of Chicago's times. His money spent in dinner, drinking, and women parties won the hoped for results. Along with the first orders from Chicago, Irv and Joe received identical, succinct telegrams, that Moe had drawn another thousand dollars from the company's expense fund.

Joe blew up to Irv. "Vat for a business are ve in? Selling shoes or vomen?"

Irv smiled. They'd been over it before. In answer to Joe he gestured with his hands but remained silent as if to repeat philosophically, "Get used to it Joe. This is how business gets done in America."

CHAPTER 20

1923

When Daniel passed his sixth birthday he was old enough to move out of kindergarten and into class 1-A. Hannah could now send her boys off to elementary school P. S. 57 with Seymour in charge of the four-block walk and she could be free to plan the day for herself for the first time since Seymour was born eight years ago. Hannah prepared to attend her first Hadassah meeting.

From the monthly Newsletter she found out the information about the Brooklyn Chapter. She phoned the Brooklyn Chairlady, Janet Cohen, and learned that the monthly meetings were held at her house on the first Tuesday of the month, from one to two-thirty. On Mondays and Wednesdays there were weekly card games of rummy and poker at various members' houses from which ten percent of the winnings were donated to Hadassah and five percent to the Jewish National Fund. And there was talk of setting up a Mah Jongg table on Thursdays.

Hannah rang the bell of Janet's home. The maid opened the door, led the way through the foyer into the large, noisy living room, where about twenty well-dressed women were chatting freely and occasional laughter would erupt. Just as the luxurious furnishings startled and delighted Hannah, a short, brusque woman walked to her holding out her hand. "Hello, I'm Janet Cohen. Did we speak on the phone?"

Hannah thought to touch hands lightly and politely as she spoke, but Janet took her hand in a firm handshake to which Hannah responded, noting too, that she was glad to feel Janet's firmness. "Yes, we did. I'm Hannah Reinerman."

"Welcome, Hannah. This is your first Hadassah meeting?"

"Yes, it is."

"Delighted to have you." Janet gestured around the room. "Plenty of seats available. Please make yourself comfortable. The meeting will start in a few minutes."

"Thank you."

Janet left to talk to someone at the low bureau with a colorful Palestinian tapestry spread on it. Some file folders were stacked on it and two women sat behind it. It would apparently serve as the business focus of the meeting.

Hannah did a quick eye scan of the room for a seat and was delighted to be among the many well-dressed women she again noted, among which was someone in surprising all-white. As Hannah moved toward a chosen seat, she heard, "Hannah!"

She turned to locate the caller and saw the woman in white running toward her. Before Hannah recognized her, she was held in a strong embrace to which she could respond only tentatively. The woman backed off to look into Hannah's face and laugh joyfully at seeing her.

"Stella!" Hannah cried out and threw her arms around her.

They finally released each other to stand grinning, a thousand thoughts, questions popping through their heads.

"Where--" Stella started, "Is this your first meeting? Are you a member of Hadassah?"

For Hannah, the white uniform didn't make sense with her questions about Stella and Arnold. She tried to answer Stella's spoken questions. "Uh, yes … I don't know."

Intent upon each other they didn't realize they were being eyed by all and that Janet had called for everyone to find seats so the meeting could begin. Janet approached Stella and Hannah. "Please hold it for later, ladies. Find seats now. We have business to tend to."

As the two walked toward chairs, Stella spoke softly and quickly. "We'll talk later, Hannah. I have a car. I'll drive you home. We'll talk."

Hannah wondered at Stella's statement, but nodded agreement, said, "Yes," as they sat down.

After the reading of the previous meeting's minutes and the financial report, arrangements for the month's rummy and poker games were read and discussed. But it turned out that Stella was the most important part of the meeting. Janet announced that Stella had finished her nurse's training and had agreed to help staff a medical clinic in Palestine for two years.

Applause broke out. Red-faced Stella stood and thanked everyone for their support.

The meeting over, Janet handed Hannah a membership application to take with her.

Hannah agreed to consider it, thanked Janet for the meeting at her lovely house and said she looked forward to next month's meeting.

Stella said goodbye to her many friends, took Hannah by the elbow and whisked her to her Studebaker parked near the house.

Before getting in, Hannah had difficulty relating her eighteen-year-old school chum to Stella chauffeuring her in an automobile. There were still horse-and-wagons on the streets.

Stella saw Hannah's hesitation. "I've been driving for a whole year, Hannah, without a mishap."

Hannah was still having difficulties putting her memories together with the grown-up Stella talking to her, a qualified nurse, driving an automobile! Hannah had come to the meeting in a taxicab driven by a man. Hannah smiled sheepishly and got in.

"I live on Kosciusko Street between Stuyvesant and Reid Avenue." Hannah stopped talking. She waited for Stella to start the car and begin driving.

"That's near where I'm rooming in Bensonhurst," Stella said. "Good. It's on my way home."

Hannah saw that Stella knew how to handle the car, relaxed and began her questions. "When do you leave for Palestine?"

"In three weeks."

"Excited?"

"Of course."

"What will you do there?"

"Anything and everything. You know we had this terrible flu epidemic just five years ago that killed 50 million people all over the world. 50 million people, Hannah, I can't even imagine that many people. Well, in Palestine they have very primitive conditions. The King of Jordan is supposed to supervise the territory and provide the necessary services. Well, he doesn't do a thing for the people there especially not for the Jews. So Henrietta Zsold set up Hadassah to do the job. She spent three years there training medical personnel. She set up a hospital in Jerusalem and two clinics in the rest of the territory. And they need more…"

Hannah had read that information about Szold's three years in Palestine in the Hadassah Newsletter, but hearing Stella relating it with such excitement and emphasis on its importance made it so real for Hannah. She felt doubly glad to be teaming up with Hadassah.

But that was as much new information about the amazing Henrietta Zsold and her organization as Hannah could absorb at one time. She sat quietly while Stella continued with a similar passion about Hadassah's work as she used to talk about her relationship with Arnold.

Hannah noted that Stella had stopped talking. They drove along in silence for a while. Then Hannah said, "What happened with you and Arnold?"

"Oh, him."

There was another long pause of silence. Hannah silently wondered whether Stella simply didn't want to talk about it when she heard Stella say with genuine sympathy, "Poor Arnold."

Hannah glanced at her friend to see Stella slowly shaking her head, her face in sorrow. "The more we expressed our love for each other," she continued, "the guiltier he felt. I thought I could change him. I was as Orthodox as he, but what could be wrong between two people if the love is real?"

Stella lapsed into a sad silence.

A silence that Hannah felt she had to respect. She noticed that they had just driven onto her block. She pointed out her apartment house and Stella parked the car in front of it. Some of the younger boys were arguing about the results of a box ball game on the large, cemented area.

"It didn't go over the line."

"Yes, it did."

"No, it didn't."

Since there had been no referee, and it was close to supper, they gave up after a few more minutes of wrangling, quit for the day and went home.

Hannah knew that her boys would be along soon from Hebrew School and if she wanted to know more of what happened between Stella and Arnold she'd better ask. She spoke hesitantly. "Did you and Arnold … before you were married …?"

Feeling no shame about it, Stella turned to look directly at Hannah. "Yes."

Hannah stayed silent a moment to absorb the shock, then said, "Oh."

"I thought real love can't be wrong," Stella continued, and I thought it would help change Arnold." Stella paused to remember her thinking at the time. She shook her head slowly. "It … didn't … help him."

Stella turned directly toward Hannah with sudden enthusiasm. "I also joined Hadassah after I graduated. I felt I wanted to do something for our people. Hadassah offered so many things that a Jewish woman can do, not just go to *schul* (synagogue) and pray.

Stella paused to wonder if she wanted to tell all. "I knew what was bothering him. I said, 'Arnold, it's all right to be in love and to express it. The rules that are upsetting you were written 4,000 years ago. We understand love better now. We understand people better. But if it still bothers you, let's get married.' "That seemed to relax him. He felt that's what our community expected."

"We waited until he graduated and his father took him on as an executive in his shipping franchise and we got married."

Silence.

Hannah waited and finally asked, "And?"

Stella talked as slowly as she shook her head. "Nothing I did as a wife, a friend, or a lover could relieve him of his guilt. I tried for two years and then gave up."

In the silence Hannah dared ask, "Divorce?"

Stella nodded and was silent.

Hannah wrestled with the shame of her friend's divorce when Stella's snickering startled her.

"I visited my mother. I had to explain to her what happened to my marriage. I had to find a way to talk about things a nice Jewish girl isn't supposed to talk about, an Orthodox girl yet, to an Orthodox mother yet. I talked about the wife's feelings, the husband's feelings, a good five minutes talking, explaining, when she caught on. 'You mean,' she said, in astonishment, 'the woman is supposed to enjoy it, too?'"

It startled Hannah to hear Stella provide an answer to her own question of nine years. But worse, how could she ever get Joe to understand. He's a good husband who makes a good living but Hannah felt helpless because she and Joe had no way of talking about this.

Stella noticed the sudden change in Hannah's face, but couldn't guess that her friend wrestled with the same problem. "So after the divorce," Stella continued breezily, in an effort to throw off her past, "I decided to get serious about Hadassah and become another Henrietta Zsold." Stella snickered cynically about the improbability of achieving such a lofty goal. "Once I got my mother to understand, though maybe not *accept* my divorce, I decided to become a nurse."

Hannah saw Seymour running toward the heavy steel storm door of the apartment house with Danny running after him. "Oh, my boys are home, Stella." Hannah called to them. "Seymour, Danny."

Startled to hear their mother's voice coming from the street, they stopped and looked at the car.

Hannah waved to them. "Here I am."

The boys rushed over. "Did you buy an automobile, Ma?" Seymour asked.

Hannah laughed. "No, it belongs to my friend Stella."

Stella leaned and waved to Seymour and Daniel. "Hello, boys."

Hannah explained as she opened her door and got out. "Stella and I went to school together."

Stella got out and came around to the sidewalk. "Hello, boys, what are your names?" She bent to shake hands with each one as he said his name."

"I'm Stella and very glad to know you." Stella turned and opened her arms to Hannah. "I have to leave, Hannah."

Hannah went to the embrace and held it for more than their friendship. She admired Stella who picked herself up after her failed marriage and embarked on an entirely new venture that would utilize, challenge, her newly found abilities. Stella had rescued her life from murky, adolescent confusion and with a clearer head was about to do something extraordinary with it.

Hannah also realized the time had passed for their old friendship. They were no longer adolescent schoolgirls. They were women, making their choices. Stella was just embarking on one. Hannah felt she had made hers by marrying Joe, the successful businessman. With Janet Cohen and the other Hadassah women in mind, and how they lived, Hannah determined again to transform Joe to look and act like the successful American that he was, and she and the boys would look like and live as the wife and family of an American success.

Seymour ran to the heavy storm door and showed his strength by pulling it open. He ran in and opened the door to the vestibule. Hannah and Danny followed.

Leaving Hannah and her two boys, Stella pulled away from the curb. Exiting from Hannah was like the final shedding of her old life. She turned the car around and drove toward Bensonhurst. She looked ahead to her Palestine adventure, her new life for which she had diligently trained.

Paul Barlin

Those years of study and field practice had opened a new world for her. Not many women she knew had achieved this much. Her pride in having climbed to this point brought the exhilaration she craved. Stella finally felt freed of the entangling cords of her failed marriage.

CHAPTER 21

1924

Raised in the cocoon of Jewish prayer that accompanied daily, weekly and annual rituals, Seymour and Daniel knew that their world was a Jewish world as ordered by God. Slowly, as they grew, the brothers became aware that the other boys on Kosciusko Street, who joined them on the flat cement playground in front of their apartment house, were not Jewish but subscribed to something else. But since religious belief had nothing to do with the rules of "Johnny On the Pony", "matching baseball tickets," "Ring-a-Levio," "Steal the White Flag," "Hop-Scotch," or "Box Ball," it never came up. Whatever belief any of the boys was raised in did not interfere with their many hours of play. The street game of the moment occupied them solely and wholly.

They only became aware of religious holidays like Christmas because for two weeks the Jewish boys had no others to play with, or during Rosh Hashanah's ten days of atonement and Yom Kippur when the Jewish boys spent most of that time in the synagogue promising to do better in the next year.

The only dividing factor among the boys was age. The older 'gang' wouldn't deign to include any of the younger 'gang' in their games of stickball or punch ball that they courageously played in the gutter. They adventurously set up their narrow, curb-restricted baseball diamond and braved the horse-and-wagon traffic, horse droppings and the occasional Model T and other automobiles. The nine and ten-year-old 'gang' left the sidewalk to the seven and eight-year-old 'kids' to make the age separation of the older and younger gangs complete. This suited Seymour just fine. It gave him another way to put Daniel down; it told Seymour's gang, if anyone asked, "That one hop-scotching on the sidewalk is my kid brother."

Starting at six years old, every day when public school let out, Daniel and Seymour walked to their synagogue's Hebrew School to sit in class for an hour to learn to read and write Hebrew, and listen to the stories behind the annual Jewish holidays. They also began memorizing Genesis in English, the first book of the Hebrew Bible. Of course, in Hebrew School, as in regular school, the two-year age difference put the brothers in different classes, to Daniel's delight because it freed him from Seymour's domination, if only temporarily.

At the Hebrew school Miss Vitlovsky, a Polish refugee, taught Daniel's class. She and her family had emigrated from Poland after Christians attacked their ghetto. Because Seymour made Daniel feel that only he, the first son, was important to his parents, Daniel automatically, looked outside the family, upon his woman teachers, as possible friendly mothers.

Miss Vitlovsky sat on the edge of her desk facing her class of seven and eight-year-old boys, or walked from side to side in front of her class saying aloud and clearly in her careful, accented English, the sentence for her students to translate into Hebrew, "The book is on the table." Or she would give them the phrase in Hebrew, "*Hasafer al hashulkhan*," for them to write the sentence in Hebrew script. Short, she wore shoes with two-inch heels on which she stepped slowly across the wooden floor repeating the sentence for the class to translate.

Daniel sat in the second row close enough to the teacher to know that she smelled nice. Daniel felt that Miss Vitlovsky shared his Jewish world with him.

It was close to suppertime when Daniel walked home from Hebrew School. Seymour had run on ahead with his friends. The playground in front of his apartment house had cleared of children. Johnny Hagen, who lived next door to the apartment house was the only one there and totally occupied himself in playing a game he'd just made up, machine gun. He ran a stick along the separated slats of his picket fence from the apartment house to the sidewalk making a loud rat-a-tat-tat noise. When he reached the end of the fence he turned around and ran the stick back.

Daniel watched John run to the end of the fence and back again. He enjoyed listening to the loud rhythmic sounds and he stayed to watch John instead of going upstairs. "Can I do it, John?" He asked.

"Sure."

Daniel took the stick and ran it back and forth. Laughing, he said, "Wow, that's fun."

After watching Daniel for a while, John said, "You wanna see a real gun, Danny?"

Daniel stopped. "A real gun?"

"Yeah."

Daniel thought how they usually played cops-and-robbers and cowboys-and-Indians. They pretended to have a gun by pointing their index finger and upright thumb and added the vocals, "Pow-pow-pow!" Daniel questioned John. "A real gun?"

"Sure, my father's a cop."

"Oh." Daniel remembered that Cowboy Tom Mix had a gun. Cowboy William S. Hart had a gun, and the bad guys they fought had guns but that was in the nickel movie on Saturday afternoon.

"Do ya wanna see it, Danny?" John sounded impatient.

"Uh … yeah, John, yeah."

"Well come on." John turned and led the way. He went to the front of his white fence and opened the gate.

Daniel had never been in the house or yard of any of his friends. He stopped to stare at the many colors of the flowers that Mrs. Hagen spent so much time with on either side of the slate walk that led to the house. There were as many colors as he could spill out of a whole box of crayons.

John called from the porch of his house. "Come on, Danny."

Daniel didn't want to leave the flowers. "Yeah," he answered but moved forward slowly.

At the porch he smelled something disagreeable he had never smelled before. "What's that?"

John had just opened the door to the kitchen. "What's what?"

"That smell."

"That's soap."

Thinking of how different the smell of the soap that he washed his hands with, he said, "Ugh, it doesn't smell like soap."

John pointed to something behind the lattice. "There it is."

Daniel stepped up on the porch and looked behind the lattice. On a shelf a large black oven pan was filled to the top with a filmy white something. The stink made Daniel gag. He wanted to run but he also wanted to see the gun.

"That's soap," John said. "My mother makes it. It's getting hard out here."

"Oh."

"Come on."

Daniel held his breath and followed John into the kitchen. The smell was almost as strong. "The smell's all over," Daniel said.

"Yeah. My mother melts the meat fat. It stinks up everything."

Daniel followed John through the dining room and into the living room.

John stopped and pointed toward the fireplace. His voice lowered to almost a whisper. "There it is. I'm not allowed to touch it."

Daniel saw a large black belt lying along the mantel. The ends hung down making it look like a black snake sleeping. He couldn't count all the bullets lined up in the belt. At the end of the belt nearest to him Daniel saw the brown leather holster. The black handle of the gun stood up out of the holster, looking ready to grab and shoot.

Daniel stared. It was heavy looking, bigger even than the ones in the movies. "A real gun?" he whispered, questioning.

"Yup."

"It's big."

"Yup."

Daniel stood digesting the frightening wonder before him.

When he had had enough, his eyes were drawn to the statue of a man hung on the wall above the gun belt, a man naked except for a cloth around his middle. His hands were stretched out wide and nailed to the wooden beam that he hung from. The whites of his eyes seemed to plead to Daniel for help, almost as if he were alive. Daniel felt so sorry for his suffering. "Who ... who's that poor man?"

"Jesus Christ. The Jews killed him."

Daniel's eyes filled with tears for the suffering man. "Why?" he asked.

"They hated him."

"Why ... why did they hate him?"

John shrugged. "I don't know."

In all of his readings in Hebrew school and regular school Daniel had never heard the name or read anything about Jesus. He looked questioningly at John, hoping to hear more. But just then he heard his name being called faintly. "Dan...ny, sup...per."

Danny knew it was his Ma calling out the window. "I gotta go," he said to John. "My mother's calling me."

His attention directed to the outside, Daniel was relieved to think of getting out into the fresh air. He hurried through the three rooms and got outside. He jumped the two porch steps, ran past the flowers and pulled the gate open. On the sidewalk he looked up. Ma was leaning out the window. "I'm coming, Ma."

Hannah pulled her head in and closed the window.

The next day at Hebrew school Daniel looked up from the English sentence he was translating into Hebrew. Miss Vitlovsky was walking slowly across the front of the small classroom. First, she'd say the sentence in English, then in Hebrew. The students were supposed to write the Hebrew script under the English.

Daniel raised his hand.

Miss Vitlovsky stopped and smiled to him. "Yes, Deniel?"

"Why did the Jews kill Jesus Christ?"

Miss Vitlovsky's earth stopped. Shock, fear, and defeat, paralyzed her face. Her stance froze. All the boys in the class, as well, were looking to her for an answer. Daniel didn't yet know that the name of the Christian Deity was the battle cry of those who burned the Jewish ghettos in Eastern Europe. But the fear and pain on her face told Daniel that he had done something terrible to her. He was afraid he would cry for her, like he felt for the man on the statue.

Behind her glasses tears welled. Vitlovsky pulled a small handkerchief from the wrist of her sleeve, lifted her glasses and dried her eyes. She stuffed the handkerchief into her wristband. "Ve dun't ... talk about det, Deniel."

Daniel looked down to finish the sentence, but he couldn't write. From the paper Miss Vitlovsky's frightened, tear-filled eyes still looked up at him. He felt so bad that he had done that to her.

CHAPTER 22

1925

In the kitchen ten-year old Seymour poured the last of his glass of milk into his mouth full of cookie paste and headed for the front door. He hated getting home late from school because he missed the fun on the street.

Hannah, busy cleaning in the living room, called, "Seymour, put your books in your room."

Seymour pretended not to hear, left his books on the kitchen cupboard, slammed the door to the apartment and sped down the two flights of stairs. He jumped the last three steps to land with a loud bang on the hard vestibule floor of tiny hex tiles. He pulled the knob of the heavy glass door, his ten-year old muscles straining to overcome the heavy-tensioned spring. As soon as the opening was big enough, he squeezed through, ran two steps and slid, the toe of his shoe banging into the steel frame of the plate glass storm door. Bracing one foot against the doorframe he pulled the brass handle with both hands. Quickly slipping through the opening he jumped the two cement steps to land with a loud smack on the sidewalk, announcing his presence to everyone.

On his right was the clamor of a Johnny-on-the-pony game. Daniel and three other boys of his team, swinging one arm in the air wild-west style, were riding the line of four bent-over ponies. The boys underneath were desperately trying not to cave in before they gasped out "Johnny-on-the-pony-1-2-3" three times to earn their chance to ride the other team. But even as Seymour looked, the boy carrying most of the weight of Danny's team of four sagged crazily toward the ground pulling everyone into a yelling heap.

Daniel's team leaped up victoriously and rushed back to the curb for another turn.

Fat Georgie, who'd carried most of the weight under Daniel's team, staggered up glumly brushing leaves and dirt from his knickers and imitation leather jacket. "I have to go to the store," he mumbled. "It's gettin' dark." His leaving would break up the game.

"Don't be a sore loser, George."

"It ain't gettin' dark yet."

"You'll get a turn soon, Georgie."

"The teams ain't fair," Georgie pouted. "You guys are heavier than us.

"Heavier!" yelled skinny Frank Harrigan, "You guys got it all over us."

Seymour wished he could show what a great player he was. He hoped Georgie would leave and they'd ask him to play. But Seymour was almost eleven. Daniel's gang was eight and nine. Seymour turned away to look out in the gutter for his own gang. Tony, the iceman's horse-and-wagon was at the curb in front of someone's shiny black Studebaker. Seymour walked off the curb and looked down the street; plenty of wagons and cars but no sign of his gang, same in the other direction. He wondered if his gang was playing ring-a-levio in the vacant lot behind the apartment house. He returned to the sidewalk to watch the game.

Georgie's team convinced him to stay in the game by letting him be the pillow, to stand with his back against the apartment house building so the first pony could bend over and pad his shoulder against Georgie's soft middle. The two other boys of the team bent over and butted a shoulder against the butt of the boy ahead.

Daniel was first for the riders. He targeted Petey, the pony in the middle. Daniel swayed forward and back while he gauged the distance to Petey's shoulders. He wanted to leave room on Petey for his three teammates.

Seymour called out, "C'mon Danny, ya' gotta come up fa' supper."

A chorus of groans and complaints rose from the eight boys in the game, the loudest from Daniel. "Not now, Sy. Can't ya' wait a while?"

"No, Ma ast me to call ya' up fa' suppa."

"Okay, Sy, right after this jump." Daniel ran and leapfrogged the back of the last boy to land hard on Petey's shoulders, but the momentum threw him to the side. He desperately clutched Petey's clothing and hung on.

Seymour wished Daniel would fall so his team would lose the rest of their turn.

But Daniel righted himself.

Seymour fumed quietly with the dirtiest word he could think of. "F---."

"Atta boy Danny," Frank yelled. He ran and vaulted. He missed so badly that no amount of clothing clutching could save him. As he sprawled on the ground a triumphant cheer rose from Georgie's team and they ran to the curb to line up as riders.

"Aw, we had three turns anyway," Frank consoled his self.

Danny looked uncertainly at Seymour. He sensed that his brother was angry and Daniel wondered if Sy would pick a fight with him. Daniel tensed and hated to feel that he always had to be on guard against Sy.

"C,mon Danny, up fa' supper," Seymour insisted.

Daniel looked up at the sun. "It's too early fa' supper," he argued.

"No, it ain't. Ma wants us to eat early."

"Awright," Daniel yielded. He turned to the others. "I have to go up," he said.

"You'll wreck the game," Harry complained. "Can't play four against three."

"I was supposed to go to the store an hour ago," unexpectedly came from Fat George. He felt in his pocket for the dollar bill his mother had given him. "My Mom'll kill me," he added. Glum-faced about his expected bawling out for being so late, he turned and started trotting heavily toward De Kalb Avenue.

A cheer went up from the rest. "Three and three, we still got a game!"

Seymour challenged Daniel. "Race ya' to the house."

Determined to win one, Daniel shot forward before Seymour got the words out.

Seymour, two yards ahead and stronger, reached the iron-grilled door first.

As Daniel came in reach of the bars Seymour bent and jutted his butt, his timing perfect.

Daniel slammed into Seymour with his abdomen. The pain fierce in his gut, he tumbled backward down the two steps hitting the sidewalk hard with his back. Despite the knife in his diaphragm and tears of rage blurring his eyes, fury bounced him up and he took off after his brother.

Seymour had opened the doors and was flying up the stairs, Daniel hard after him.

The apartment door swung open and slammed shut in front of Daniel but Seymour didn't have time to latch it. He ran the long hallway into their bedroom, slammed the door shut and wedged his foot at an angle against it between the bottom of the door and the floor.

Daniel heard the bang of their bedroom door. He raced down the hallway and threw himself against it. The middle sagged open but the bottom, braced by Seymour's foot, held.

The door snapped straight and bounced Daniel back. He charged it again hitting it with his whole side. The door thumped, banged and crackled as if the grain were splitting, the noise frightful.

Hannah rushed from the kitchen. "God in Heaven," she screamed in Yiddish. She rushed down the hallway yelling at Daniel, "What are you doing? What are you doing?"

Daniel clamped his jaw and charged again, hissing, "I'm gonna get him. I'm gonna get him." He threw every fiber of him against the door.

"Stop it! Stop it!" screamed Hannah. "You're breaking the door!" She reached to grab him.

He slapped her hands aside.

She swung a blow to the side of his head and landed hard.

Shocked, he sought his mother's face to ask "Why?" and saw her hatred blazing at him. Daniel panicked as if hit again in the diaphragm. He sucked desperately for air but all went black and he fell. He sucked a hoarse, rasping groan and his lungs suddenly filled with air. Thankful, he felt grateful that he would live. A wail of relief yet the pain of aloneness broke in sobs from him. He knew he belonged nowhere, was loved by no one.

Though Hannah felt pity for the helpless body of her son, pity was snuffed by her anger. She did nothing to ease his suffering. Whenever her boys fought she became an uncontrollable tempest. It infuriated her that she knew nothing of how to end their fights except call on God. It infuriated her that she understood nothing of why they fought.

Though contrite for having hit Daniel and pitying him in his collapse she had too much rage and could not soften. She thoughtlessly turned it on her first son. "Seymour, come out of there."

Surprise slowed Daniel's sobs. Would she really get angry with Seymour?

It was quiet behind the door.

Angered even more by his refusal to respond to her, her voice growled in her throat. "Seymour!"

Daniel stopped his sobs. She had never targeted Seymour before. He stared at her. She looked like she was really going to give it to him.

Behind the door Seymour was equally stunned.

But Hannah was stunned most of all. Her too quick and overwhelming anger at the boys meant that she felt no love for any in her family, not husband, not Daniel, and now not Seymour; she had no fulfilling source. An unexpected well of tears burst in her. When she spoke again her voice choked. She tapped a fist weakly against her chest as when praying her atonement on Yom Kippur. She looked upward and wailed. "O God, why do you do this to me?"

Daniel continued to stare at her, his awe at her suffering interrupted his. His mother was a crying child like himself.

Behind the door Seymour heard his mother's voice crumble and then her sobs. Stunned, he stood paralyzed.

Recovering, he opened the door slowly, to confirm what he had heard. Yes. He stared, astonished, frightened.

Hannah beat on herself for having stayed in the marriage. She inveighed against herself in Yiddish so the boys would not understand. "Bessie was right. I should never have married him. She told me. Bessie too, had Orthodox parents. Fool. Fool. Why did I stay in this marriage?"

But marriage vows were sacred and not to be broken by silly disagreements.

CHAPTER 23

1925

Working his way up toward street level, Joe Reinerman gripped the banister to help pull his self up the stairs of the De Kalb Avenue subway exit.

The crowd of fellow passengers, eager to get out of the cold and into their homes bumped or brushed past him to scatter quickly.

Not only did the fatigue of a ten-hour workday weigh Joe down, but his extra 35 pounds did not add to his buoyancy. Reaching the top of the stairs he stood a moment to catch his breath, then automatically turned to his right to buy the Hearst Journal from the newsstand of the wounded war veteran. Without scanning it he folded and slipped it into the pocket of his coat. As he set out on the trek home he smiled imagining Seymour and Danny running to him, taking the paper out of his pocket and arguing over who gets which part.

He turned the corner onto Kosciusko Street and responded to his automatic alert as to where to step his feet on the uneven slate slabs; worse now because melted snow had turned the dirt spaces to mud. But after ten years he had become accustomed to the inconvenience of the uneven sidewalk. The line of maple branches immediately overhead reminded him of Count Levidov's forest outside of Tchernivakh. Joe chuckled. "Heh, heh, it's a long vay from Tchernivakh, Russia to Brooklyn in America."

Joe had good reason to be enjoying Brooklyn, USA. His shop was in the midst of another successful year. Moe, and Ben and Harry, the two new salesmen, were continuing to have an unusual selling season and for the next month Joe would be pushing his production workers to get the shoes out in time for the retailers' selling season.

Joe's day now was from 7:00 a.m. to 6:00 p.m. He had asked his fourteen day workers to start at 7:30 instead of 8:00 without offering them extra pay. He sensed that it had provoked angry talk that could lead to a work stoppage. Walking the uneven slate sidewalk toward the apartment house, Joe questioned whether to change his mind. A work stoppage in the middle of the season could lose him thousands of dollars. Yeah, he thought, I'll give them the half-hour extra.

Suddenly Joe felt very hungry, as if as he had opened the storm door of the apartment house and could smell Hannah's cooking.

In the light of the flickering gas street lamps some boys were running back and forth. Joe wondered if Seymour and Danny were among them.

Suddenly one of them shouted, "Hey Sy, hey Danny, ya' fodder's comin'."

Danny started running first but Sy's longer, stronger legs got him to his father ahead of his brother. "Hi, Pa," he yelled. With a quick move he slipped the newspaper out of his father's pocket just as Danny bumped and wrapped his arms around him. "I get half, Sy," said Danny. His tone was sullen as if he expected to be cheated out of it.

"Sure, sure," said Seymour. He straightened and broke Danny's grip. He slipped the two sections of the paper apart and gave Danny the one with the headlines.

Danny raised a frustrated howl. "You've got the jokes."

"Ya' wanted half, dincha'? Ya' got it."

Joe felt helpless. Seymour, the older, always got what he wanted with the smaller Daniel. He shooed the boys ahead of him. "Opstairs now, it's dahk already."

Hannah and the boys had already eaten. While Joe took off his jacket and loosened his tie and collar Daniel hurried to him and hung on to one arm. "Checkers tonight, Pa? You promised me. You played with Seymour last time."

"I kent play mit dirty hends. Let me vash, Denny. After supper ve'll play."

After Joe ate Hannah cleared the dishes and wiped down the kitchen table.

Joe found his *Der Tag* on the kitchen cupboard where Hannah usually put it for him and sat down at the table to read. He still read the Yiddish language section first for his news of the day. Later he would scan the English section headlines to see how they matched up.

Seymour had commandeered the desk in the boys' room as usual, to do his homework. But he left the door open to hear anything happening that he should know about.

Daniel, on his knees on the carpet at the coffee table in the living room, copied his assigned list of new words from his schoolbook into his notebook.

Hannah washed and rinsed the last of Joe's supper dishes and found a place in the full dish rack for it to drain. She wiped her hands on her apron as she walked to the table and sat down opposite Joe, who was still reading. "Joe, put the paper down. We have to talk."

Reluctantly Joe lowered the paper. "Something important?"

"Yes, in two weeks we're going to the Opera House for the Jewish National Fund. Hadassah is selling tickets for it. It's a big affair and you don't have a suit to wear."

"I vear a suit every day."

"You're not going to a fancy affair at the Metropolitan Opera House in that suit you wear to the shop every day."

"Vat's wrong mit it?"

"It's old. It's dirty."

"So I'll send it to the cleaners."

"For God's sakes, Joe. You're a successful businessman. Spend the money for a new suit and look like one."

"I got to put on all the fency menners?"

"Yes, that's what successful businessmen do."

"I leave that to Moe, him, mit da suits and cigars."

"Joe, I'm not going to sit with you in the Metropolitan Opera House with all those well-dressed people if you don't buy a new suit."

Joe thought about it. "All right, how much is it?"

"About a hundred dollars."

"A hundred dollars!"

"Yes."

"For a suit?"

"Yes."

"I'm not the president."

"That's what a good suit costs. You're a successful businessman, Joe. I'm not going to let you buy schmattas (rags) anymore."

"It's already a hundred dollars a ticket. Dat's three hundred dollars for vun affair."

"It's for the Jewish National Fund, Joe. We're buying land for Jews to live in Palestine. Where else can they go?"

"All right, all right, I'll buy a suit."

"Good. We'll shop this weekend."

Joe nodded and picked up his paper again.

"Joe, we're not finished yet."

Annoyed, Joe slapped the paper down. "Vat?"

"Joe, the boys fight too much in that one room."

"Nu, boys fight. So?"

"They should be in separate rooms."

"Ve gonna rent anudder room? I grew up with Moish and Avram in one room."

"That was Russia, Joe. We're in America now. We should rent a bigger apartment."

"Dere's a bigger apartment here?"

"No, Joe, it's on Ocean Parkway."

Joe stared. "Ocean Parkway?"

"Yes. It's closer to the ocean."

"Fa' swimming?"

"Don't be silly, Joe. Ocean Parkway is now a boulevard. It runs all the way from Brooklyn Park to Coney Island. You should see how beautiful it is. The Hadassah women told me about it. Two of them have moved there already. Horse and wagons are not allowed anymore, only automobiles."

"Who's got an automobile?"

"You talked about getting one. You said you were tired of the subways. You gave Moe one to use for the company and he has another one for his family. You know how convenient it makes everything." Hannah stopped for a breath then added, "You can drive us to the Catskills for our vacation. We wouldn't have to bother with the train anymore. And at the new house on Ocean Parkway there's plenty of room for parking."

"Vat house?"

"A new apartment house, all in red brick. It's beautiful."

"You van't us to go through the *hegdish* (chaos) of moving to live in a fency red brick house? Dis is no good anymore?"

"Joe, we've lived here ten years. In a year-and-a-half Seymour will be Bar-Mitzvad. The boys are growing. They need to be in separate rooms."

Joe started to object but Hannah anticipated him. "I know. You were three brothers sleeping in one small room. That was Russia, Joe. You're a successful businessman now. You can afford to give your family new, clean space."

Joe ended the argument with, "I'll t'ink about it." He forewarned Hannah that she didn't win yet. "It's not gonna happen tomorrow."

CHAPTER 24

1926

Joe first bought the car, a 1926 Studebaker. He rejected Henry Ford's Model T as did most American car buyers in that year because Ford had refused to change anything on his machine since he first produced it 18 years ago. Although Ford steadily reduced the price from $850 to $250 in 1920, it was still the same black box on four wheels. A common joke of the era was, "When you buy a Model T you can have any color you want, as long as it's black." No other colors or body designs were available, whereas other car companies offered luxury-looking tidbits on their cars that pleased American buyers; red, blue, green, or yellow as well as black and early attempts to streamline the body. The new designs excited buyers.

Model T sales had dropped so drastically that Ford cancelled its production in 1927. He redesigned a spiffier Model A to be his new offering.

Leo, the mechanic who serviced the Reinerman Bros.'s Model T, taught Joe how to drive. As wise an instructor as he was a knowledgeable mechanic, for the final test he directed Joe to a neighborhood of narrow, two-lane streets.

Leo knew that cities like New York didn't plan for broad streets while automobiles were still only an oddity among the horse-and-wagon traffic. But by the roaring twenties the number of autos on the streets of New York convinced city planners as well as the rest of the population, that the city had best be redesigned around automobiles being the major item in personal transportation.

The main thoroughfares connecting vital business districts demanded the city's immediate widening efforts. However, the slow process of redesigning the remaining city streets to accomodate the projected use of the automobile usually left city planners one-step behind. In local residential areas, where driving space was eaten up by horse-and-wagons and cars parked on both sides of the streets, the two lanes for traffic were just two narrow lanes. Leo made sure that Joe spent time driving on those narrow streets until Joe seemed comfortable with the challenges of oncoming traffic and an unpredictable horse.

At the end of his lessons Joe proudly parked the Studebaker in front of the apartment house on Kosciusko Street.

Seymour recognized his father at the wheel and called out, "Hey Danny, Pa bought a car!" All the games on the playground ceased and the boys rushed over to see the new car up close.

Joe got out and went to the sidewalk.

The boys stepped back.

"Danny, Seymour, don't let anybody touch."

Seymour spoke up. "Right, Pa."

"Den come up for supper."

Danny repeated, "Right, Pa."

Joe made an effort to utilize the car for his family. He pretended that Friday was the end of his week that he didn't work half a day on Saturday. After their week of school the boys were off for two days. Friday evening, the end of the week, was a good time for a ride in the new car. Joe felt glad and proud to comply when after Friday supper Hannah said, "Joe, drive us to Brooklyn Park. It's nice there, by the water."

"Yeah, yeah, give us a ride," the boys chimed in.

"Sure," Joe agreed, "In' the car everyvun."

It was a balmy summer evening and twilight would last until nine o'clock. There was no need to bother with extra clothing. The boys raced down the stairs and into the back seat of the car.

Before starting the motor, Joe turned, as well as his extra weight let him, and cautioned the boys with a raised finger. "No fighting in the car, kinder (children)."

"Okay, Pa," Seymour said.

On the first ride in their own car Seymour and Daniel's eyes were glued to the window on each side all the way to the park. Periodically they would bounce their behinds up and down on the seat to feel its springiness.

Joe found the parking area near the water. On the grass between the car and the lake was a larger than life bronze of a lioness and her two cubs.

As Joe parked Seymour called out, "Look at the lion!" As soon as the car stopped moving he opened the car door and started running.

Danny followed.

On her three-foot pedestal the lioness stood half raised as if to look out over the jungle growth to guard the safety of her small brood of two. Her front legs were straight, raising her head higher to see farther. Her rump rested on the ground. One cub clung to her left shoulder. The other cub hung on to her right midsection.

Joe and Hannah remained in the car and smiled to see the happy excitement of the boys. Especially did Hannah feel relaxed that the boys were not fighting, and there was room on the statue for both.

Seymour reached up, grabbed the cub on the left side and worked hard to pull himself up and sit horseback style just below the lion's shoulders.

Daniel grabbed her tail and climbed steadily to finally sit on her reclining rump.

Seymour raised one arm and circled it as if he were swinging a lasso like he saw in the cowboy movies and accompanied it with a "Whoo-ee, whoo-ee."

Daniel sat smiling, rocking slowly back and forth as if his horse was loping along.

Friday night out at the lion statue in the park became a weekly event for the family while the warm weather lasted. For the boys it celebrated the end of a week of school and the coming two-day vacation. At one of the last park sojourns in mid September Hannah said, "Joe, while it's still light let's take a ride down Ocean Parkway."

"Okay."

Hannah rolled down her window and called to Seymour and Danny. "C'mon boys, we're going for a ride."

The ride on the Parkway was a subtle but transforming experience for Joe.

Joe had started with his fear-ridden shoemaking apprenticeship in Russia where his focus on each task to get it right had to be intense because a mistake endangered his tenuous position. His Christian masquerade uncovered, Joe fought for his life and managed to flee to America.

Proving his skills to shoe contractor Lefkowitz meant that he could go on to other challenges his new country would throw at him. He judged his success in America by the amount of money his work made; enough to rent a new apartment for Moish and Papa Duvvid, to support Hannah and the boys, a new apartment in Brooklyn, summer vacations for his family in the Catskills and a new car.

Having carried the entire responsibility for the success of his contractor's shop, and now, with Moe, the much larger factory that made the whole shoe, confirmed that Joe had never had time for other than his work. He had a job to do, problems to solve, or new ideas for his work to consider. He left the pursuit of social graces, which he considered as putting on "fency menners," to others. He considered his long days of work and worry to be ordinary, expected. His fervor to succeed, to provide for his family, never left him. His nose focused closely on his work, it excluded his spending time to meet people and relatives socially. Hannah had to remind him about family get-togethers.

In the early years in his new land Joe was doubly careful to observe the times for Orthodox prayer rituals. But even they had not withstood the intense focus of his expanding work schedule. He saw the inside of a synagogue only on the High Holy Days of Rosh Hashanah and Yom Kippur. During his half-day in the factory on Saturday, The Sabbath, instead of his weekly religious observance, he spent the half day checking the results of the past week's work and making sure that the materials on all stations were ready for Monday morning. God didn't seem to be upset with him since Joe continued to be able to provide good things for his family.

The Friday evening jaunts to the park were a new, but small, sample experience of how it felt for Joe to release his work-focus for a moment.

After a few minutes on the wide boulevard Joe became aware that he was moving his head from side to side to check for possible obstacles on either side. He suddenly realized that it was not necessary because the two lanes going in his direction were kept separate from the two oncoming lanes of traffic by a two-lane-wide median divider; a pedestrian walkway and saddle-riding trail furnished with an occasional bench for pedestrian comfort that ran down the center of the boulevard's length. Also adding to his feeling of how unusually wide the boulevard was, the buildings on either side were set back forty feet from it instead of the usual twenty feet. Open space, open space created by wise city planners to withstand the increasing density of rapidly growing Brooklyn.

So much space, Joe thought as he drove, *so much space.* He felt relaxed and happier, though he may not have understood his change from the usual tensions of driving on narrow streets. It felt good; he liked it. Joe's reaction to the expanse of Ocean Parkway could have served as the subject of the vaudeville comic's joke about the man who banged his head on the wall repeatedly. When asked why he did it, he replied, "If feels so good when I stop."

The boulevard's loosening effect on Joe gave Hannah an advantage when she would talk to Joe about their moving into a new, five-room apartment in that large redbrick, four-story building two miles farther down.

Hannah tested the waters. "Isn't this something, Joe?"

"Yeah," he said.

Joe sounded impressed. Hannah smiled.

One block before the object of Hannah's desires Joe braked the car to let cross traffic pass.

Hannah alerted him. "Joe, stay on the right side and keep your eyes open for the large, red-brick building."

Joe drove more slowly. Halfway down the block the red-bricked, four-storied structure was suddenly there to tower above the shorter residences they had just passed. Fronted by gardens, protective chain-link fences outlined the two spacious entrances of the imposing building.

As they approached the end of it at the corner, Hannah said urgently, "Turn here, Joe, turn right."

Joe turned.

"Stop, Joe, park here, park here."

Joe sweated maneuvering the car and parked, but he objected. "Vat for? You know somebody here?"

"No, I just want you to think about our living here."

"Living here!" He turned his head to stare at her. *"Du bist mishuggar.* (You're crazy.) The rent must be a t'ousand dollars."

"No, Joe. It's only a hundred and fifty."

Hannah's information stunned Joe. "You know?"

"I asked. Moe moved his family into a bigger apartment in the new Bronx building."

"Ve should be crazy like Moe?"

"What's crazy about living in a more comfortable apartment?"

Joe looked at the majestic structure. He felt it to be beyond him. Awed, he said, "In such a building?"

"Why not? We're not good enough, Joe? Jews have come up in America. Get used to it, Joe. We've got as much money as the rest of them."

"I should t'row it avay on such a rent?"

"Throw it away?" Hannah turned and gestured out her opened window, her tone mean, accusing. "Living in such a house is throwing it away?" Hannah pulled her hand in, turned partially to Joe and spoke as if it were her whole life's agenda. "Joe! That's what our money is for!"

Hannah's grandiloquent plan for the family attacked Joe's structure of frugality. In the tense silence he questioned her plan to spend his money. To check whether there was any sense to her plan, Joe recalled Irv's report of Reinerman Brothers' gross income for last year, 1925; 69,000 dollars; and for the first half of 1926, already 36,000 dollars. Moe was deliriously happy with their season so far. When Irv saw that Joe's enthusiasm was still tempered by the thought that all the money owed them might not be paid, he added a sarcastic addendum to his report. He looked directly at the skeptical Joe and said, "that is, Joe, we will have 36,000 dollars for the first half if they all pay their bills."

Joe had to agree that they were having an unusually good year, but he also remembered Papa Duvvid's meager two rubles pay for a day's work in the Count's lumber mill. It did not permit him to celebrate as boisterously as did Moe.

Meanwhile, Hannah's face slowly flushed red in remorse because the tone of the argument with Joe had grown nasty and the boys had heard every word. She knew she should have waited until she and Joe were in their bedroom with the door closed, or the boys were down in the street. She said, "Let's go home, Joe."

Silently defending his self against Hannah's arguments, Joe turned the car around. Driving back on Ocean Parkway was no longer the pleasant experience.

Hannah didn't give up. She still determined that she would live in a place suitably luxurious to host the Monday and Wednesday card games for Hadassah. Held in private homes, they provided a small but consistent stream of money to help the Jews in Palestine. Hannah couldn't match Stella's dramatic move to do clinical work in Palestine, but then Stella didn't have two boys to take care of, yet Hannah could be part of providing urgently needed funds by hosting card games for Hadassah and the Jewish National Fund in her new apartment.

CHAPTER 25

1927

At dawn Joe got out of bed and went to the bathroom. When he returned he expected to sleep for another hour. Instead Hannah was up with her robe on and acting like her day had started.

Joe asked her, "Vat are you doing up so early?"

"It's a long drive to the Bronx and there's still snow on the roads."

"Joe looked at the clock. "It's only five-t'irty."

"You have to shower. I have to shower. I have to get the boys up and see that they're washed and dressed in their good clothes and I have to make breakfast for everyone."

Still Joe stood in his pajamas as if silently debating something.

Hannah was annoyed. "Joe, this Saturday is a *Yontif* (holiday). Moe and Lily's Jesse is getting *Bar- Mitzvahed* (confirmed)." Hannah suddenly thought to check on their gift for Jesse. "Did you get the five-dollar gold piece?"

"I got it."

"Is it nicely wrapped?"

"I told him make it special for my nephew's *Bar-Mitzvah*."

"You have it?"

Joe got annoyed. "Of course I hev it. It's a'ready in my coat."

"Awright, awright," said Hannah soothingly. "I was only checking up on it.

Joe still hadn't moved.

Hannah guessed at what he was thinking. "Joe, you're not going to the shop today."

Now Joe sounded angry. "Stop vid da shop already. I know I know."

But Hannah continued, "The shop won't fall apart if you don't go in to check. One Saturday you can forget about it." She changed quickly to

133

prevent him from blowing up at her. "You want to shower first or shall I? I'd better go first. I have a lot more to do this morning than you do."

Relieved that it was over Joe moved toward the bed.

"Don't go back to sleep, Joe."

"I'm just gonna vait for you to finish."

"The service starts at ten. We should leave by eight."

"Two hours ve need to drive?"

"It's in the Bronx, *yenner velt*, (another planet). And we've never been to their *schul* (synagogue). We have to find it."

Joe got into bed while saying, "Ve'll find it. Ve'll find it." He laid down, his hands behind his head on the double pillows. "Go. Go shower."

Joe felt pride in his driving ability that got his family to the synagogue on time. He was also glad to again be part of the Sabbath Service, which he did entirely from memory. After the service, for all of the synagogue's congregants there was a celebration of music, dancing, food and drink downstairs in the large reception room. But for Moe and his wife Lily's immediate relatives Lily had arranged a private party with catered snacks and drinks at their new, larger apartment.

Lily, 55 pounds heavier than when Moe courted her, proudly walked everyone through each room. What stunned Hannah was that the walls in each room were painted a different color. Going from room to room Hannah puzzled at the change of mood she clearly felt. But she thought that purple in the guest room, blue in the master bedroom, pink in ten-year-old Muriel's room, gray in Jesse's, and yellow in the dining room was a gimmick that she would not imitate. What did stun her was the size of the apartment. She had counted six rooms and each stuffed with all the furniture it could hold. Hannah wondered at the cost of it all.

On the long drive home Hannah couldn't resist continuing her campaign for the new apartment. "Joe, how did you like Moe's new apartment?"

"Too expensive."

"He told you how much?"

"No. But vat else?"

"Joe, you make as much money as he does."

"Of course, ve're partners."

"So?"

"So v'at?"

"So if your kid brother can afford it so can you."

"You need six rooms?"

"Six would be nice."

"You'll get lost in so much. I could move the whole factory into six rooms."

"The biggest they have in the Ocean Parkway building is five rooms."

"Too much."

Hannah raised her voice. "Five rooms is not too much. The boys are growing. We're four people now."

"Too much money," Joe corrected.

"It's not too much money. You want to live right you pay for it. Moe and Lily are paying. Lily hired a decorator even."

"A decorator?"

Hannah mocked her sister-in-law. "Fency shmency Lily, she could never think of a different color for every room. Of course she hired a decorator."

"She had a different color…?"

"You didn't notice? And how much furniture? I can live with half that much. How much do you think it cost them?"

Joe clammed up and concentrated on his driving. They were crossing the bridge over the East River. Soon they would be back in Brooklyn.

Hannah noticed Joe silently shaking his head. She spoke sarcastically. "You're thinking of the *shtetl* (hut) in Tchernivakh, Joe?"

"Maybe."

"But you say you're an American now, Joe?"

Her question insulted him. He turned his head and gave her an angry look.

But Hannah stubbornly carried on. "So live like one."

"I'm livin'," he retorted angrily.

"Even Irv, your accountant, who makes a lot less money than you is living in a new apartment, almost as big as Moe's."

Hannah carried her campaign into the summer. Unlike Stella she hadn't trained for anything. All she could claim for achievements was to show she was the wife to a successful husband and mother of his children. She continued to drive Joe to step upward to show his success, which now included renting a five-room apartment, one, finally that Hannah considered luxurious enough to share with her card-playing Hadassah friends.

On a Friday night in early summer Hannah forgot that Joe had promised to play checkers with Daniel and she let the boys play on the lion statue until it was almost dark. It was a hot, humid evening. There was no reason to rush home to a stuffy apartment.

When they did get home, Hannah turned the light on in the kitchen, opened the window and said to the boys, "Open the windows in the living room and let some air in."

Seymour pounced on the folded *Journal* newspaper that Joe had put on the kitchen cupboard and prepared to escape with it into the living room.

As always, Daniel felt cheated. He argued his plight. "I get half," he said loudly. Daniel hoped his complaining voice reached his mother and she'd help make it fair.

Joe had retrieved his *Der Tag* and was reading at the kitchen table.

"Danny," said Hannah, "go into the living room with the paper, and no fighting. Papa and I have to talk."

In the living room Daniel was the underdog as usual and Seymour repeated his dominance over the jokes.

Hannah sat down opposite Joe at the table. "Joe, put the paper down. We have to talk."

Joe put the paper on the table. He looked at Hannah apprehensively and hid behind his Yiddish. "*Vus yetzt?*" (What now?)

"We've talked enough about moving."

"You talked."

"Joe, I want us to move this summer, before the boys go back to school in the fall so they don't lose any time in their classes."

Joe knew nothing about his boys' school schedules. He remained silent.

"Joe, what I want in this marriage is important too."

"It's not enough for you?"

Hannah raised her voice. "I want a place big enough that I can invite my Hadassah friends to."

"Dey gonna pay da rent?"

"It's too crowded here."

Joe pretended to look around. "Vhere is it crowded?"

"When I shop on De Kalb Avenue there's hardly room to walk anymore. And when we go there to *shul* on Yom Kippur we almost get pushed off the sidewalk."

"My fency lady doesn't like to be pushed?"

"Joe you make enough money so we can live better."

"Dis is not good enough?"

"No, it's not good enough."

Joe felt attacked. Angered, he sprang up and spoke loudly. "Vat vould it take to satisfy my fency lady?"

Outside, around the narrow courtyard windows lit up.

Hannah stood up to take the offensive and topped his volume. "We can live better than this, Joe."

Outside, heads popped through opened windows.

"Joe, for God's sakes, take your nose out of the shop and see how people with money are living! My brother Sam, the furrier just bought a new house. My sister Lena's Milton--"

Joe interrupted her in an equally loud voice. "You had notting ven I married you. You vere living in a tenement."

"I dragged you from the tenement so I could have your baby in a clean home."

"You had notting," Joe repeated. "You vere sleeping in the same bed mit' your sister."

"And you didn't even know to change your suit when you go to the shop when I married you. I had to show you how to dress to meet people. And tell you to take a bath more than once a week."

"Who did I see in my shop? Only two *Talienischers* (Italians) who voiked fa me."

Hannah topped Joe with all her anger. "But you slept with your wife every night!"

A woman's voice shouted at them, "So kill each other already and let the children sleep."

Shamed and embarrassed, Hannah turned and slammed the window shut. When she turned back she saw Joe pick up his newspaper and hold it in front of his face as if hiding. Hannah turned to see what Joe was hiding from and saw nine-year old Daniel in slippers and pajamas, the folded checkerboard in one hand, the box of checkers in the other.

Daniel's small, scared voice asked, "Wha ... what's ... wrong?"

"Uh ... nothing, Danny," Hannah said. "We ... we were just ... talking."

"No ... no checkers tonight, Pa?"

Joe lowered the newspaper. "Uh ... no, Denny ... it's late ..."

Hannah spoke. "Play with Seymour, Danny."

"He beats me. He changes the rules."

Joe wanted to be a hundred miles from Hannah and from Daniel whom he had hurt so by breaking his promise. But as long as his son stood there Joe sat. Joe hoped what he said next would end it. He spoke softly. "Ve'll ... play tomorrow, Denny." The kitchen air felt stuffy to Joe. Breathing it gave him no relief. But he sat waiting for Danny to leave.

Daniel turned and walked slowly out of the kitchen.

Joe picked up his paper hoping that would discourage Hannah from talking to him.

When he heard the door of the boy's bedroom close Joe put the paper down, left the kitchen, went out the front door, down the stairs, out the storm door and finally into the cooler air of the summer night. He had thought he would walk, but instead he stood looking at the huge maple tree's large four-pointed leaves dipping playfully in the breeze.

CHAPTER 26

After dumping her pain-driven anger on Joe, Hannah still determined to make their move happen. She used the only two weapons left to her. When she put Joe's dinner on the table she didn't sit and talk with him but busied her self in the living room, or with the boys, to leave Joe eating alone.

Eating by himself in the kitchen, Joe felt quarantined. He chewed but Hannah's cooking had no flavor.

In bed she turned away from him to sleep as far from him as the double bed permitted.

Four days of her boycott was enough for Joe to reconsider his opinion. In the office, when Moe got off the phone, Joe asked him, "Moe, how much rent do you pay fa' da' six-room palace?"

Moe stared for a moment trying to understand the word 'palace.' "Oh, you mean my apartment."

"Yeah, da' six rooms?"

"A hundred and eighty a month with the landlord's stipulation that it's going to one-ninety next year, starting January."

Joe made a pained face. Disbelieving, he shook his head and questioned Moe, "Almost two hundred dollars?"

Moe was quick to justify it. "Look what I have, Joe."

Joe was as quick to agree. "It's nice. Fency."

Moe smiled and shook his head. He pitied Joe's inability to enjoy his money.

"Dey raised my rent too," Joe said. "I pay eighty-five now. Ten years ago it vas forty-five."

"That was ten years ago, Joe. The world's different. The war's over and America is the richest country in the world."

"The var?"

"The World War. Since it ended the country's been riding high. Even Prohibition can't stop anyone from celebrating. I can always treat buyers

139

to drinks in a speakeasy. Why don't you give Hannah and the kids a break and move outa that hole in the wall?"

"Hannah talked to you?"

"Hannah? No. But I saw. The last time we had *Seder* (Passover) at your house, with your family, my family and Papa Duvvid, we could hardly fit in."

"You didn't tell me."

"So I'm telling you. Get a bigger place. Enjoy your money. Our investments that Irv put us in are making money. Business is great. Enjoy America, Joe.

"Ahm enjoying."

"So smile, Joe. We have a business that's doing better every year. In America, Joe, you're not little boy Yussel in Tchernivakh running from the Christians."

Joe waved a hand that drove away those unpleasant memories. It also gestured an end to the conversation. He left the office to check with the cutters in the factory to make sure they had started to work on the order that Moe brought in yesterday.

But the conversation with Moe stayed with Joe as he drove home. Joe found himself nodding in agreement with Moe's argument as he silently did a repeat of their conversation. The rent for the new apartment was not really a problem. Why shouldn't he give Hannah the pleasure of their big change for the better?

After he finished supper Joe sat at the table waiting for Hannah to clear his dishes.

Hannah sat in the living room listening to the news on the radio. She guessed that Joe had finished eating and she came back into the kitchen to collect his plates and put them in the sink.

Joe had finished but hadn't taken his newspaper from the cupboard. Instead he was working to clear his teeth with a toothpick.

Hannah returned to the table with a damp rag to wipe it down, but before she started Joe said, "Nu, you vanna talk?"

Hannah froze. She didn't know what was coming. "What about?" she asked, and remained standing near the table.

Joe leaned back so he could look up at her, smiled and asked, "Vat vould you like?"

He knows the answer to that, Hannah thought. Peeved, she kept her silence. She leaned over instead to wipe down the table, but stopped when Joe asked, "You don't vanna talk?"

"Only about one thing."

"So sit down."

Not believing him, she searched his face.

Joe made a motion as if to get up and leave. "So, it's goodbye, you'll see me later. Yes?"

Still holding the rag Hannah slowly sat down opposite him.

Joe sat back down. "You vanna look at dee apartment?"

"The one on Ocean Parkway?"

"Yeah."

"Yes."

"Nu, so let's go Sunday."

Hannah struggled silently with disbelief while staring at him, managed, "What … what changed your mind, Joe?"

Joe shrugged his shoulders and grimaced a silent "I don't know." He reexamined his last conversation with Moe for a reply, but out of the tumult of many thoughts that it stirred in him he finally settled for only one word in answer to her question, "America."

Hannah thought it a strange answer but didn't spend the time to understand it. She confirmed, "This Sunday, Joe, after tomorrow?"

"Yeah."

"All right, good … goo--wonderful! Wonderful, Joe!"

Joe grinned to see that he had made Hannah so excited again.

Mr. Drexel, the building manager walked the Reinerman family from his office to the large lobby where the shiny, stainless steel rectangle in the far wall announced the elevator door. Drexel pressed the button for the car. Waiting, Hannah looked at the unusual lobby furnishings. On the wall facing the entrance hung a huge square of red fabric that started high overhead to display its appliquéd, oversized, coat of arms in dramatic black, white and yellow. It dominated the large lobby. The eye looking through the tangle of crossed swords and muskets stared unflinchingly at the building entrance as if keeping guard over everyone's comings and goings.

The dramatic hanging extended down to just six inches above the glossy top of a long, narrow mahogany table with thick, deeply carved legs. An oversized throne-like chair with curving arms graced each end of the table. The chairs of stunning mixed-color upholstery seemed to be waiting for the trumpeted entrance of the king and his queen.

Though awed by the dramas the medieval décor suggested, Hannah had no background to fill in the details. Instead, she had come into the building with her head overflowing with pictures of the modern-day room furnishings advertised in the *Journal* newspaper; beds, couches, chairs, drapes, all of endless patterns and styles for her to choose from.

Inside man Joe, whose daily concerns encompassed bundles of tanned leather, cut, processed and finally finished into ladies shoes within the four walls of his factory loft, had no response to the medieval dramas the lobby offered. But he did relish the unusual large, silent space of the lobby. The high ceiling and far walls offered him a quiet open stance dramatically different from his factory loft of constant noise, motion and his urgency to check details, to see that tanned leather was faultlessly turned into stylish shoes. The oversized space of the lobby, where he had no responsibilities, relaxed and expanded his usual tense physical stance.

The elevator door opened. Drexel stood aside and gestured the hesitant Reinermans in. Drexel waited until the door closed and pressed the button marked '3.' The slight upward jerk that started the climb made Seymour and Daniel move closer to Joe and Hannah. Their parents smiled at the boys' reactions to having their first ride in an electric elevator.

The car stopped. Drexel walked out and stood aside while the boys hurried out and Hannah and Joe followed. In the hall Drexel led the short walk to the apartment entrance. He inserted his master key, swung the door open and stood aside as the four Reinermans eagerly filed in.

Seymour and Daniel, after standing in awe for a moment at the sudden bright daylight flooding into the large empty space with shiny wooden floors, scattered to search out the limits of their new home and to guess at what room would be his.

Excited, Hannah stood in each room imagining the furnishings she would fit into it and how she would arrange the card tables for the Hadassah games.

Joe walked around with a smile on his face, thinking how much he liked the sunlit space in each room of the apartment and contemplated the wonder of his coming this far from the hut in Tchernivakh. But he quickly thought of what he had accomplished since then. *Of course, of course,* he thought, pleased with his factory that permitted him this new apartment. *It makes sense. You have the money you buy a different life. It makes sense.*

Joe found Hannah in the kitchen space. "Nu, Hannah, good enough?"

"Oh, yes, Joe."

Joe smiled with satisfaction. "Money makes everyt'ing possible. So let's tell the manager."

They found Drexel at the entrance where he'd been waiting for them to decide.

"Ve like it," said Joe. "Tell me again da terms."

"First and last months' rent, $250 damage deposit, and signing a one year lease."

Joe nodded. "Good. I'll make out a check."

Excited, Hannah felt she was fulfilling her dream. *Wasn't it every girl's dream?* She thought. Her thoughts quickened to catch up to the speed of details churning in her head, details to establish the reality of her new life. Mentally she tried to grab an advertised couch, chair, drape, table, and fix it in its new place as a chore to be done, but there was too much that had to be done first; *the packing, the movers, where was the school for the boys, a synagogue so Seymour could study for his Bar Mitzvah. Could she make a party after the Bar Mitzvah as elaborate as Moe's Lily? Also, Seymour had only one more six-month semester in elementary school, where would his Junior High be in this new neighborhood? How would he get there?*

As they walked to the car Hannah was breathless with the many self-assignments her wishes challenged her with. Four more weeks of summer the boys would still be home. They could help with some things. Certainly they could pack their own clothes and books in boxes. Hannah hoped Bessie Grablowski could give her time with furnishing-each-room ideas, even though Bessie was busy now with her selling-insurance career. First, Hannah reminded herself, *the packing and the movers …*

CHAPTER 27

1927

On the first Monday after Labor Day Moe and Joe sat at their desks in the office waiting for Irv to finish fidgeting with ledgers to find the one labeled, Gross Income, 1926. The Reinerman budget year was from September to September. Moe and Joe couldn't understand why it didn't follow the calendar year, but they left it in Irv's, their CPA's hands. The business partners were anxious. Finally they would know what kind of a year it had been.

Joe noticed the streak of sunlight shining through the office's one window. Seemingly unblemished by the dusty film on the glass and dirt on the windowsill, the unstoppable sunbeam lit a bright path to the other side of the room and spotlighted the section of shelves where the best of their earlier design samples were displayed. Joe smiled. The dust film on the window reminded him of the plate glass window of his first shop on Canal Street that he had asked Mrs. Wolansky and Shmuel to make shine so people passing by would notice and read the lettering on the glass, **Joe Reinerman, Leather Work** in Yiddish and English.

Joe smiled too, to remember the years that he had chosen to remain nursing at the breast of his Yiddish language, *Mammaluschen*, and to stay among the stores and streets of Manhattan's Lower East Side that breathed his Yiddish culture. Then, in those early days immigrant Yussel still needed to be surrounded by things Jewish. But his compulsive need to make the whole shoe made immigrant Yussel gather up his courage and dare to compete in the open world of American business.

Joe observed Moe holding his inevitable cigar, unlit whenever Irv was in the office. Moe looked American, Joe thought, almost as soon as he stepped off the boat. Even though Moe had enjoyed his *Bar Mitzvah* in Riga, he never was religious. He didn't wait for God to tell him anything.

The Bible was not Moe's bible. He found his cues from the goings on around him. Two brothers, so different ...

Joe thought of the greatest challenge to his Orthodoxy, Mrs. Wolansky. Joe's smile broadened to recall his first and only time with her, also the first time he questioned his ironclad tenets of Jewish Orthodoxy, a major upheaval in his life. But he was surprised that he no longer felt any physical excitement when he thought of her. It was a time, an important something, a crucially important something that had happened to him but now had passed. *Really?* He wondered. *Had it passed? Could such a volcanic event fade quietly into his past?*

Joe reckoned the number of years and all the changes to his life that had happened since then. Musing on the wonder of that day with Mrs. Wolansky, he had to conclude that all that had happened to him since had cooled the hot lava of that volcanic eruption to leave it as part of the silent landscape. Joe enumerated events that had followed since; starting his own contracting shop, taking Moe in as his partner, breaking out to create the whole shoe, organizing the factory routines, the years of improving production, marrying Hannah, his two boys, moving to Brooklyn, moving to an even fancier apartment ... "So much, so much since," he mumbled, "no vunder, no vunder ... "

Irv's inevitable fanfare whisked Joe from his reverie.

This time Moe was there to cut Irv short. "Enough with playing radio announcer, Irv. Tell us, in English."

But Irv continued to have his moment. "...and we are pleased to announce that the past year, 1926 ..." Irv paused to build the suspense.

Moe reached to the sample stock shelf behind him, grabbed a shoe and drew his arm back threatening to throw it. "Let's have it, Irv, or..."

Irv ducked down and talked rapidly, "... 1926 was their best year yet, totaling eleven percent higher than last year, gross total for the year in dollar terms, 74,629 dollars." From his scrunched down position Irv threw a fist into the air and yelled, "Yea!"

Moe put the dusty sample back on the shelf and brushed off his hands. With the satisfaction of congratulating his self, he thought, *Boy, I sold a lot of shoes last year.*

Joe's pleased response was a mumbled, "Hmph, I didn't know I could make so many shoes in vun year."

Irv straightened up and cheered in his natural voice. "Hooray, Reinerman Brothers. You had a great year."

Grinning, Moe turned to his brother. "What do you think, Joe?"

Grinning back, Joe said, "I like it." He thought about Irv's report for a moment. "Vat's not to like about making money?"

Yet it was about more than the money. As Joe sat relishing Irv's report, it meant that his production methods were working. His decisions, whatever his sweat when weighing the what-ifs and maybes of needed quick choices, even when arguing with Moe about them, his almost instinctive judgments about production methods had been successful in meeting the needs of his market.

Joe suddenly understood why he had wanted to take on the challenges of making the whole shoe when he was already a successful uppers contractor. His apprenticeship in Russia had taught him, and kept telling him during the years he had the contracting shop on Canal Street, that he could do more than make only part of the shoe. Despite his nervousness as a fourteen-year-old shoemaker's apprentice in Riga, with the added, unremitting tensions and fears of being discovered to be a Jew, he had come to know the satisfactions of making the whole product, from the start of outlining the customer's foot to installing the final buttons or laces as required. Those satisfactions he missed when stitching only the upper of the shoe. He had made a good living stitching uppers but money success had not been enough for him. He had a pride in his hands-on abilities to make the whole shoe that he had to satisfy.

Joe looked at Moe who was still grinning over Irv's report. Moe could talk like an American and knew how to treat buyers. Those two items alone won him his partnership with Joe and they also won him his apartment of the fancy-colored six-rooms. Without Moe's personal skills of talking about Joe's shoes and partying the shoe buyers with liquor and women, very few boxes of finished pairs would find their way to the shipping room. So, two brothers, as different as a horse and a cat, yet together they were producing Irv's successful reports year after year.

And what success! Joe, still full of adjusting to the many new details of the move to the apartment on Ocean Parkway and driving the new route each day to the factory on Bridge Street, he thought excitedly, *Did anyone ever think that Yussel from Tchernivakh would live in a brand new five-room apartment in Brooklyn, in America, and drive to work in an automobile?*

Labor Day, America's seasonal turning point, when moneyed, middle-class families returned home from their vacations. America looked ahead to the fall holidays, the new retail-buying season had again come around. Like Irv said, "Does the sun rise every morning?" Moe had already successfully wholesaled Joe's shoes to the retail stores and enough women shoppers had the money to pay the increase to the twelve-dollar a pair price tag. The Reinerman Brothers could look ahead to another good season.

Spolio, the designer had already begun experimenting with new designs for the next sample season that followed.

*   *   *

The Reinermans' big move to their new apartment had been accomplished in time for the boys to register at their new school and catch the beginning of the semester. Daniel began 11th grade and Seymour settled into the second half of 12th grade.

Hannah and Joe sat down at the kitchen table to talk about finding a synagogue to belong to so Seymour could start his studies for *Bar Mitzvah*. "First," Hannah began, "not Orthodox." She raised her hand and slapped the table.

Her gesture of finality startled Joe as much as what she said. He had lived all his life thinking himself an Orthodox Jew, his family automatically the same and Joe decided the religious matters for the family.

When he recovered from Hannah's statement he asked her, "Since ven do you decide?"

"If I go to shul with you, Joe I don't want them to hide me with all the women behind a curtain as if there's something wrong with us and we shouldn't be seen. We can't even see the Rabbi or the Cantor. And I don't need a *mikvah* (bath for ritual purity after menstruation and childbirth) before I pray.

"Vat's wrong vit a mikvah?"

"We have a beautiful apartment with a full bath and I know how to clean myself."

Joe sat up, alert at the unexpected argument. "Vere … vere did you get dese ideas from? Dere vas a mikvah even in the Bible."

"That's what's wrong, Joe."

Stunned, Joe looked at her. "Now the Bible is no good?"

"The Bible is good, Joe, but times have changed in 4,000 years."

"V'ere still Jews, Hannah."

"Yes, but being a Jew in America is different from being a Jew in Tchernivakh, different from living in a *shtetl* (ghetto hut) in Europe. They had no plumbing. They carried in water from the pump outside. So they took a mikvah bath before synagogue. Were in America now, thank God. We have a new, five-room apartment with all the plumbing we need."

As much as Joe resented being told by Hannah how to be a Jew, Hannah's argument stirred up old guilt feelings in him. His intense work schedule didn't allow him to see the inside of a synagogue except on the High Holy Days. It had been that way for years. And he remembered when he sat in his contractor's shop arguing with himself that he failed to say daily and weekly prayers in the synagogue because he had to supervise the two workers in his shop until six. He had excused his Orthodox lapses because his work required more of his time. Living in America, he had rationalized, a Jew's life is different, thank God.

On this, Joe was surprised to find himself in agreement with Hannah. *Yes, we do live differently in America.* He looked at his wife with new eyes and a wry smile, but spoke with some sarcasm. "Nu, boss, so vat kind of a synagogue should it be?"

At a Hadassah meeting Hannah had been surprised to hear that none of the women in her chapter belonged to an Orthodox congregation. On holidays those who were religious went to either a Conservative or a Reform synagogue. The thing that really set Hannah against Orthodoxy was the curtaining-off of the women during services, separating them from their men. "Why, Joe?" she asked him, "Why do they do this to women? Is there something wrong with us?"

Joe was at a loss. He had never thought about it.

Hadassah had been an education for Hannah. The women with their modern dress and study and career encouragement had discussed and agreed that some rituals were sparked by the fears and customs of the *shtetl* Jews of the European ghettos and really didn't apply to living in America. American women had the right to education, careers, and to sit with their men during religious services and were not to be hidden by a curtain during services. And at Hadassah, for the first time, Hannah had listened to a delicate discussion that challenged Orthodoxy's attitudes about women and menstruation, which regarded women as unclean during this time.

As if this neighborhood that they had moved into agreed with Hannah, there was no Orthodox synagogue in this newly built section of Brooklyn. Apparently no Jewish families were asking to join such a synagogue. Joe wondered where Seymour would learn about his passage into the Jewish community and where the family would attend for the High Holy Days. Remembering the religious customs, rules and restraints that he had lived with on Manhattan's Lower East Side made him feel that Orthodoxy would be too ... too Orthodox for these younger, more Americanized, middle-class Jews that he saw around him in the wider spaces of his new neighborhood. Although he could not verbalize it, he agreed with this new generation who were quick to shed Orthodoxy's highly restrictive parochial tenets, especially those that meant the demeaning of women.

Joe felt those changes in his religious life had been necessary to his work despite the promise of piety that Joe had made to God in Riga.

In contrast, couples in the Conservative and Reform Congregations worshipped together and welcomed the Hebrew to English translation of the prayer books that left the choice of prayer text to the individual. The Reform Congregation went further, carrying on all of the service entirely in English.

Orthodox prayer text, though unrelentingly in Hebrew, presented no barrier to Joe, who had started in childhood to memorize it. But he knew that Seymour and Daniel, born in America, would never find the time to learn the translations, if that even interested them. Conservative texts in Hebrew with English translations on the opposite page, or Reform with services entirely in English would serve Joe's American Jewish family better. Knowing he would talk to God at least during the High Holidays, Joe chose the Conservative synagogue.

Hannah agreed saying, "With an English translation of the prayers I'll know what I'm saying to Him."

*   *   *

Hannah called Bessie Grablowsky and asked her if she could help with ideas for added furnishings for the new apartment. Since her father died Bessie had launched herself out of Orthodoxy to join other self-supporting women who opted to find their place in America's vibrant economy. Although middle-aged, Bessie's choice to guarantee herself financial independence reminded Hannah of Stella's breakout from a religious woman's accepted subordination to her husband into an individual career.

Bessie was delighted to drive over to view Hannah's big step-up in the world. She congratulated Hannah on her choice of apartment. They spent an hour over tea and Hannah's honey cake about the possible pieces of furniture to be bought. Hannah thanked Bessie for taking the time to help.

CHAPTER 28

1928

Hannah walked into the kitchen to speak to Mary, her fulltime colored maid, who was peeling and cleaning vegetables for the dinner's soup. "Have your lunch now, Mary, and then you'll set up for the card games."

"Yes, M'am."

Mary was a middle-aged Negro woman of lighter than usual coloring who had been recommended to Hannah by Sally Blanken, one of the Hadassah women.

"The soup you can do later," Hannah continued, "when the ladies leave. Be sure to put the cushions on the folding chairs for them. You'll put a small plate of the hors d'oevres out first. Put it on one of the small end tables and move it close to their card table so it's convenient but doesn't interfere with the game. Let the ladies nibble on those while they're playing. Then you'll bring out the nut and candy mix."

"Yes, M'am."

"Can you handle setting up two tables?"

"Yes, M'am. I'll do them first and then have my lunch."

"That's good, Mary."

Hannah started to leave the kitchen, but then turned back. "Two tables instead of one give us a lot more things to do."

"Yes, M'am, they do."

"Of course I like the idea that so many want to play at my house."

"Yes, M'am."

"I was lucky to find four more matching cushions at Alden's Furniture Store."

"Yes, M'am."

"You know what to do now, Mary?"

"Yes, M'am, I do."

"Good,"

Hannah turned and squinted at her wrist to see the time on her tiny diamond watch and whispered to herself as she walked out of the kitchen continuing to plan the day. "A whole hour is enough time for Mary to finish the setup." She walked into the living room and thought about the day's busy schedule, and that she would have to talk to Joe about summer camp for the boys. She recalled that she had asked the Merskys, the camp owners to come next Tuesday after dinner, seven o'clock, to tell the Reinermans about their Tunis Lake Camp for boys. Hannah frowned. *I wonder how Joe will react to the idea of Seymour and Danny being away all summer. He's so busy at the shop he hardly sees them anyway. But he will complain to me about spending the $350 for each one.* Hannah thought of an added financial obstacle, the train-fare for each boy to and from the Catskills and the fifty-dollar charge for the camp uniforms. Hannah decided not to talk about the added expenses, if possible. Hannah continued the imaginary conversation as if she were already arguing with Joe about the cost. *"... Every time we argue over the cost of things you finally admit that money isn't a problem anymore. But out of habit you'll always argue about my spending ..." Yes, I'd better talk to him tonight to start preparing him for the Merskys.*

Hannah turned to look into the dining room at the table already set up for four, for the family dinner. *Joe said he'd be home at six tonight, but with him I never know ... It'll be a good experience for Seymour and Daniel to be at camp for the summer with other Jewish boys.*

Hannah went into the dining room to see if all the details of the settings were in place to serve the family dinner. Mary had set it up first thing when she arrived in the morning before starting on her other chores. The white tablecloth set off the silver flatware, the crystal glassware and the gold-edged dinner porcelain. The table radiated elegance enough to be the stunning demonstration table at Macy's. Hannah had suggested to Mary that she ready it before the ladies arrived. From the card tables in the living room they could look into the dining room and it would certainly add to the décor of the apartment.

Joe's timing worried Hannah. *It will be a family dinner if Joe does get home at six, or the latest, six-thirty. The boys can't wait any longer than that. Of course, when Joe gets into busy season I can't expect to make everybody wait for him.*

The added work for Mary and the difficulties of the timing made Hannah question the formalizing of the big meal of the day for everyone at six. *Maybe a formal family dinner is not possible with our kind of family,* was her second thought. She continued skeptically, *Maybe Macy's is trying to import England's formal upper-class dinner to upper-class America just to sell a lot of fancy stuff.* Hannah suddenly had a mild backlash of remorse when she thought of all the money she had spent on the crystal glassware and the porcelain dinner plates edged with the tiny gold leaf pattern. *But the sterling silver flatware,* thought Hannah, *I really did need,* to relieve herself from some of her guilt.

Looking around at the dining room table and chairs, Hannah thought, *Whew, a busy day, the Hadassah card ladies and the family dinner. I told Mary if we keep the formal family dinner idea, she can come in later in the morning to make up for staying late to do the cleanup.*

The doorbell rang. "Oops," Hannah said aloud, "The ladies are here," and she hurried to greet them.

By three-fifteen the ladies had had enough of sweet nibbles and rummy and poker. They gathered their wraps and purses, reminded each other about the Hadassah meeting at Janet's next week and left.

Hannah counted Hadassah's share of the games' coins into the leather drawstring moneybag that Joe had made for her, $6.55. With the $5.84 from the previous bi-weekly games it totaled $12.69. Pleased to bring such a sizeable amount to the next Hadassah meeting, Hannah stored the leather bag in her dresser drawer in the master bedroom.

Twelve-year-old Daniel came home first.

Hannah reminded him. "We won't eat until six, so have your milk and cookies now and do your homework."

"Okay, Ma."

Fourteen-year-old Seymour had made the soccer team at Montauk Junior High. He stayed for soccer practice but did get home before six.

And Joe was on time.

Hannah thought, *Hallelujah.*

Joe came out of the bathroom rolling down his sleeves and sat down at the head of the table.

The boys quickly followed and sat down opposite each other.

Daniel said, "I'm starved," and reached for a slice of bread.

Hannah spoke sharply, "No, Danny, not yet."

Danny made a face and settled back in his chair.

Hannah picked up a small hand bell and tinkled it loudly.

There was a pause and Mary came in carrying a tray with four bowls of soup. Everyone sat waiting until all were served. When Hannah picked up her spoon everyone followed and began to eat.

The boys felt so constrained by the formal atmosphere that lasted throughout the meal, when they finished they felt they had to ask permission to leave the table.

But Hannah's family agenda for the evening had just begun. "I want you to stay and listen. Papa and I are going to talk about our plans for you for the summer when school ends."

Joe looked as surprised as his sons and didn't continue his routine of finding his paper to sit at the table and read. "Vat plans?" He asked Hannah.

Mary began clearing the table.

"Janet Cohen from Hadassah sends her son Stevie to a wonderful summer camp for boys."

"Da' whole summer?"

"For July and August."

"Dey gonna sleep dere fa two months?"

"Yes. Stevie is not even as old as Daniel, but he has a wonderful time."

Businessman Joe asked the inevitable question. "For how much?"

"Three hundred and fifty dollars."

Joe looked at Seymour then Daniel and then asked, "For both?"

"No. Each."

"Each!"

The boys' eyes widened to hear the amount their mother was ready to spend on them.

Danny mouthed '350 dollars' silently. Yet his second thought recognized one of the rare times he felt treated equally with Seymour.

"It's for the whole summer, Joe. Joe, I can't deal with them when they fight."

Joe looked at Seymour. "Dey fight?"

Seymour suddenly felt he was on the spot for always finding some way to put Daniel down.

Daniel felt glad to have his father look questioningly at his brother. He thought, *Maybe Pa will realize that Seymour always does something to start it.*

"Yes," said Hannah, especially when there's no school. "Boys fight, Joe. Did you and Moe always get along?"

Joe snickered. *"Mishugganer* (crazy) Moish." He asked Hannah, "Vat dey do in cemp fa da whole summer?"

"They have sports, they swim, they hike. I'd have to spend that much money just to feed them for those two months."

"Mmm," Joe looked at his sons. "So, *boychiks?*" (child's pet name).

Daniel nodded tentatively. "I think I'd like it, Pa."

Seymour nodded more affirmatively. "I'd like it, Pa."

Joe looked at Hannah. "You know dese people?"

"Janet Cohen told me about them, Mr. and Mrs. Mersky. I called them and asked them to come Tuesday night at seven."

"Here?"

"Of course here. You'll come home on time Tuesday."

The appointment with the Merskys gave Hannah the excuse she needed to put an end to the cumbersome formal family dinners. "Let the rich do it," she mumbled, "it's a pain in the neck. Mary will have time to do the other things that need doing and I'll have time for other things.

On Tuesday night Hannah had Mary make a goulash, a one-dish meal. Joe was on time. The family ate supper as before, in the kitchen. The meal was over and cleaned up by a quarter to seven. Hannah sent the boys to their rooms to finish up any schoolwork that had to be done. Joe went into the living room to listen to the news on the radio. Hannah gave Mary the welcomed news that formal family dinners were no more and Mary could go back to her earlier schedule.

Mary thanked Hannah and started to tell Hannah how the earlier schedule would help her take care of her grandchildren while her daughter was working.

Hannah felt obligated to stand in the kitchen and listen to Mary's troubles, and felt liberated when the doorbell rang. "See you first thing in the morning, Mary."

"Yes, M'am, I'll see you then."

Hannah went to the door, greeted the Merskys and ushered them into the living room. She introduced them to Joe.
***

The Merskys and the head counselor of each age group were on the train with the campers returning from Tunis Lake Camp when it pulled into New York's Grand Central Terminal. Disembarked, all seventy-eight boys grouped according to ages as in camp, stood on the platform beside the stilled train, the eight-year olds in the lead while the Merskys checked off the names to make sure all were accounted for. Each counselor led his group toward the large waiting room where the parents were anxiously waiting to see what kind of changed child would return to them.

Happy voices erupted as each group of boys found their parents. After the hugs and kisses, excited voices of campers pitched on high told of some camp incident off the top of his head where he had excelled or made the summer notable. Voluble campers, glad to tell their stuck-in-the-city parents of their high adventure in the mountain-sweet air of the Catskills, continued talking as the family went off to find their parked car.

CHAPTER 29

1929
Irv, compiling the income figures at the end of the high selling season in early July, hinted to the brothers that this could be their best season ever.

Neither Moe nor Joe thought that was so unusual because they had had a continuing run of "the best season ever" for the last seven years. Armed thus with yet another repeat, the brothers simply added it to their habit of anticipating great news. When Irv would sum up the year's income after Labor Day they expected yet another year of "The best season ever."

Moe, feeling giddy about their making what felt like unlimited amounts of money pressed Irv to go further and guess at the total income figure, but Irv, who enjoyed holding all the information cards in his hands, laughed at Moe's request with, "You don't pay me for guesswork." Irv slapped the ledger. "I'll get the final figures from the books, in September."

Bubbling happily because his investment was making money, Irv graced the brothers with more good news. He looked at Moe, then Joe to get their attention. "Do you know what the market is doing?"

"Going up," volunteered Moe.

"Yes, but do you know how much?" challenged Irv.

Moe grimaced and shrugged his shoulders. The stock market was Irv's specialty not his.

Joe waited attentively. Impatient, he finally asked, "Nu?"

"The market opened at 332 this morning, the highest it's ever been."

"So ve're making money?" Joe asked, grinning."

"Right," Irv said, proud of his market savvy. "Our $5,000 is worth about 8,950 dollars for each of us.

Joe shook his head in disbelief of so much good luck. "Only in America … " Enjoying his good feeling, Joe grinned, shook his head again and went out into the factory.

*   *   *

Seymour and Daniel were enthusiastic about returning to Tunis Lake Camp for a second summer and Hannah and Joe were glad to oblige. They saw no financial obstacle to spending the money and since the boys enjoyed it they were glad to meet with the Merskys and sign the papers for another summer.

The summer came and went and Daniel and Seymour were home again a year older telling Ma and Pa about having had another "great summer at TLC". Refreshed, the boys were back in school after Labor Day.

*   *   *

A week after Labor Day, as usual, Irv looked at the Reinerman brothers sitting at their desks. Irv was ready to tell them what their gross income for the year '28-'29 had been. Irv paused, looked at Moe, then at Joe … then, almost not believing the results of his figures himself, he spoke slowly, "$91,758."
There was a moment of silent disbelief.
Moe threw his arms into the air and shouted something like "Wow!" to the ceiling.
Joe slapped his desk and giggled into himself, then threw his head back and laughed. *What a world,* he thought. *What a wonderful world. Everything good happens in America.*

*   *   *

Listening to the CBC radio newscast Monday eve, October 28 1929, while waiting for Hannah's "Dinner is ready, Joe," Joe became mildly interested in the news item that "… most of the European stock markets had had a bad day…" Walking toward the kitchen he wondered what it would mean for so many people to have lost a good part of their investments. *But that's in Europe,* Joe thought, *far away.* He remembered Irv's words when Irv invested their $5,000 for each of them, including Irv himself, *"This money fund is as safe as the rock of Gibralter. I did the research."* And then his most recent report of *" … the highest it's ever been."* Assured, smiling, Joe went into the kitchen and sat down at the table.

Joe arrived at his shop the next morning at his usual seven a.m. and the single freight elevator that served all purposes in the building lifted him to his shop on the third floor. He crossed the short hallway to the door that opened into his reception room, his office and then his shop. He started to turn his key in the first lock and realized it had already been opened. He tried the second lock. They had both been opened. Panic struck him. *Was somebody in there? Was he being robbed? Or did he forget to lock it last night? No no no, somebody opened it.* He stepped inside cautiously and listened. He heard faint noises. *From the office? Is somebody in the office? But there's nothing to steal, a few dollars in petty cash.*

There was a sudden noise and a man's voice talking loud but he couldn't figure what he was saying. Joe stepped carefully toward the receptionist's station until he could peek in through the glass upper half of the door. He saw Irv frantically clicking for the operator, then yelling into the phone. "Froelich, Froelich Investments, Burton 2184!

Alarmed at the panic in Irv's voice, Joe hurried in and asked, "Vat … v'at's heppening foist t'ing in da morning , Oiv?"

Irv lowered the phone a bit to talk just above it and yelled, "The market is crashing. Joe, crashing."

"Da shoe market?"

"No, the stock market."

With a sick feeling in his gut Joe stood with his mouth open and he saw his $9,000 fly away and disappear. *And Moe's, and Irv's, too.* He sank into one of the visitors' chairs.

Irv yelled into the phone again. "Get me out, Frank, all three." "I don't care what it is, get me out, all three … As soon as it opens … Do your best, do what you can." Irv slammed the receiver down and fell back in his chair.

After a moment Joe asked, "Vy did you use Fanny's phone. Something wrong with yours in da office?"

"First phone I came to. Every second counts."

"Ve lost it?"

"I'll know at the end of the day when Frank calls me back and tells me what he was able to do."

"T'enks God, ve're still selling shoes. Ve'll still make a living."

Irv looked at Joe, but decided not to enlighten him. "Yeah."

Joe got up and said, "Nu, so let's make shoes." He opened the door to the office where all was familiar. The desk and phone of each of the three waited for them as usual. After a moment Joe said, " "Stocks, even good vuns, don't make shoes." He went out into the factory to check on the work routines for the day.

Irv, who had earned his Master's in Business Administration, kicked himself from here to hell for letting his greed blind him so that he didn't get out at the peak of the bubble, that he didn't foresee the stock bubble breaking. Added to his woe was the fact that he had lost money for Moe and Joe. They had trusted him. When the Dow peaked at 381 on September 3 they had each doubled their $5,000 investment. Today, questioned Irv, after the crash? It could be zero, he thought in panic. "We'll see. We'll see," he mumbled tensely. "The ticker will be late, maybe as late as seven tonight." Irv beat on himself. "Damn!" He reached up to the wall behind his desk and pulled off his framed MBA that he had proudly hung there and dropped it on the floor. The glass cracked in many pieces. He kicked the mess under his desk, out of sight.

Joe stayed on the factory floor until the work crew showed up. He went over details with some of them and returned to the office where he was surprised to find Moe already there. Moe usually came in by ten or eleven. "Vy so early, Moe?"

"Nobody wants to talk business as usual when the market's crashing."

"So, vomen still need shoes."

Moe was about to explain to Joe, whose head was always, and only, in his factory, when he saw Irv behind Joe signaling with his hand and shaking his head as if telling Moe, *"No, don't tell him the connection between the two."*

Moe got the message. "Yeah, women still need shoes," he agreed in answer to Joe.

On September 3, 1929, at the end of a six-year meteoric rise, the stock market had peaked at 381 and seemed like it would never again go down. Economist Irving Fisher proclaimed that the stock market had reached a permanent plateau. Yet in contradiction, the market moved slowly downward until October 28 when it plunged over 100 points. The crash continued the next day, dubbed 'Black Tuesday.' For that week of the stock market's crash the nation lost 30 billion dollars.

The market continued to slide even further until November 13 when it seemed finally to have bottomed out at 198, down almost 200 points from its peak.

As if riding the fervent prayers, wishes and hopes of the many desperately trying to recoup some of their losses, the market enjoyed a slow but steady rise of a hundred points to 294 in April 1930.

It was at this point in 1930 that neither Moe nor Irv had to tell Joe how the frightening convulsions of the stock market would diminish his business of selling his shoes. Workers were laid off. People weren't buying, not shoes, not anything. It was as if the entire population had agreed to stop spending what little they had left. Sales in the stores ceased. People who were not already bankrupt because they had over-borrowed to make a killing on 'sure thing' stocks, were savoring any pennies they had left.

Retail sales at a standstill, storekeepers had no interest in building their inventories. Almost universally across the nation, stores idled with what inventory they had and ordered nothing further. Orders already in progress for Reinermans' shoes were cancelled, which stopped work on shoes in various stages of being finished. Joe had no choice but to lay off the rest of his 38 man and woman work force telling them he hoped it would be temporary. Moe and Joe apologized to Irv, their accountant-bookkeeper and Fanny, the receptionist for taking them off salary. If they were needed they would be called in on an hourly basis.

At supper that evening Joe and Hannah were silent until Seymour and Danny finished eating and left the table. Hannah looked at her husband and said, "How bad is it, Joe?"

"It's bad," he said, nodding his head to affirm his words. I t'ought dere vould be vun or two orders for Easter," Joe shook his head, "but notting, not even vun." Joe sat, thinking hard about where possibilities for income might be. He silently shook his head in the negative because he didn't see any. "Maybe ... maybe fa Christmas—"

Hannah panicked. "Christmas!"

Joe looked at her, nodded to affirm what he had said. "Dat's all I see, Hannah, dat's all I see."

Christmas was too far away to offer any hope. Hannah chronicled to Joe her downhill slide. "I let Mary go, also the Thursday cleaning girl. I told Janet from Hadassah that I can't host the card games anymore. She said she was sorry that things had turned so bad for us."

Joe nodded as if to accept Janet's sympathies. Curious, he asked, "Vat does her husband do?"

Hannah stiffened. That was something her Hadassah friends didn't even whisper about so as not to offend Janet.

"You won't tell, Joe?"

"Who vould I tell?"

Hannah hesitated further, then whispered, "He's a bootlegger."

Joe stared at Hannah, disbelieving. After he recovered he said. "Vell, *he* von't hev to give up *his* house."

"No."

They were silent again, each fearfully facing the further changes to their lives. Both had known poverty and the meanest of tenement dwellings. They silently asked themselves, *are we going back to that?* As Hannah continued her voice broke, "Our lease ... here goes for ... another two months."

"Dat ve cen pay," Joe said. "but den ve move. Somet'ing cheaper vill save us money."

Hannah bit her lip to keep from crying.

The Reinerman's next apartment was four rooms in the bottom floor of a duplex in an older, crowded section of Brooklyn, rent $65 which they paid out of what was left of their savings. Seymour and Danny once again shared a room and desk and slept in the same bed.

CHAPTER 30

1931

In March, 1931, 4,000 banks failed across America. The Reinerman Brothers declared bankruptcy along with thousands of other businesses. But neither Moe nor Joe could harbor the thought that they would be out of the shoe business. They agreed that each would raise, beg, borrow, or steal, half the money to buy back enough machinery and pay the bills to start again. They naively thought that this was just an unusual dive in their annual business cycle, that like every year, the good season comes around; it goes around, it comes around.

Moe made an agreement with Sydney Oliphant, the landlord to let them use half of their original space at one-third the rent. Moe drove the hard bargain because the first and second floor businesses in the building had already failed and vacated, and no one else was knocking on Oliphant's door. Sid accepted Moe's offer.

Despite their low expenses their income was still no match for the bills. Moe and Joe took no salaries. One order came in for two styles, 10 pairs each, for Easter. Joe hired Silvio Valanti one of his former workers whom he knew could do all the operations to make the whole shoe from start to finish. Production would be slower but there was time enough to fill the order and using one man was the cheapest way to go.

Simultaneously, Moe set out to phone every known contact and any new ones that were worth a call.

Joe, known for 'the best hand-turned shoe in the business', still believed that he could continue to make a success of a business that had prospered for twenty-seven years. Joe's compulsive need to prove that his skills in making shoes could compete with anyone's blinded him from seeing that the depression of the thirties was catastrophically different from the annual, cyclical 'slow season'. His continued hope for the shop was that crack salesman Moe, could drum up a few orders for the Easter season to carry them over into the next cycle.

After a few days of calling Moe began to get the message. Moe, who prided himself about being sharp on business trends, was just beginning to realize that this was not the usual slow season of the annual cycle.

While Moe was working the phone a bit of unforeseen luck dropped into Joe's lap. Beulenberg the Boot Maker fitted people whose feet were not equally paired and required two different fitting shoes in oxfords, ankle high half boot or calf high full boot. Perhaps the abnormal foot had been caused by a birth defect, an accident or a war wound and it had to be fitted by an individually crafted piece of footwear.

Joe's apprenticeship experience in Russia had been just that, making shoes individually for each foot, for man or woman.

Three of Beulenberg' workers had serious cases of the flu and were quarantined in their homes. When Beulenberg heard about Joe Reinerman, he called Joe. Satisfied with Joe's work Beulenberg offered him a week's work at 10 dollars a day.

After the week only one of the ill workers was able to return to work. Beulenberg asked Joe to stay on for another three days. Joe was delighted to oblige and tell his family that he would make enough to pay off the eviction notice.

Meantime the one order at Reinerman Brothers was almost done and Moe's phone calls had brought nothing else in. The brothers knew their second attempt at continuing the business wasn't working. Moe thought about giving it up and asked Joe to sit down and talk it out. Moe also invited Irv to sit in hoping Irv's financial experience would serve to convince Joe that whatever it was that had happened to America's economy it was a waste of time and money to expect any business investment to pay off.

Joe was glad to sit down and talk. What else?

*   *   *

Washed and dressed, Daniel readied himself to say his morning prayers before breakfast as he'd been doing daily since his *Bar Mitzvah* three years ago. He opened his velvet prayer bag and took out the leather straps, one to circle his left arm length seven times in support of its small sealed box of Hebrew prayer script on his upper arm. The other strap was a headband that held its prayer box as a beacon in the center of his forehead. Daniel tightened the prayer box on his upper arm. About to circle his arm seven times with the rest of the strap, Daniel stopped. Although Pa didn't talk about how tough things were and Ma would turn her head to hide her tears, Daniel knew that the family might be forced to move again because they had so little money left. He suddenly couldn't see the relevance in devoting himself daily to a God whom the Jews first recognized 4,000 years ago, in view of what had just happened to his family. *If God was so good and so all-powerful why did He let them take Pa's business away?* Daniel couldn't make sense of his religious family being hit with such hard times. Nor could he see any reason to continue saying daily morning prayers. Daniel returned the leather straps and prayer scripts to the velvet bag, pulled the drawstring tight and continued to get ready for school.

Not so Seymour. Favored in the family as the first son who would take charge of the family's business affairs and holiday prayer rituals when Pa was gone, Seymour had no such conflict about saying his daily morning prayers. Without questioning, he considered morning prayers part of his inheritance that he had to maintain.

Seymour had graduated from Madison High and immediately registered at City College for a two-year Business Degree. He never questioned that he would function in the world of business, as he never questioned his being required to say his daily morning prayers. Being the important first son of his religious Jewish family it was a given.

Despite the extraordinary economic catastrophe that continued to grip America, Academia's Business Administration courses still taught that the annual business cycle for consumer goods would prevail. Seymour himself had begun to question traditional economics because the stock market continued its frightening slide and didn't stop until a year later in July 1932, when it hit forty-one, its lowest level since the 1800s. But Seymour felt that he needed a business degree whatever might happen. He saw the degree as the way to begin learning the process of making a living in the business world dressed in a shirt-and tie, and for his eventual handling of his family's affairs.

Seymour had grown up knowing the family's closeness to the shoe industry. Looking for an unskilled job he knocked on shoe jobbers' doors before and after classes hoping to land his first job as a stock clerk. His thought was that if he found a job, he would hang on to it and switch his day classes to the slower road to a degree by attending night school.

His first year came and went and he had found nothing. He registered for his second year at City College and kept hoping to find something, more impatiently now, because he was worried about the eviction notice.

When Seymour told his father what his plans were, Joe suggested Seymour try *Princess Shoes*. "Tell Dave Feigenbaum you're Joe Reinerman's son. I treated him good."

"Thanks, Pa. I will."

Seymour impressed Dave Feigenbaum. Going to college and sticking with it until his BBA meant the boy wasn't job-hunting to blow spending money on the fun stuff. Obviously more serious than just a kid off the street, Feigenbaum wondered if Seymour could qualify for a project he had in mind.

Although Dave already had one youngster keeping his assigned shelves accurately stocked, to Seymour's work he added the bookwork of recording daily his stock in, stock out, stock on hand. Seymour was excited to bring home his first $12 for the week, but more, being encouraged by Dave to take his first step in managing a business.

Although Daniel no longer strove to keep the door open to his God, he had unknowingly and totally absorbed other tenets of his family's Jewish Orthodoxy, one of which said that a boy and girl may not touch until they marry. Since this took talking about sex off the table for Orthodox families and their adolescent offspring, they did not feel remiss for not attempting some guidance to prepare their children for the sexual phenomena. This meant that Orthodox children were permitted to detour around a huge chapter of knowledge, which could have provided them much help as they groped their way attempting to ride the frightening rapids of puberty and adolescence.

When out in the more permissive world of daily life what they did learn about sex was haphazard, often incorrect and often dangerous to them or to their partners. But Daniel and Seymour had never heard the word 'sex' in their house, not unexpected from parents who could not verbalize in any way about the sexual contact between themselves.

At fifteen Daniel still didn't understand how babies were born. His fellow students gathered for their algebra class with all the chatter and laughter allowed before the bell rang. Tess, a fellow student approached Daniel extending a slip of paper toward him. Other students who knew what was written on it moved toward them to watch.

"Danny," Tess asked, "can you tell me the answer to this equation?" On the paper was written: AB over LC + 9 months = ?

Danny puzzled over it, gave up and extended it back to Tess shaking his head in the negative.

"Don't you know the answer?" Tess queried, disbelieving.

Snickering broke out from the students gathered round, watching.

Daniel looked around and realized they were laughing at him. His face flushed in shame.

Tess took the slip and pushed it toward him. "Read it again," she said, as if Daniel surely must know the answer, "you do know what it means."

More students gathered round to add to the suppressed laughter.

His face aflame, and although he shook his head in the negative, he yielded to Tess' insistence and took the paper again.

But looking at the imitation equation didn't help him any further. He offered it back to her.

But Tess pushed it toward Daniel again and whispered the answer for him, "A baby," just when the door opened and Mr. Barker, the teacher came in one step ahead of the bell.

Tess gabbed the slip of paper, pushed it into her bra and dived for her seat like the others.

Daniel found his seat and sat, confounded.

In his senior year at Abraham Lincoln High School Daniel was still too shy to make any physical contact with a girl. He turned down the party invitations of his classmates. His only outside-the-class activity was sports. He loved that feel-good, able-to-do-anything exuberance that competitive sports gave him. He took pride in his excellent physical development. But he didn't make the connection between his intense activities and his turbulent hormones. In the school there was little or no public discussion of the physical and emotional maturing generated in youngsters by their adolescent hormones. If any of the Social Sciences had dared to show itself in the curriculum texts, shocked Victorian attitudes would have trapped and gagged it to silence. Hormone remained a word in the dictionary, which few investigated. Daniel was unaware that sports siphoned off some of the pressures of his natural maturing, which he declined to otherwise engage.

During his senior year at Lincoln High he captained the soccer team and was a suddenly rising star of the fencing team. Those two major letters plus his two more for two seasons of baseball earned him four major Ls in all. Socially shy, struggling to ignore his hormones, he planned to register at Brooklyn College as soon as he graduated.

CHAPTER 31

1933

Moe and Joe sat with Irv, in the office gloom of a single overhead bulb. Since the first bankruptcy, Irv came in for an hour or two if there were entries to be made, but only if there would be a check for him. This time however, he was glad to join them because he had something important on his mind that he had to tell them.

In the small shop beyond the closed office door Silvio operated his stitching machine finishing the last pieces of the one order. Joe clung to the rhythmic, rattling sound like an exhausted swimmer to a life preserver.

Irv shook his head. "It don't look good." He felt stupid about his observation of the obvious, but it was a way to begin. He smirked self-consciously, "I don't have to tell you guys that." Silently he grappled with the latest news on his mind, hesitant to tell the brothers.

Moe and Joe were smoking. Since Irv had been laid off Moe and Joe didn't bother to honor his rare presence by not smoking. Joe now smoked the cheaper Lucky Strikes, and Moe smoked his cigars down to two-inch stubs. Two years ago he threw half-cigars away. Now he smoked his butts until he felt the heat on his lips and feared for his moustache, which showed nicotine stains. By the time he discarded the stub the chewed end had disintegrated. He constantly interrupted his words to pick soaked tobacco shreds from his lips and teeth and rub them off his fingers on the rim of the ashtray.

Irv, still the non-smoker, waved the stench away from him. The smokers ignored the silent hint. "After I sit with you guys," Irv chided, "I have to send my suit to the cleaners. Edith can't stand the smell."

The brothers didn't get it. To them the stench was comforting.

"Of course, these days," Irv continued, "I hang them on the line and save the seventy-five cents."

After Irv finished nobody talked. The clammy silence thickened. The one machine had stopped. Joe wondered whether Silvio was mounting a new spool of thread, or had finished the few pieces and gone home.

Irv reached and touched the closed ledger on the desk. "Whaddaya wanna do about this?" he asked gently.

Joe didn't hear. He was listening for Silvio's machine to start.

Moe fumbled with his jacket, pretending to brush ashes from it.

Uncomfortable with the silence, Moe talked. "What can we do? There are no orders out there. I've worn the phone out."

Irv tried to lighten the inevitable disaster he felt he had to drop on them. "Is that why they're taking the phone away?"

Joe inhaled his cigarette, then threw his short arms upward, cigarette ash floating down like star dust. "Vun more," he said with an emphatic nod of his head.

Moe and Irv looked at him. "One more what?" Moe asked with his precise articulation.

"Ve give it up vunce more," Joe said grimly.

"Bankruptcy and start again?"

"Yeah," Joe said without joy.

"You're crazy," Moe said.

"Vy 'crazy'?"

"Aren't you in debt enough? I am."

"Vun more," Joe said stubbornly. He couldn't think of his life without the shop.

"Joe," Irv interceded gently, "it's a shrinking market out there; shrunk, flat, finished." His hand raised and slapped the desk they were sitting around to emphasize its finality.

"I dun' believe dat," Joe argued. "Vomen gotta hev shoes."

"But they can't pay the price," Irv argued, and added pointedly, "not your hand-turned price."

Reinerman shoes sold for eleven dollars a pair when the market was good.

"Ve'll make it cheap fa dem," Joe countered, "Seven dolla's."

Silence.

"Six dolla's," he bargained, working for an agreement.

"You can't make them cheap enough," Irv insisted, finally seeing a way to tell them that the worst had happened for them.

"Vat's 'cheap enough'?" asked Joe. He looked for an answer from Irv then Moe.

"Four dollars a pair," said Irv.

"Wholesale?"

"Retail."

"RETAIL!" Moe and Joe reacted like two astounded puppets hooked to the same string.

Only Yiddish could express Joe's astonishment and frustration. *"Du bist misshugga,* Oiv," (You're crazy, Irv) he hissed, and with an angry gesture cut Irv off. "Who makes fa' two dolla's wholesale?"

"Italy."

"Italy? Vad dey make it from, *bupkas?"* (beans)

"Leather. And it's a good-looking shoe. Marshall Fields is buying them, and Ohrbach's." Irv stopped because he saw the pain of the two men, his friends, at having cut their legs from under them. And worse, he knew that Reinerman Bros. was doomed, never to rise again.

Joe listened again for the machine. He heard the outside door close. Silvio had gone home. Joe wiped away his terror with an angry gesture of one short arm. "Vun more!" he insisted angrily, as if demanding it from someone.

Irv threw up his hands and held his silence.

Moe jumped in. "The money, Joe. Who's gonna lend you the money this time?"

Joe shook his head rapidly, refusing to listen. He lit another cigarette. He slapped the arm of his chair and stood up. "I'll find it!"

Irv, in pain for Joe, shook his head in a last effort to stop him. "Joe, you're crazy," he said quietly. "You're throwing good money after bad."

"Joe," Moe said emphatically. "I can't take on any more debt."

Joe turned to him and raised his hands in an accepting gesture. "All right, Moish, I'll find it."

In the silence, the partners of twenty-seven years thought about what had just been said; it was the end of their partnership.

Moe put out his cigar butt in the ashtray and rubbed his finger free of tobacco shreds on the rim.

Joe inhaled deeply, held it and blew out thin smoke. He bit his lips.

Irv stood up slowly. "I'll go hang out my suit."

Joe tried to go on alone. He went to relatives who had lent him money before.

"Joe, you're crazy," Al said to him. "The market is dead. Wait."

"Vait? Ve gotta eat, Al! Vait fa' vat?"

"Joe, not again," said Phil.

"Vat else, Phil? Vat else?"

Joe choked down his pride and pleaded with Harry Lurner, the bootlegger. "Just a small shop, Harry. I dun' vanna be 'big' anymore."

"Joe, shoes are no good now. *Shmattas* (clothes) are no good. Hats are no good."

"So vat's good, Harry? How do ve make a living?"

"Alcohol, Joe. Dey'll wear rags, walk wid holes in deir shoes, go without a hat in the snow, but money for alcohol dey got."

Desperate, Joe thought of the college fund for Seymour and Danny. Not needing Hannah's signature, he decided not to tell her.

The fund totaled $1,852 dollars. Taking it Joe felt like a thief. He vowed he'd pay it back each month even before he took a salary. He told no one. *If I pay it back, who has to know?*

At the auction, the few buyers were not interested in the Reinerman machinery. The new Italian methods had buried the hand-turned shoe. Joe was able to buy back four machines. The auctioneer carted the rest off to his warehouse. He would have been smarter to sell them for scrap.

Joe opened his new business under the name 'Brooklyn Shoe Company.' Sid, the landlord, insisted on the first month's rent in advance. Credit for lights, water and gas was a problem. To prevent the utilities from refusing him credit, he had Hannah apply for his company under her maiden name, Henneberg.

It was only after he lost his business for the third time that the bewildered Joe Reinerman accepted the fact that a catastrophe had happened to his beloved American economics. He finally understood that it was time for his hand-turned shoe to leave, to make way for the Italian machine that had resulted in a revolution in the shoe industry.

Despite his feeling of being thrown aside by an industry that he had fought with and won his place in for 27 years, and despite his inability to verbalize it, Joe still felt a strong affinity to make shoes that fit the feet. Finally accepting the fact that the ladies' hand-turned shoe business was dead, Joe hoped that Beulenberg might be able to use him again. Not stretching and shaping leather to fit a foot he felt he was nowhere, useless.

CHAPTER 32

1933

Daniel graduated from Abraham Lincoln High School in June. Always the worry about eviction, the family made no hoopla about it. Graduation was not a *Bar-Mitzvah*, simply another day that closed out one era for 17-year-old Daniel so he could go on to the next, to something of his choosing. It would be his decision. But since there were so few opportunities for him, he would have to find his own way. No longer did he feel he had to discuss his next move with his parents. He felt eager to step out into the world.

Joe and Hannah knew little or nothing about colleges. They had heard only that if you have the money, put some aside for it. Maybe your son could be an architect, or a doctor, or a lawyer. He could make a better living if he is trained for something.

Daniel remembered the one time his parents discussed it with him, when the family had plenty of money with which to make choices, and Daniel had only to decide in which direction he would go. His mother had given him a mixed compliment for his quick, articulate tongue. "With a mouth like yours, Danny," his mother said to him, "you ought to be a lawyer."

But Joe, who was impressed by the wonder of Manhattan's skyscrapers, said, "No, Denny should be an architect."

Neither Hannah nor Joe foresaw the lack of economics that Daniel would be living in.

On July 1 Daniel decided to spend the day in Manhattan to see if any jobs were available. On the way home he planned to take the subway local to Joralemon Street and register for Brooklyn College. At the subway entrance he bought the *New York Times* for a nickel from the street level newsstand as he did every day, folded it and held it tucked under his arm as he glided down the stairs, one hand zipping along on the banister. On the train the morning crush was past, there were plenty of seats on the express to Times Square. Danny unfolded the paper to see the day's news. The headline in three-inch type leaped out and riveted his attention,

"1/3 OF NATION HUNGRY"—FDR

Daniel remembered that all four of his family sat glued to the radio last night listening to Roosevelt's fireside chat. The whole country was focused on the president and his proposals to help the country get through this worst of all crises in America's history. Daniel tried to read the report of the arguments raging about the government bills that Roosevelt was trying to get Congress to pass, but his fears of the eviction notice with which the family had been served intruded constantly to remind him that he needed to look for a job. Daniel finally gave up on Roosevelt and went to the job possibilities.

For the first time in his daily reading of the New York Times Daniel turned to the Classifieds. At this early point in the depression, businesses continued to shut down and there were no calls for skilled workers. But there were bank runner jobs. No matter how bad the economy, banks had to have runners daily to carry the papers of a deal that had to be signed by another bank or loan institution. Postal mail that took two to three days was not even considered.

But Daniel was in for another shock that caused added turbulence to his inexperienced youthfulness. Of the eleven bank runner jobs listed all were marked 'Christian Only.'

"All?" was Daniel's silently probing question as he searched for an unmarked job opening in the barricade that blocked him.

"Yes, all," was the answer of the Times Classifieds.

Daniel was doubly kicked in the gut; that his favorite source of information, *The New York Times* teamed up with the banks to deny him even an interview, and that the larger world, in which he knew he wanted to find his place, would not receive him.

Hitler's *"Kristalnacht,"* the Nazi's first, nation-wide attack on Germany's Jews was in the news. But that was Hitler, the maniac, in Europe. America? America, too, hated the Jews? And he read it from his reliable source. Dazed, Daniel decided he'd better get off at Joralemon Station and register at Brooklyn College. He knew the City's new college wouldn't shut him out.

After registering, Daniel decided to go on to Times Square anyway to see what his job possibilities were in Manhattan.

Daniel got off at Times Square Station. Eager, he hurried to the wide staircase that led to the street and bounced up the steps two at a time. Outside it was early enough in the July day for the air to be fresh and cool on his face, But the Square had become a gathering place for shabbily dressed, homeless men. On each corner a man stood by a box of apples and a sign, "Apples 5 cents." Others were standing idling in groups. Individuals strung out in a line sat on the sidewalk, their backs against the buildings. Below the Square he saw that a double line of men had already begun to form at the door of the Gospel Mission for their free midday meal.

Around the Square on the sides of buildings tall giant-sized signs advertising Coca Cola, Burma Shave, Nedick's and others blinked their thousands of bulbs into the sunshine. Atop the buildings the thousands of blinking bulbs on signs also shouted to pedestrians for their attention. At street level, curious shops of all kinds branched out into the areas immediate to the Square.

Daniel started walking. A large wooden sign marked 'Race Records' squeaked just over his head as it swung in the breeze. Its unique message of Southern Blues blared out the open door to America's Northeast and to the tourists who probably had never heard this kind of Americana. Daniel stood fixed, listening to the passion of the singer, stirred by the sobs in his voice.

Daniel came upon one of Bernard McFadden's Pennyteria restaurants. A scrawled sign was taped to the inside of the storefront window, "Busboy Wanted."

"A job," Daniel thought excitedly. While he stood a moment to work up his courage, he noticed a billboard sign atop the low building. The painting on it showed a man's face of stern Anglo-Saxon features looking as fierce as a hell-and-brimstone preacher, extending his arm and a pointing finger to the waving field of grain in the foreground. Along the earth line at the bottom of the painting it read, God's Whole_Grains.

Daniel looked through the store window again to see some men standing and eating at higher-than-usual tables, no chairs. *So they can't sit around,* he thought, *and clutter up the place.* Daniel went inside and headed for the man in a white apron standing behind the small food counter. "You have a job? Daniel asked.

"Yes."

"What do I have to do?"

"Pickup the dishes and bring them into the kitchen and wipe down the tables."

"What does it pay?"

"A dollar a day and one meal, six days a week."

Daniel's excitement disappeared. He knew he wouldn't work for a dollar a day but he was curious about the name of a restaurant called 'Pennyteria.' Daniel knew that the Horn and Hardart Auomat was popular in Manhattan because it charged less, lots of food items for two or three nickels. *But food for pennies? How cheap did the Depression make them go?*

At the Automat, the cashier loaded the customer with a handful of nickels in exchange for a dollar bill. In the restaurant along a wall small, closed glass doors sealed slices of pie or cake or a sandwich in its individual compartment. Two nickels into the slot opened the door of a slice of pie or cake, three nickels for a cheese sandwich. There was also a long bar where a cold salad plate or a hot portion of meat could be had for fifty cents.

But Daniel had never heard of Bernard McFadden or his Pennyteria. *Food for pennies? Obviously it caters to the poorest,* he thought, *that's how bad things are.* Daniel asked the man, "What kind of food do you serve?"

The man gestured down to the small bowls of food between them, behind the glass barrier, stewed raisins, cooked oatmeal and something that looked like a mix of different grains. In a dull voice he rattled off, "Raisins, three cents, oatmeal, three cents, God's whole grains, five cents."

Daniel thanked the man and left.

Out into the sun again he turned onto 44th Street, two blocks above the square where the shop advertising was more reserved, in tune with their uptown clientele. But a few beggars were also on the street hoping to squeeze some coins from the stylishly dressed lady shoppers. Daniel came to the *Schrafft's Candies* shop and restaurant. Elegant boxes of candies were displayed in the window on one side of the entrance. In the window on the other side was the usual daily menu printed with as many French words as might be understood by uptown Manhattanites. Beside it was a neatly printed sign on yellow poster board that read:

DISHWASHER WANTED
COLLEGE GRADUATE PREFERRED

Stunned by the sign, Daniel froze. A dishwasher couldn't make more than $15 a week. Four years of college to earn so little? Suddenly the meaning of the drama that had happened to his family was written in the five words of that sign. Though too inexperienced to understand all its implications, he knew the Depression was a cyclone that had blown away all that they'd had, stripped the country's landscape bare. His father's business gone, his family no longer had anything of worth. Even if he were to graduate college, which is what every young man is told to aim for, four years of study would be worth no more than a dishwasher's job at *Schrafft's Candies.*

Daniel thought of the men idling around Times Square, himself locked out of a bank runner job by the 'Christian Only' label, the *Schrafft's Candies* sign calling for a college graduate, and the job at McFadden's not worth taking. *The Depression,* Daniel thought, punning, *is enough to depress anybody.* He found himself walking slowly toward the subway entrance; so much for his chance of a job in Manhattan on a sunny day in July.

Daniel enjoyed his studies in the liberal arts. The news in *The New York Times* occupied him on the train before and after classes with its write-ups about the pros and cons of the impending passage of the 21st amendment to the Constitution. This would repeal the 18th amendment, which for 14 years had attempted to prohibit the sale of alcoholic beverages. President Roosevelt had pushed hard for the 21st amendment knowing that it would result in a desperately needed spurt of business activity, crimp the power of the criminal gangs controlling alcohol activity in every large city, and put a stop to the killings and murders of the gang wars.

Surprise! Repeal of prohibition would also land Daniel his first job.

Hannah, aware that Janet Cohen's bootlegger husband would soon be legit and busier than ever distributing liquor legally, phoned Janet in a plea for some kind of work for Daniel during the three weeks of his college's Christmas vacation.

Janet promised to get back to her.

Prohibition was repealed on December 5, 1933 and liquor poured into the cities like a dam had burst.

After a few days Janet called Hannah back and gave her the details of where Daniel was to report for his interview. "When he gets to the Griffler Wine Company tell him to ask for Phil, my husband."

Hannah thanked Janet profusely.

Daniel had passed his midterms and felt free to forget about his last week of classes before the Christmas vacation in order to make himself available for as much time on the job as possible. At his interview he told Mr. Cohen that he would be free for a full three weeks through New Year's Day.

"Good," replied Cohen. He was a pudgy man with slicked blond hair. His white silk shirt and blue silk tie made him look even softer, but a look at his face told you his mind raced as did his speech to get the items of his daily schedule done. "You'll be working on a small truck," Cohen said rapidly, "helping Saunders, the driver to deliver cases around the city."

Daniel nodded.

Cohen stopped talking to look Daniel over to assess his strength whether he was strong enough to carry a case of 12 fifths of whiskey on each shoulder when making deliveries. Carrying two cases at a time into the saloon meant that each truck run could cover more territory more quickly. Cohen pointed to a stacked load of Jack Daniels against the wall. "Can you carry two cases at a time, one on each shoulder?"

Confident, four-letter man Daniel walked over to the stack.

Cohen followed.

Daniel hoisted one case to his shoulder and turned for the second.

Cohen lifted one to his other shoulder.

Standing straight, Daniel held on to the two, and said, "Where do you want them?"

Cohen laughed. "You'll do. Your driver," Cohen continued, as Daniel returned the cases to the stack, "is Jack Saunders. He's worked with me for a long time. He'll show you the ropes. You and Jack'll get here at eight in the morning to load up and work until you deliver all the cases. Your pay will be twelve dollars a week. Six days. Sunday, you're off unless I need you."

Excited, Daniel nodded. "Fine," he said.

Riding home on the train Daniel concentrated to put the details of his job together so he'd be better prepared. But his excitement about making the money needed to stop their eviction bubbled up constantly and kept throwing his thinking off track.

CHAPTER 33

1933

Joe finally understood that in the Depression only cheap works, *very* cheap. Standing in the BMT train to Manhattan, he knew if he wanted to still make his living from shoes, he had to accept the revolution. With the coins in his pocket the only money to his name, he got off at Canal Street and took the local to Prince Street.

Dave Feigenbaum's 'Princess Shoes' was an old loft just below the garment district. Dave made a business of selling shoe irregulars wholesale to low-end stores. He used to buy odd lots of shoes from 'Reinerman Bros.' Odd lots and seconds had been of no value to Joe, so he'd let Dave have them for practically nothing. Joe pulled the weighted-pulley cord to start the elevator for the slow ride up to Dave's floor.

When it finally arrived Joe grabbed the cord and held on to stop it at the floor level and stepped off into Dave's shop where Seymour was unloading shoe boxes from a shipping carton and stacking them on shelves. Surprised when he saw his father, he said, "Hey, Pa, what 're you doing here?"

Joe grinned and tried to joke. "I came to see that you're doing a good job for my friend Feigenbaum. How's it voiking out, Seymour?"

"Good, Pa, good."

Joe walked to the partitioned square that was Dave's office. Dave was there alone.

Though surprised to see Joe, Dave held out his hand and greeted him with, "Pretty soon I'll have all the Reinermans working for me.

They shook hands. Dave spoke in sympathy. "Sorry to hear it, Joe." Everyone left in the industry knew that the Reinerman brothers had gone under. Dave was shocked to see how Joe had aged. "Tough. Tough, Joe," he sympathized. "I'm just holdin' on." He pulled the secretary's chair around the desk and invited Joe to sit. His secretary came in only one day a week.

Joe opened his coat and pushed his hat back on his head. He had lost weight because he was eating about a third of what he used to. His face was unsmiling and sallow. His lips had disappeared into a thin line. His teeth clamped themselves stubbornly when he wasn't speaking. The spread of his nose seemed greater, making his face more solemn. "You still here, Dave?" he said, trying unsuccessfully to think of a joke.

"Holdin' on, Joe," Dave repeated, "just holdin' on." He was feeling awkward. When Joe had money, he'd been generous to Dave. Now Joe had nothing.

"How's my son doing?"

"Fine. Seymour's a good worker."

"Good. Irv, my accountant," Joe started, "vas telling me about de Italian shoes,"

Dave perked up. Joe had jumped into his territory. "Yeah, Joe, I don' know how dey do it."

"You like dem?"

Dave spread his hands wide. "Terrific! Classy shoes! Cheap!"

Joe felt again that sinking feeling when the competition was better than him. "You buy dem?"

"Dat's all I buy. Dat's all ya' c'n sell now."

Joe pointed to the large window through which he saw Seymour working. "Dat's vat dat shipment is?"

"Dat's what every shipment is. Who c'n afford anyt'ing else?"

"C'n I see v'at it is?"

"Sure, Joe." Dave went to the large window and raised it. "Seymour, let me have three different styles."

Seymour selected boxes from three different shelves and handed them to Dave. Dave brought them to the desk, opened one and handed the shoe to Joe.

Joe turned it in his hands, responding, as always, to the feel of tanned leather. It was a simple, bright-red pump with a three-inch heel. Curious about the construction, he raised the edge of the inner lining. Stitching was not apparent. Puzzled, Joe looked at Dave. "V'at is it? A paste job?"

"Something they call a 'weld'. Dey put it in da' machine, dey come down once, boom, it's done. Dey save t'ree operations."

Defeated, Joe nodded then shook his head side to side. "No vunder dey sell it cheap." He sighed sadly then turned the shoe over to run his stubby thumb along the sole. He handed the shoe back to Dave. "Dey vear good?"

Dave shrugged his shoulders. "Fa' four dollars? Of course."

Joe was shocked. "Four dolla's! No vunder, no vunder." It was clearer now why he was out of business, why he had been foolish to try a second time, never mind the third. He shook his head. "How cen dey do it fa' four dolla's?"

Dave threw up his hands. "I don't know, but it makes a great item. If it wasn't for this, I'd be out of business, too."

Joe lit a Lucky Strike.

Dave moved the ashtray to him.

"You voik on fifty pa'cent?" Joe asked.

"Mostly. A few cents more or less."

"You make out?"

"It's slow now. I'm hopin' orders'll pick up for Easter."

Joe nodded. He blew out smoke. "You hev styles?"

Dave reached for the other two boxes. He brought out a two-tone blue with a one-inch heel.

Joe fondled it enviously.

From the third box Dave brought out a high-heeled ankle strap design and handed it to Joe.

Joe held it up. "Also four dolla's retail?"

"Four twenty-five. On sale, three ninety-five."

All handsome looking shoes, Joe shook his head, finally accepting that the revolution had made it 'another world' in the shoe industry. "You hev more styles?"

Dave waved a hand toward the stock shelves. "Fifteen, twenny styles. All pretty. All cheap."

"Sizes?"

"Anything you want."

Joe crushed his butt in the ashtray. "Dave, ya' vanna help me open a store?"

Dave held up his hands in protest and grunted cynically. "Joe, Joe, I got enough headaches."

"Me, Dave," Joe said, tapping his chest with his finger tips, "I'll take da' headaches. You supply da' shoes."

Relieved, Dave flung his hands freely. "Sure, Joe." He happily envisioned a sale to stock Joe's store, until Joe said, "On consignment."

Dave stopped with his mouth slightly open. He was about to tell Joe that he didn't sell on consignment. But on consignment meant that Joe didn't have a nickel and Dave felt sorry for him. When he looked at Joe's face, Dave knew he couldn't say no. Joe had favored him with great deals in the past. He hoped Joe wouldn't want too many. "How many pairs, Joe?" he asked slowly.

Joe pushed his lower lip forward and shrugged his shoulders. "Fifty pair?"

Though it cost him to move them out and then back again if they didn't sell, Dave nodded slowly in assent. He silently calculated the sale if Joe were to sell them. "Okay, Joe," he said quietly. "When do you want them?"

"Foist, I'll find da' store, a few blocks from Abraham & Strauss at Borough Hall. Den I'll sell dem twenty-five--t'oity cents cheaper. I'll open op fa' Easter."

Dave nodded, glad it was Joe and not himself trying to start a business. He stood up and offered his hand. "Okay, Joe, let me know."

Joe shook Dave's hand gratefully and nodded.

CHAPTER 34

1933

Because the Reinermans fell behind in December's rent, by the 15th they received an eviction notice again. If they didn't pay the full amount of $120 for the two months, they would be evicted January 31.

By 1933 evictions had created hundreds of homeless families. To slow the rising flood of people thrown onto the streets the city passed an emergency notice that landlords must give tenants two months' notice. Not enough. It was an attempted kiss in a hurricane. Desperate people joined the Workers' Alliance, which was picketing city offices demanding a six-month moratorium on rents. The city's response was to urge charity organizations to set up more shelters and food lines throughout the city.

Desperate, Hannah sat down with a pencil and paper. Daniel's expected $36 for his three weeks on the liquor truck plus Seymour's $30 a month for the rest of December, and his $60 for all of January would give them $126 by the end of January. Hannah went over the figures again to make sure. Yes, just in time they could pay off the eviction notice. Knowing she had some food in the freezer compartment, Hannah breathed a little more easily. Where would they have found the money to move to another apartment and pay a first month's rent in advance? *If Joe could get a few more days with Beulenberg the boot maker,* Hannah prayed silently, *his ten dollars a day would let us catch up again.*

When Daniel got home after his interview with Phil Cohen there was more news. His mother sat at the table with him while he ate his lunch. "Bessie Grablowsky called," said Hannah.

Daniel frowned until he remembered who Bessie was. "Oh, yeah, Bessie" he said.

"She's moving to Manhattan," Hannah continued, "to be closer to her office. You know, she's already a big shot in the insurance business."

Daniel said, "Yeah," and waited.

"She said she would like to help us out."

Daniel waited then asked, "How?"

Hannah spoke slowly, carefully, not knowing herself what to think, wondering whether she was a failure as a mother to her sons and as a housewife to Joe. "She wants us," Hannah continued slowly, "the family, to move in with her." Hannah looked at her younger son, wondering whether he understood what she was saying.

Daniel puzzled over it in the silence, then asked, "The whole family?"

"No, not the whole family, you and Seymour and me."

Daniel waited, but his mother was silent. He finally asked, "And Pa?"

There ... there's no room for Joe."

"No room—What's Pa gonna do? Where's he gonna live?"

"I'll talk with him tonight, when he comes home."

Daniel thought a moment. "She's gonna charge us rent?" Daniel decided he didn't like Bessie.

"No," said Hannah, "no rent."

Surprised, Daniel stared. "Just like that, it's free?"

"Well, yes and no."

Puzzled, Daniel looked at his mother and waited for an explanation. I'll ... I'll work for her."

Surprised, Daniel asked, "You'll work?" Daniel didn't understand. *Ma never worked. She's always home.* "Doing what, Ma?" he asked

Hannah stumbled over the words. "I'll ... I'll clean her apartment and ... and make dinner." She added quickly, "Like ... like I do in my house. I've always done that."

Daniel stared at his mother trying to get used to the idea that she would be working as Bessie's maid. He finally asked, "Does Seymour know?"

"No, he went to work early. I'll tell him when he comes home."

"Manhattan," Daniel mused, "Seymour will be closer to his work."

Hannah nodded.

Daniel thought a moment. "When does she want it to happen?"

"She's moving after the first of the year."

Daniel sat quietly, absorbing this big change to his life, his family's life. Then he said, "Why don't we get evicted and save the money?"

Puzzled, Hannah looked at her son.

"Yeah, Ma, if we're gonna move in with Bessie we can keep the money we have and let the landlord evict us. We'll move into Bessie's place."

Hannah thought about it then smiled at her son. "Smart boy, Danny."

After the boys went to sleep, Hannah sat up with Joe. "Danny figured it out," Hannah said.

"Vat did he figure?"

"He figured out we should stay here until we have to get out and then go to Bessie's. That way we can keep whatever money we have. If Koppelman evicts us he can't expect us to pay him rent."

Surprised at this morsel of good news, Joe nodded.

After being thoughtful Joe reiterated, "You'll voik fa Bessie?"

Hannah looked at Joe and nodded. "I won't mind. She's a good friend. It gives us a place without rent.

"Nu," Joe said, "at least *you'll* hev a job." He sat in silence for a moment then added, "And the boys 'll hev a place."

Hannah nodded" What will you do, Joe?"

Joe thought a moment then said, "*Lantsman fin Kurland* (countrymen from Kurland) I hev plenty. I'll find more than one at the synagogue. I'll get a room in Manhattan, on da Lower East Side."

"Beulenberg hasn't called you?"

"Not yet. Not yet."

"If he calls you we'll be all right."

Joe nodded. "Yeah, if he calls."

"When you get settled, Joe, be sure to give him a number."

"I vill, Hannah, I vill."

"There's time yet, Joe. We have almost a month before the eviction. Let's go to bed."

Joe nodded and got up.

*   *   *

Daniel's driver, Jack Saunders was a busy little Black man who never smiled. But he knew every detail of his trucking job precisely. He was in the office getting his papers for the day's run. Daniel was glad to wait for him in the large storeroom surrounded by endless cases, out of the winter wind.

Jack came out of the office into the storeroom with a stack of invoices clipped together in his hand. "We're gonna do the Yorkville run today," Jack explained, "da whole east side of Manhattan."

He handed the top invoice to Daniel. "Dat's da last delivery of the run. Dose cases go in da truck foist. I'll lift the garage door and back the truck up close. You hand the case to me 'n' I'll load it."

It took them better than an hour to load the truck for its 32 stops.

Daniel wondered how long it would take them to drop off the whole load.

When the last cases were loaded Jack rolled the truck forward and Daniel pulled down the garage door. He was glad to get into the passenger seat and relax.

But there was more for him. Jack lectured him about the paper work. "You're the invoice man. Take only da' top invoice from da' clip, only one. When we deliver da' cases to da' bar you ask him to sign to show he got 'em. And make sure he puts da' date down. When you get back in da' truck ya' put dat one on da' bottom and take da' next top one into da' next bar.

Daniel listened carefully and finally nodded that he understood.

Jack rolled the truck forward and waited for his helper.

Daniel got out, closed the garage door and got in again.

Jack rolled the truck down the short driveway and waited for his chance to slip into a lucky space between the rolling cars. Impatient, Jack let loose the vilest cursing Daniel had ever heard. Jack cursed the f+=*&^%$# drivers who wouldn't let him into the traffic. When he did roll in the long lines with the other drivers he cursed the f&*+=$#@ cop directing traffic because he held Jack up longer than he did the cross traffic. Jack had the same loving words for the F=*(&^%$ newly-installed traffic lights. Of course it shocked Daniel, more so because he was enjoying seeing parts of Manhattan he'd never seen.

After spending many hours of the first day with his driver, and hearing Jack's comments just as vitriolic as they'd been in the morning, it made Daniel wonder where all Jack's bitterness came from. Daniel's only experience with a Negro man had been in the Catskills when he was nine years old, where Joe had driven the family to spend their month's summer vacation. Eddie, the maintenance man, a tall, broad-shouldered Negro sang and walked with a rhythmic bounce while doing his chores. Rather than play games with the other kids, Daniel thought it more fun to follow Eddie and listen to him sing, "I took Miss King out walkin' all on a Saturday night," while picking up paper scraps around the guest buildings or sitting in the wagon behind Bobo, the dray horse taking the kitchen's cans of garbage to dump in the land fill a mile up a dirt road.

Daniel liked sharing Eddie's chores and he hoped he would see Eddie again on the family's vacation next year.

Now, as Jack's truck-helper, Daniel also had to learn about some smaller details of his job, liquor bar protocol. When they put the three cases down on the far end of the bar at *Rosie's,* their first stop of the day, Bodie, the barkeep asked his usual, "Whad'll ya have?"

Not savvy about saloon routine Daniel was puzzled. He didn't understand the question.

Impatient to keep their deliveries moving, Jack swung the back of his knuckles lightly across Daniel's arm. "Take something, kid."

Daniel frowned. *Take something?*

Bodie, seeing the kid's confusion said, "Whaddaya drink?"

Drink? Oh...uh ...

Jack nudged Daniel toward the bar stools. They sat.

Sitting on a bar stool, forearms on the bar, Daniel caught on. "Drink? A glass of milk," he said.

Embarrassed for his helper, Jack overrode him quickly. "Two beers, Bodie."

Daniel managed to drink down his first beer.

After spending many hours of the first day with his driver, Jack's comments continued to spill just as much vitriol as they had in the morning. It made Daniel wonder again what could have happened to Jack.

Each day leading up to Christmas the job turned into a frantic rush to service the saloons. Tavern customers' drinking increased as the day of the Lord's birth approached. Daniel stopped counting the hours from when Jack handed him the stack of invoices in the morning to when he got back on the subway train to go home exhausted, at night.

Christmas, The Day of the Lord sufficiently awash in liquor, the rush was on again to service the last day of the old year. Jack and Daniel put in the hours to make sure there would be enough for the tavern customers to drink on New Years Eve.

On the Saturday of Daniel's third week Phil Cohen gave him $24 instead of $12. In response to Daniel's surprise and excitement Cohen said, "That's for doing a good job, kid. Too bad you're going back to school next week. I could use you here."

Daniel felt profuse gratitude. "Thank you, thank you, Mr. Cohen."

CHAPTER 35

1934

Dave Feigenbaum walked with Seymour toward his office. "Sy," he started slowly, "are you learning anything in school?"

"Well, yeah. I'm getting my two-year BA Certificate at the end of June. That's the end of the semester."

Dave kidded Sy about his favoring FDR. "Can you tell me why we're still in a depression after Roosevelt's wrestled with it for two years already."

Seymour realized Dave was pulling his leg for his idolizing of FDR. "He needs more time, Dave. We've been blowing up the economic bubble for ten years before it went poof. "

"Is that what you learned at school?"

"Yeah. Of course that's only a part of it."

"What are your plans?"

"My plans?" Worried that Dave might be thinking of letting him go, or shutting down *Princess Shoes*, Seymour shrugged. "I'd like to keep working, if that's okay with you, Dave."

"Yeah, that's what I wanted to hear. My brother-in-law, Ben Sorenson has been talking with me. He lives in McKee's Rocks, outside of Pittsburgh. You remember I sent him a small shipment of the Italian shoes. They sold fast. He thinks they're a great item. But his operation is small. He'd like to expand. I talked with him about you taking over the shoe jobbing operation for him, if you're interested."

Seymour's eyes went wide with excitement. "Yeah, sure. What will I have to do? In McKee's Rocks?"

"His shoe-jobbing operation is like mine." Dave interrupted himself. "It ain't gonna happen tomorrow, Sy. I just wanted to know if you're interested. If we decide to go ahead with it I'll let you know."

"Okay. Thanks, Dave."

*   *   *

Back at classes again in January, Daniel was still debating with himself 'College or Job.' As the subway train doors closed Daniel found a seat, put his two texts and notebook close beside him and opened the New York Times to 'Help Wanted'. He skipped the 'Christian only' ads for bank runners to check out those accepting 'unskilled'. There were none. But there was one job listed for 'waiter, experienced'. Daniel remembered the summer he waited tables at camp. *I'm experienced,* he thought excitedly. He noted the address. Manhattan. *I probably won't get back to Brooklyn College in time for my first class. But that's all right, a job's more important.*

In front of the restaurant a huge crowd of men bulged onto the sidewalk. Daniel slowed his running as he saw them. He stood at the edge for a moment then decided he would never make it to the interview. *All these men for one job,* he thought despondently. It was another blow that made him realize how bad the situation was and how meager his chances of getting a job. He turned and walked back toward the Union Square subway entrance thinking, *I'd better get tomorrow's Times well before eight-thirty in the morning.*

Walking nearer to Union Square he heard a voice blaring out over a loudspeaker. Curious, instead of passing the Square he turned in and stood behind a crowd of men standing before a raised platform, hands jammed in their pockets against the cold. Over the head of the speaker a streamer in large red letters read WORKERS' ALLIANCE. The speaker was ending his oratory by again enunciating the services the organization performed. "We are putting pressure on the government to control rents, stop evictions, establish more food distribution centers, and provide welfare services to the unemployed. Sign up in the Worker's Alliance. Join with us to help you."

Scattered applause and some cheering followed.

Next, a speaker for the Communist Party took the microphone. "We are telling our members and all others who need the Alliance's services to join the Workers' Alliance. In unity there is greater strength for each of us and for all of us." More cheering and applause followed.

Before the meeting could disband a young man and woman hurried to the center of the stage and in broad pantomime played out a scene in which a woman welfare worker asks the man the dumbest questions to find out if he qualifies for government help. The man's smart-ass answers had the crowd laughing. When the two actors left the stage there was loud applause.

At the news stand five-thirty the next morning Daniel picked up a copy of the *Times* when the bundle was dropped from the slowed-down truck. Daniel opened his paper to read the classifieds as he walked back to his house. There was nothing listed that he could do, so he rode the subway to school. Daniel hadn't told his family that he was actively looking for work. He hoped to surprise them.

Five-thirty in the morning at the newsstand became his routine. But even five-thirty in the morning wasn't enough of an advantage for Daniel. Crowds were still getting to the job sites before him. He didn't realize that those people were getting a late evening edition of the paper the day before in which the want ads were already listed. Being unskilled, with no specialty to offer, Daniel became discouraged. He decided to try something different.

Riding to class the next morning, Daniel searched the want ads. Three of the bank runner jobs were still offering $15 a week. Nine paid only $12. If he got one of the $15 ones, with what Sy was making, they could pay the $60 a month rent. Daniel checked the bank runner ads carefully. No change. Every bank and agency listed still said 'Christian Only.' Daniel raised his head to remember his reflection in the mirror. *I don't look Jewish,* he thought. *How will they know?* He recalled playing the part of the Irish heroine's grandfather in a musical at camp. His brogue of the old Irishman had been convincing. The audience applauded loudly when he exited.

Daniel reread every word of the bank runner ads, weighing each to choose one. He finally chose the Acorn Employment Agency.

It was only eight in the morning but the line of applicants at the door of the agency extended halfway down the block. Daniel was among the first twenty-eight allowed in to crowd the small area of the agency and fill out applications. The rest waited their turn outside the closed door. Inside, the young woman handed Daniel his application along with her repeating "Fill it out over there."

"Over there" was a wide shelf along the wall to write on, with a long groove to hold a scattered number of pens and an inkwell set in a hole every three feet. Six young men were standing at the ink-spattered shelf filling out forms. Waiting his turn, Daniel moved out of the way against the wall and looked over the application. In the upper right hand corner, in bold caps, it read **CHRISTIANS ONLY**. Daniel gulped, but decided again that he would lie. He read on. After 'Name', 'Address' and 'Phone no.' it asked 'Church Affiliation' and 'Name of Pastor'. Daniel felt lost; he didn't even know how to lie about those. He looked for the girl to ask her if he could take the application with him, but she had apparently gone back into the office. He folded the application, put it into one of his books, and slipped out of the agency. He was relieved to get away from the crowd and the tension of lying. He bounced down the old wooden steps, which squeaked with the weight of him.

After classes that day, he rode home on the subway and put his books in the room he shared with Seymour. He was glad his mother wasn't home. He walked along Webster Avenue looking for a church. He found one five blocks from his house. The large sign on the lawn read 'Webster Ave. Presbyterian Church, Rev. Oscar Appleton, Minister.'

Daniel stood there memorizing the information. Finally, he turned away from the sign and repeated it out loud. He turned back again and studied the cross atop the tall spire, fixing in his mind how it rose above the sharply peaked, shingled roof. He studied the sign again as if he were memorizing lines for an acting role then panicked when he realized that it read 'Minister' and on the questionnaire it asked for 'Pastor'. Were they the same? Johnny Hagen used to talk about his 'priest'. Was that the same? He decided he'd ask his English instructor at class the next day. As he was about to turn away, he realized that there was more information on the sign; 'Services, 10a.m., Sunday School, 10-12 n. *Should I memorize that too?* He decided too much is better than not enough.

Two days later, after questioning his English instructor, Daniel understood the difference between a Catholic and a Protestant, and that minister and pastor were the same.

Sy had already left the house at six-thirty for work. Daniel got out of bed. To save on stove gas and electricity he took an egg out of the icebox, cut a slice of bread and put them on the steam radiator to warm while he washed and dressed.

He was ready to leave at seven for an eight-thirty interview at the agency. He stood in front of the mirror in the bedroom, with his hands in the pocket of his coat, studying himself from each side to see if he could pass for a Protestant. He had combed his wavy black hair carefully. He placed a finger under the tip of his nose and pushed lightly upward. He turned sideways to check his profile. It would be better if his nose turned up, than if it suggested a Semitic downturn. He took his finger away and stepped backward for a final overall check. Nothing he could do about his nose. He remembered that when he was fourteen he used adhesive tape to hold his nose in an upward position while he slept. But it hadn't helped; at seventeen it suggested a slight downturn like his father's.

On the subway he tried to read the *Times* but the words were whirled away by his turbulence. He folded the paper and put it on his lap. Anticipating the questions the interviewer would ask, he fingered the edge of the application that stuck out from his notebook, worrying whether he could carry it off in the interview, and then on the job, if he got it.

As the thundering train rattled and bounced him, he comforted his fears of the interview by remembering how well he did on his job on the liquor truck during Christmas vacation. Daniel remembered the national hubbub when President Roosevelt repealed prohibition on December 5th, 1933, in time to celebrate Christmas. Finally released from the restraints of the Volstead Act, the country wallowed in alcohol. And Daniel and his driver, Jack, were in the middle of it. In the morning they loaded the truck from eight to ten, then delivered the heavy cases until nine at night, to saloons throughout the five boroughs. Christmas eve, they delivered the last case at ten. After a day off for the Day of Christmas the rush was on again to supply the taverns for New Years Eve. Daniel fortified himself for the interview by reminding himself. *Mr. Cohen thought I did a good job. He gave me an extra week's pay.*

In a Yorkville bar in the German section of Manhattan Daniel accidentally heard the first inkling of what others thought of his appearance. Daniel wore a heavy sweater, a raglan-sleeved wool overcoat and a visored trucker's cap with earmuffs against the winter cold. Five-foot eleven, slim and muscular, he carried a case of 'Early Times' on each shoulder. As Daniel strode toward the bar's storeroom, two men at the bar turned to watch him. As Daniel was leaving the tavern for the remaining case, he heard one of the men say in German, "*Schoene Yunge.*"

The German was similar enough to Yiddish so that Daniel understood the compliment. But he didn't realize that it was being said of him. He heard it again as he brought in the last case. Then Daniel realized he was being complimented. Remembering the incident Daniel smiled and felt better about the coming interview.

On the train as he rode toward his interview Daniel thought of that liquor-truck job because Yorkville Germans supported Hitler. The man would not have complimented him if Daniel had looked 'Jewish'. He was encouraged.

Daniel bypassed the long line of applicants outside the door of the Acorn Employment Agency. Most were pressed against the building to minimize their exposure to the January wind. Some were blowing into their cupped hands or stamping one foot then another against the cold. Daniel had turned in his application the day before and was told to return the next day at 8a.m. for his interview.

Daniel opened the door and stepped in carefully to avoid bumping anyone in the crowded room. He felt the bulkiness of his thick overcoat in the tight space. He made his way to the young woman on the other side of the room sitting at a small desk and typewriter in front of Mr. Anderson's office.

"I'm here for my interview," he said to her.

"Name?"

"Daniel Reinerman."

She picked up the list, checked it and gestured toward the door. "Go right in, Daniel."

Daniel opened the door, closed it behind him and stood face to face with Mr. Anderson standing in front of his desk already giving Daniel the once-over. Anderson's thick, blonde hair was center-parted, the two halves pasted down. His upturned, pointed nose seemed trying to escape his pasty complexion. A glistening blue tie outdid his pale blue eyes. His round paunch strained for more room against three confining buttons of his jacket. He picked the top sheet from a small stack on his desk and glanced at Daniel's answers. His inquisitor's eyes left the paper to check Daniel's clothing and appearance and settled to watch Daniel's face. "Daniel Reinerman?"

"Yessir."

"What church do you go to?"

"The Webster Avenue Presbyterian Church."

"Who's the pastor?"

"Reverend Oscar Appleton."

"How often do you go to services?"

"Sundays."

"What time are services?"

"Ten o'clock."

Anderson paused to look at the rest of Daniel's application.

Relief washed over Daniel. His answers came out just as he had rehearsed them over and over. He felt comfortable enough to add, "Sometimes the pastor starts a few minutes late."

Anderson looked up and started to smile but cut it off and checked the paper again. "Reinerman, what nationality is that?"

"German, Sir, German Protestant."

Anderson looked down again. "You're at Brooklyn College?"

"Yessir."

"What will you do if you get this job?"

"I'll quit school, Sir. I need this job."

Anderson nodded and looked down at the paper. "I see that you worked on a delivery truck."

"Yes."

"Why did you leave?"

"It was only a Christmas vacation job, three weeks."

Anderson paused in his rapid questioning, reached sideways to lay the application back on the stack. Back to Daniel's face, he engaged Daniel's brown eyes.

Daniel stood quietly, more assured now that his well-rehearsed repertory could answer a next question.

Anderson's eyes looked up at Daniel's thick black hair. "Do you have a hat?"

Daniel was getting the idea. This was a white shirt-tie and jacket job that needed a hat to complete it. But he didn't own the conventional fedora. His mind raced to salvage him from a sinking feeling. The sudden thought of borrowing his father's rescued him back up to the surface. "A ... yes."

Anderson walked behind his desk and leafed through some smaller forms. He went through them slowly, selected one and reread it slowly. He compared it to Daniel's application. "You live in Brooklyn?"

"Yes."

"This bank is in Manhattan. They pay $15 a week.

Daniel nodded.

"I want you to go home and get your hat for the interview. Anderson stopped, interrupting himself to check his wristwatch. "No, it'll be too late for the interview. Go to a barber shop and get your hair cut shorter."

Daniel nodded compliantly but worried that his mother couldn't spare the 75 cents.

"Be sure you wear the hat. It's gray?"

"A ... yes."

Anderson nodded. "Good." He extended the slip to Daniel.

Daniel took it and continued listening.

"Take the BMT express to Union Square. It's only two blocks from the station. Ask for Mr. Silverwell. It's all there on the paper."

Daniel nodded. 'Yes, yes. Thank you."

"That's all."

Daniel felt a mix of exhilaration and fear as he elbowed his way through the crowded room. His careful plan had worked. He had outsmarted the all-powerful gentiles. But he reminded himself that he didn't have the job yet.

Outside the agency he bounced down the creaky wood steps and buttoned his coat against the cold wind. Haircut and hat still had to be taken care of. Hurrying toward the subway entrance he decided to skip his classes and go straight home.

Daniel bounced up the stairs of the duplex two at a time. "Ma! Ma! I got the job!" He was so excited with the success of what he had done that he couldn't help overstating his case.

"I'm in the kitchen, Danny."

Daniel dodged around the dining room table and stood in the kitchen doorway. His mother was salting some raw chicken parts at the sink. "Ma, have you got 75 cents?"

Hannah turned her head to look at her son. Her thick black hair was pulling loose from her bun. The skin under her tired brown eyes sagged. "What for?"

"A haircut. I gotta get a haircut."

"A haircut? You just had--"

"I know, Ma, but it's too long."

"So why didn't you tell the barber to cut it shorter?"

"The man at the agency says it's too long. And I gotta get a hat."

"You got hats."

"Not the right kind. Like Papa's."

"Who's got the money?"

"I'll borrow Papa's."

"What'll he wear?"

"Just for a day, to get the job."

"What'll Joe wear? It's cold out."

"He can wear my wool cap. Just for a day. I need it to go to the bank interview."

"You're gonna work in a bank?"

"Not *in* the bank, as a runner. Carry papers from one bank to the other."

"In my purse you'll find change. It's on the dresser. Don't take more. I'm shopping tomorrow."

"And I have to wear a suit with a shirt and a tie."

"You have, you have. You don't have to buy anything." Hannah looked critically at her son's hair. "It's not wild, Danny."

Ma, if he wants it shorter I'll cut it shorter. Ma, It's a job."

All right, all right. In my purse."

The forty-eight dollars Daniel earned for three weeks on the delivery truck he had given his mother to hold for the rent. As Daniel rushed by the kitchen on his way to a haircut, Hannah called out, "Danny, maybe we should buy you a hat."

Daniel stopped. "Save it for the rent, Ma. I'll use Papa's, if it's gray."

"Gray? Of course it's gray. Gangsters wear black."

Daniel returned to the house with his hair cut.

"It's short," Hannah commented.

"Well, that's what they want. Is Papa home?"

"It's too early. You didn't go to school today?"

"No, I was too anxious about the job."

"That's all right?"

It's not like high school, Ma. They allow a couple of absences as long as I do the work."

"You wanna eat?"

"Yeah."

After eating, Daniel went to his room that he shared with Seymour. He opened his Ancient History book and tried to study but the words danced away from him. Anticipating tomorrow's interview, trying to imagine the further questioning, the Ancient History book disappeared.

He came to the unhappy conclusion that job and college don't mix. *But if I don't take the finals next week I'll lose the whole semester. But the money*—Again he added his 15 dollars to Seymour's 15 to Pa's 20 for two days of bootmaking plus the $48 that Ma was holding. Well, they had the rent for this month—*if I get the job*. It was the twelfth of January. They should have paid it on the first.

The battle of job versus finals upset him. Losing the whole semester is no way to start college. He wondered if he could take the finals even if he did get the job, but then he remembered the sign in the window of *Schraft's Candies*, where the fancy uptown ladies met for a lunch of tiny sandwiches; the sign that read

DISHWASHER WANTED
COLLEGE GRADUATE PREFERRED

Four years of college to be a dishwasher? Daniel shook his head and decided in favor of the job even if he lost the whole semester.

As soon as his father came home Daniel was on him to try on his hat.

"V'at? Mine het? V'at for?

"I got a job."

Joe's tired eyes widened behind his glasses. "You got a job? Vunderful. V'at kind job?"

"Bank Messenger."

Joe nodded approvingly. "You need a het?" Joe took it off and held it out. "You got a het."

Eager, Daniel put it on. It fell over his eyes.

Joe laughed as he took off his coat and jacket.

But Daniel's sky had fallen. He spoke in a tortured voice as he lifted it off. "It doesn't fit, Pa."

"Ve'll fix it. Ve'll fix it.

"How?"

Joe started rolling up his shirtsleeve. "Everyt'ing can be fixed." He repeated it as he rolled up his other sleeve. "Put it away now, Denny. I vanna vash. I vanna eat." He turned toward the bathroom.

After dinner, Hannah cleared the dishes and wiped down the table. Joe brought his copy of *Der Tag* to the table. "Get da het, Denny."

Danny went to the hall closet for the hat.

At the table Joe tore the Classifieds page in half.

Daniel put the hat on the table and sat down to watch.

Joe measured the width of the sweatband with his thumb and made folds of the paper accordingly. "Everyt'ing can be fixed," he mused as he worked. He guessed at the length he needed and tore off the rest. He tucked the folds under the sweatband and triumphantly handed it to his son. "Now try it, Deniel."

Daniel put it on. It sat high on his head like a comedian's costume His agony of being doomed to fail was in his voice. "It's too small, Pa."

"Ve'll fix it. Ve'll fix it." soothed Joe. He retrieved the newspaper stuffing, undid three thicknesses and tore them off. He replaced it and handed the hat to Daniel.

Daniel put it on. It fit. With a whoop he hurried to the full-length mirror in the hall.

Joe followed.

Daniel gleefully tried on the hat at different angles. He even turned the whole brim down instead of just the front.

Pleased that he had solved the problem for his son, Joe chuckled at Danny's theatrical shenanigans. "Not like det, Denny."

"I know, I know, Pa. I'm only acting." Daniel squinted his eyes and mugged an angry face. "Edward G. Robinson," he said, and pointed a gun-like thumb and index finger at the mirror. "Yeah, ya rat, da las time you double-cross Al Capone. Bam!"

Joe laughed, turned and walked toward the kitchen.

"Thanks, Pa," Danny called out. He returned the hat to the closet shelf and followed his father.

Joe sat at the table opening the rest of *Der Tag*.

About to sit down, Daniel saw the paper scraps on the table. "Oh my God!" he whispered. Aghast, he froze above his chair.

Startled, Joe put down the paper. "Vat, vat is it?"

Hannah turned from the sink, questioning.

Daniel pointed to the scraps covered with the Yiddish Alphabet. "It's Jewish."

Hannah asked, "So?"

"Of course it's Jewish," affirmed Joe, "it's from *Der Tag*."

"It can't be Jewish, I mean, it mustn't be Jewish. What if someone looks under the sweatband and finds a Jewish paper?"

"What mustn't be Jewish?" Hannah asked.

"I can't be Jewish for this job."

Joe's face clouded. "You can't be Jewish fa dis job?"

"No, Pa, they won't hire me. They hate Jews."

Joe jumped up and yelled, "Tell dem to go to Hell!"

Daniel backed away from his father's anger but pleaded, "Pa, Pa, I won't get the job."

Joe swung an arm erasing Daniel's plea. "I dun't care."

Daniel pleaded his case. "Pa, Pa, it's a job."

"Not anudder void, Denny. I'm you fodda." He swung his fist down and banged the tabletop.

Joe ended the argument but Daniel stifled his tears and fought on, thrusting verbally at his father. "If you did it why can't I do it, Pa?"

Joe, not comprehending, stared. "Vat? Vat did I do?"

"You said you were Christian so you could work. Why can't I do it?"

Daniel saw his father's mouth open, but the sounds didn't follow. Instead, Joe's stubby index finger touched his chest then stretched out to point at a vague angle. "You're ... you're talking about Kurland? Back den? Under the Czar? You t'ink it's the same? *Pisher*, (kid) you don't know. Here, ve don't hev pogroms. Your *zaydeh* (grandfather) raised me to be a good Jew. He cried ven Uncle Herschel said the only way I could learn a trade was to be a Christian. To voik I had to be Christian. So I learned. I learned Jesus. And I learned the trade. In two years instead of three. But dey found out I vas a Jew and I had to run for my life. And in America--" Joe's head waggled with his remembered success and prosperity. Joe smiled, glad to tell his son what America gave to their family. "I sent you and Seymour to camp. And violin lessons and piano lessons and a fine apartment on Ocean Parkway with the best furniture and your mother's fine dresses. So ve lost it. Everybody lost it. The millionaires are still jumping out windows. But not Joe Reinerman. I'll make it again. And here ..." he pointed emphatically to the floor between him and Daniel, "...I can be a Jew and do it."

Joe waggled his finger at Daniel. "You don't hev to lie like I did. Dis is America, Denny."

"So why don't they want Jews?"

Joe's gesture swiped the offending gentiles away. "Dunces. Dey don't know any better. Dere are udder jobs."

"No, there aren't."

"So you'll work with me in the store."

"What store?"

"Ven I get it. The shoe store."

"Pa, we need money now."

Joe stamped his foot and shook his stubby body angrily. "Don't you t'ink I know dat? I'll get it. I'll get it."

Hannah spoke up. "When, Joe, when?"

Joe whirled. "You, too? I'll get it. I'll get it."

Daniel couldn't yield his job. "It's not different, Pa."

"It *is* different."

"Have you read the ads, Pa; Christian Only, in the *New York Times?*"

"Dey don't kill Jews in America."

"No, they starve them."

"Dere are udder jobs."

No, there aren't"

Joe banged the table again. "No, Denny, in America you're a Jew. Dot's it."

Danny ran to his room, slammed the door and flung himself on the bed.

Seymour came home late from his evening class and woke Daniel. "Put your pajamas on and go to sleep."

Daniel changed, but before settling down for the night, without saying anything to Seymour, he set the alarm to ring on soft for 4:30 a.m.

At 4:30 the alarm buzzed. Daniel shut it off and slipped out of bed carefully to avoid waking Seymour. He took a page of the *New York Times* out of the wastebasket, gathered his clothes and went into the kitchen but did not turn on the light. He put an egg and a slice of bread on the radiator to warm. He washed and dressed in the bathroom then got his father's fedora from the hall closet. In the kitchen he took out the Jewish paper from under the sweatband and substituted the *Times*. For breakfast, he chewed on the bread and slowly drank the warmed egg.

Wearing the fedora he tiptoed to the hall closet and put on his coat. Finished, he turned to look at himself in the mirror. Pleased with his white shirt, tie and jacket appearance, he smiled, touched the turned down brim front of the hat, waved to his image and whispered, "Hi, fella."

Excitement swelled in his chest as he stepped toward the door. Without a sound he unlocked it and stepped outside. He closed the door softly behind him.

CHAPTER 36

1934

In the First National Bank of Manhattan, Daniel leaned across Mr. Silverwell's desk and handed him the information form from the Acorn Employment Agency. Daniel stood, hat in hand, while the personnel manager glanced at the paper.

Almost immediately, Mr. Silverwell's blue eyes looked up to inspect Daniel's. They were brown. The personnel manager wished that Anderson had sent him another blonde haired, blue-eyed candidate for the position, but he had to admit that this youngster's being in college in these chaotic times weighed well against undesirable physical characteristics. This youngster had serious intentions, ambition.

Forced to stand and wait, Daniel thought he'd walked into a Hollywood movie and was being interviewed by the white-haired actor, Charles Coburn. Mr. Silverwell had that soft, fatherly look except when the hard blue eyes attempted to look into and search Daniel's mind. His pressed gray suit was impeccable, as was his starched white shirt and wine-colored tie. Everything about him seemed perfect. The leather corners of his desk blotter were beautifully scrolled in gold. Daniel touched the knot of his own tie to make sure it was in the center of his collar.

Though hesitant, Mr. Silverwell decided to accept Daniel for the job. His runner had quit two days ago to join the CCC and documents had piled up. "Sit down, Daniel."

"Thank you." Daniel sat on the chair in front of the desk.

"The bank is open for customers from ten to three. Your hours are from eight to five, Monday through Friday."

Getting the job caused such turmoil in Daniel's head he was afraid he wouldn't hear what was being said to him. Daniel nodded, not only to show that he understood, but that he was agreeable to whatever the conditions of work were.

"Can you be here by eight o'clock in the morning?"

"Oh yes, sure."

"Good. Your pay is three dollars a day. However, the first two weeks we take off three dollars for the agency fee. Payday is Friday. Your wages will start from today, Wednesday."

Daniel nodded, trusted his voice. "Yes, sir."

"Can you start now?"

"Sure, Mr. Silverwell."

Mr. Silverwell reached for the thin portable file carrier on the far side of his desk. Inside were sealed manila mailers, each with a white slip clipped to it. "These are documents that have to be delivered to various financial institutions. They are arranged in order, from the top down. The directions are on the white slips."

Daniel nodded with mounting excitement.

Mr. Silverwell opened a drawer, took out a flat gray steel box with one hand, and a fountain pen from his inside breast pocket with the other. He wrote smoothly on a petty cash form, then offered the paper and pen to Daniel and took a dollar from the box. "You will get a dollar each day for subway and trolley fares. When you finish delivering these you'll report to Mrs. Hogan. Return any change to her. From now on, she will be your dispatcher. She will also give you your pay at the end of the week."

Nodding, Daniel signed the petty cash slip and nervously fumbled the dollar into the money slit of his wallet. He looked at the first white slip. Familiar with the subways from his job-hunting forays, he understood the directions, slipped the paper into the pocket of his coat and returned the sealed mailers to the folder. He suddenly felt familiar with what had to be done. For three weeks he'd sat next to Jack Saunders on the liquor truck, arranging the pile of white slips on his lap, as they delivered cases of liquor to tavern after tavern.

Unused to coping with a hat, Daniel dropped it as he stood up. He retrieved it and took the folder of mailers under his arm. "Thank you, sir," he said.

Mr. Silverwell's lips compressed and he nodded curtly.

Daniel headed across the polished-marble lobby floor toward the large, carved wooden doors that kept the noisy world from disturbing the precisely considered transactions of the bank. He didn't feel his feet walking.

Outside, the precious folder locked underneath one arm, he pulled his hat down against the icy wind, dug his hands into his coat pocket and strode toward the BMT subway. Gleefully he squeezed the pacquet of mailers, hugging himself at the same time. *$15 A WEEK! $15 A WEEK!* He flew down the subway stairs, changed the dollar at the change booth, dropped a nickel in the turnstile and breezed through.

When the train thundered into the station Daniel felt that it roared out his triumph.

He made his eight deliveries and returned to the bank at 1:30 with the signed copies.

Mrs. Hogan had four more deliveries for him. She was an attractive woman, in her late thirties. She had married into one of Manhattan uptown's better families but her loving Jason de Witt turned out to be an incurable alcoholic. Ten years of personal misery and social embarrassments left her no option but divorce.

Daniel thought her eyes seemed sad. Her pince-nez glasses that held themselves on the bridge of her nose intrigued Daniel. Without the usual frames, he kept expecting them to fall off. Her dark brown hair, showing traces of gray, was caught loosely in a bun. Her finely printed blouse, buttoned up to the middle of her neck, seemed a pedestal for the tilt of her head. She sat at a desk about ten feet from the entrance to Mr. Silverwell's office, creating her own executive space. Daniel thought she was pretty, but formal looking, like a schoolteacher.

"Did you have any difficulties, Daniel?" She asked him as she accepted the signed copies.

He was surprised at the warmth in her voice. He liked her immediately. "No, Mrs. Hogan. Everything went fine."

"Good. Here are four more. Do you have enough change?"

"Yes."

"Did you stop and have lunch?"

"Lunch? A ... no. I was anxious to get through."

"Well, you mustn't skip lunch, Daniel. Stop for a sandwich."

"Yes, M'am." Daniel was grateful. He hadn't given himself permission to take the time. He was starved.

Mrs. Hogan walked with him to the front door. "If you return after three, the front door will be locked. There is a bell at the side," she said, pointing. "Push it and I'll open the door for you."

Daniel nodded and left.

His first delivery being in the Times Square area, he stopped at Chock Full 'O Nuts for a nineteen-cent, cream cheese-and-nut sandwich and a five-cent orange drink.

When Daniel returned to the bank at a quarter to four, Mrs. Hogan took him downstairs into the filing room and explained the alphabetical filing system for the stack of transacted forms. "This is where you will work until five," Mrs. Hogan explained. "And if you do this as well as you do your deliveries, Daniel, we'll move you up to the next step."

Excited and happy, Daniel turned to look at her, meeting her warm smile with a shy smile of his own. Surprising him, still smiling, she touched his face with her warm hand and held it there for a moment exciting Daniel's hormones. Her hand moved to his shoulder and slid down his arm, to make even clearer her sign of approval. Daniel was sorry she had to leave.

At five o'clock she looked in on him. "That's all, Daniel," her voice sang quietly, "time to go home."

Daniel walked with her to the front door where the tellers bundled in coats against the weather were waiting to be let out. Mrs. Hogan unlocked the front door. She exchanged good nights with them as they left. Outside, they scattered like peas let out of the pod, tightening mufflers, gloved hands holding on to their hats against the whip of the wind as they hurried to transportation.

Thursday morning there was a larger pile of deliveries. Mrs. Hogan gave Daniel two dollars from petty cash for his train and trolley fares. "And don't forget to stop for lunch, Daniel," she said sweetly.

"No, M'am, I won't. Thank you."

Daniel felt that she liked him. Thrilled to know that he was succeeding, he bounced out of the bank toward the subway.

John Anderson of the Acorn Employment Agency usually checked an applicant's references before sending him out on a job interview. However, Thomas Silverwell, a very important client of the agency, had been suddenly left without a runner. The kid, Andrew Clancy, had been accepted into the CCC, the Civilian Conservation Corps and had left the bank without giving notice.

Stunned and upset, Mrs. Hogan had asked Clancy when she gave him his last pay envelope, "Why the CCC, Andrew?"

"Free meals and clothing," he replied, "and thirty dollars a month."
As he went with her to get his pay he added, "And out of the crummy
tenement my mother lives in with six kids." And Andrew was gone.

Of all the applicants for the position of bank runner, John Anderson
thought Daniel Reinerman the most likely. He seemed straightforwardly
honest, intelligent and pleasant. And important client, Silverwell, had
agreed with Anderson's choice by hiring Daniel.

On Thursday, Anderson made calls to check Daniel's references. Yes,
he was a student at Brooklyn College. Yes, he'd worked on the truck for
the Griffler Wine and Liquor Company during Christmas vacation. But
the Webster Avenue Presbyterian Church had no 'Reinerman' family in
its congregation.

"Are you sure?" Anderson asked the secretary.

"I'll look again, Mr. Anderson, and I'll also look under new
members."

Anderson waited, drumming his fingers.

"No," she finally answered, "no 'Reinerman'."

Dazed, terrible thoughts were spinning in Anderson's head. *Is the kid a
Jew? If so how the hell did he get past me? I can spot the kikes a mile away.*

Wait, Anderson reasoned to himself, *maybe the kid's name is 'Reinerman'
and the family's name is something else.* Anderson pulled Daniel Reinerman's
application and checked. No, it didn't say anything about another family
name.

Anderson decided to call the Reinerman house.

Hannah answered. "Hello."

"Is this Mrs. Reinerman?"

"Yes."

"Mrs. Reinerman, this is the Jewish National Fund calling."

"Ye-es?"

"We're at the beginning of the year, and the beginning of our campaign
for Palestine-- "

"Wait. Wait, young man. I don't like to interrupt you, but, unfortunately,
this year, we are not in a position to make a donation."

"I'm sorry to hear that. Have you made donations in the past?"

"Of course. We were big givers. We sat in the hundred dollar seats in
the Metropolitan Opera. I played cards every Tuesday for Hadassah."

"Thank you for your time, Mrs. Reinerman."

Sharp-witted Anderson hung the receiver, but didn't release it.
Paralyzed by both fury and fear he didn't know what next to do. The

Council of Financiers favored his Acorn Employment Agency because he guaranteed them that he'd screen perfectly for White Protestants. If he told Silverwell that he'd blundered, John Anderson's name would be wiped off the Council's list of the twenty-two banks that utilized his services. Immobilized, Anderson imagined himself fleeing out the door and down the squeaky steps as the building collapsed behind him.

But what if I don't say anything to Silverwell, he asked himself, feeling like a lemming trying to avoid the inevitable? *But then I'd always worry that Silverwell might find out the damned kid is a sheenie. I'd be dropped for incompetence, stupidity or lying. Maybe,* he thought hopefully, *the kid is a lousy worker and he'll get fired anyway.*

Anderson picked up the receiver and gave the operator Silverwell's number.

Mrs. Hogan answered.

"How are you, Mrs. Hogan? ... That's good. Is Mr. Silverwell there?"

"Just a moment, John."

Silverwell came on. "Yes, John."

"Hello, Tom. How are you?"

"Fine. What's on your mind?"

"Just checking to see how the new boy is working out."

"Excellent choice, John. I hope we can keep him."

Despite the sick feeling in his gut, John plunged in.

"I...I've run into a...a slight problem about him."

"Oh. What's that?" The disappointment was very clear in Silverwell's voice.

"He lied about being a member of the Webster Avenue Presbyterian Church."

"Didn't you know that before you sent him over?"

"I usually check references, Tom before sending someone out, but you were in such a hurry. He seemed able and pleasant."

"Yes, he is, John, able and intelligent. Mrs. Hogan said, " '...one of the best we've had'."

"Well, I ... I'm glad that he's working out well."

"I'm glad you checked anyway, John. That's what we pay you for."

"Yes. Yes sir."

"Is he a member of *any* church?"

"I don't think so, Tom." Anderson waited anxiously in the pause.

"Well," Silverwell began softly, "a lot of our youngsters don't attend church regularly. Maybe, when I get to know him better, I can get him to do that."

"Yes, well, all right. I...I'm glad he's working out. 'Bye."

" 'Bye, John."

Feeling sick, Anderson slumped in his chair. His pain exploded. "Damn!" His fist thumped the desk. "That f ----- Jew!" He bounced up. "Slimy kike!" Anderson didn't know what next to do, but he did know that he must have a replacement ready. He opened his door. "Priscilla!" he called sharply.

His secretary jumped. "Yes, Mr. Anderson."

"Come in here, please." Anderson walked behind his desk trying to calm himself.

Sitting down, he blew out air and then spoke to Priscilla. "Find me a blue-eyed, blonde-haired applicant for bank runner. No, find three of them. Have them fill out applications and be ready for interviews."

"Yes, Mr. Anderson."

"Drop everything else. Do this first."

"Yes, sir."

While he waited for the applications, he tortured himself over what to do about Reinerman. Even if Silverwell never found out about Reinerman, Anderson couldn't leave him on the job. That damned Jew had gotten the best of him. Anderson had to get rid of him. Not only for personal vengeance, but the financial structure of his agency was endangered. If word got out that he had let a Jew slip by him he was through.

An hour later, he was checking references of three applicants who had aryan-looking characteristics. He chose the best two of the three for interviewing and phoned Silverwell.

"Hello, Tom, I've done some further checking on the Reinerman kid ... you know how thorough we are, and the news I'm afraid, is not good. The 'little' problem is a 'big' problem. I think you'll want to make a change."

Anderson took advantage of Silverwell's confused silence to impress the banker with his agency's astuteness. "I have two absolutely sound candidates, either one of whom will serve you well. You can interview them as soon as you wish--"

"Wait a minute, John. What did you find out about Reinerman?"

Anderson lowered his voice. "He's a Hebe."

"WHAT! How the hell did you make such a mistake?"

"Tom, I'm sorry. You know it's never happened before--"

"Don't you ever, *ever,* send me anyone without checking references. DAMMIT! That's what we depend on you for!"

"Yes Sir. It will never happen again. I have two excellent applicants--"

"Let me talk to my dispatcher. I'll call you back."

Silverwell phoned Mrs. Hogan's desk. "Jennifer, will you step in for a moment."

"Yes, Tom."

Closing the door behind her, Mrs. Hogan was surprised to see that Silverwell's bland pallor had turned pink and his mouth moved in angry spasms. He swung his chair to face her. "We have a problem with that Reinerman kid, Jennifer."

"A problem? He's one--"

Silverwell held up his hand and stopped her. Though they were in the privacy of his office, he lowered his voice. "The damn kid's a Jew!"

Mrs. Hogan acted as if he'd struck her. She went white and groped for the arm of her chair. "Oh, my God!" When she recovered she asked, "How did that happen, Tom?"

"Anderson didn't check references until after we'd hired him. His excuse was that we were in a hurry."

"We were, Tom, but not that much of a hurry."

"John's got two replacements. I'd like you to sit in on the interviews with me."

"Of course, Tom."

They sat, silently defending themselves against their defeat.

Mrs. Hogan finally said, her lips tight with anger, "they're trying to rule the world. Henry Ford was right after all."

Silverwell recovered. "Well, it's the first time we lost a skirmish. And we can correct it almost instantly. It's only one more day. Let him finish the week. We'll start clean again on Monday."

"I'll take care of it, Tom."

"And I'll set up the interviews for today."

"Fine. I'll be available."

Daniel returned to the bank at two forty-five. Mrs. Hogan was not at her desk. He looked for her at the various teller stations, but did not see her. After he waited a while, she came out of Mr. Silverwell's office with an angry look on her face. She turned toward her desk and saw Daniel. Her chin went up in a haughty gesture that distanced him from her.

Daniel was surprised and wondered what had happened to her.

Without taking the time to sit, she picked up three manila envelopes and handed them to him. "If you finish after four, you needn't return to the bank. I'll see you in the morning."

"Yes, m'am." Daniel put the mailers into his folder and left, feeling sorry for Mrs. Hogan's unhappiness. He vaguely wondered why she didn't mention the filing.

Friday was a busy day for Daniel. Banks try to tie up unfinished business before the weekend. A second batch of deliveries was ready for him on Mrs. Hogan's desk when he returned after lunch although she wasn't there. Daniel popped the envelopes into his folder and was off again.

Friday was payday! His first payday! The thought of getting his first paycheck buoyed him as he walked. He rode the trolleys and trains to his deliveries counting the dollars he'd earned, and how much more he would earn in the weeks to come. He wondered whether it would be cash or a check. No matter. Nine Dollars! And Mrs. Hogan liked his work. He had a job!

At four-fifteen, he returned to the bank and rang the outside bell.

Mrs. Hogan opened the tiny panel to see who it was. Daniel heard the lock click. He depressed the handle, pulled the heavy door open and followed Mrs. Hogan to her desk.

Mrs. Hogan sat down and with one of the keys from her ring, opened the top right drawer. She thumbed through sealed envelopes, selected the one marked 'Daniel Reinerman' and handed it to him. Her face was unyielding. "Your pay."

Daniel's face lit up. "Thank you!" he breathed, as he took it. He pointed toward the filing room entrance.

"That won't be necessary," Mrs. Hogan said with quiet firmness. "You're free to go."

"Oh, thank you." Holding his envelope, Daniel took one step back. "Well, good night."

Mrs. Hogan said nothing. Gave him only the curtest nod.

Daniel, too excited over his pay to wonder about Mrs. Hogan's severity, turned away. As he walked toward the door, he slid the pay envelope into the breast pocket of his jacket.

On the subway platform Daniel was swept into the train with the rush hour jam, but he didn't mind. Holding on to a pole he secretly bounced up and down on his toes, responding to some inner song. Despite the crush of people in the train, Daniel slipped a hand inside his jacket and fingered the smooth pay envelope. Feeling giddy, almost silly, he smiled. What a prize to bring home!

When the crowd of people on the train thinned out he swayed from the toes of one foot to the toes of the other, as he used to do as part of his warm up before a soccer game. His young body had responded to his three days of walking to deliver the bank papers by building his energy and muscle.

The doors opened for the 18th Avenue station near Bensonhurst and Daniel hurried along the snow-patched platform toward the stairs. He was almost running when he reached the duplex five blocks away. He flew up the stairs. The tang of fish baked in lemon juice smelled good. "Ma, Ma! Are you home?"

"I'm in the kitchen."

"Money, Ma, money!" Daniel danced into the kitchen waving the envelope.

Hannah turned from the stove and watched Daniel tear open the envelope. As he took out the one-dollar bills and handed them to his mother with a "Here, Ma", a piece of white paper fluttered to the floor.

"Only three dollars?" his mother asked.

Daniel, bending to pick up the slip of paper, stopped and looked up at her. "Three dollars?" He checked the bills in his mother's hands. "Not a five?" He looked at his mother. "No, all singles. Only three?" he questioned again, disbelieving.

Confounded by the small amount Daniel walked the kitchen trying to understand it. Slowly he understood that Silverwell took out the two weeks of agency fees all at once. Puzzled and deflated, he explained the arithmetic to his mother.

"You dropped something," Hannah reminded him.

"Yeah," Daniel said, and bent to pick up the small square of paper.

It was printed at the top in flowery script, 'From the desk of Thomas Silverwell'. Below the delicate line that divided the heading from the message, in the beautifully clear penmanship of Mrs. Hogan, Daniel read, 'Your services are no longer required as of the date above.'

Thomas Silverwell per J.H.'

Daniel straightened up slowly, his eyes glued to the paper. He read it silently twice more and then began muttering to better understand it. " '...

no longer required, as of ... *today!'* " Daniel groaned, then called out for help. "Ma! I'm *fired!*"

"Fired? You just got it."

Daniel turned as if to ask Mrs. Hogan 'Why?' Then realized she wasn't there and he no longer had access to her. Never would have again. Tears welled in his eyes. He turned and walked slowly out of the kitchen toward his room. He had long since given up expecting to have emotional access to his mother ... or to Seymour ... or his father. Getting the job on his own, and losing it, told him again that he didn't have anyone else's shoulder to cry on but his own.

CHAPTER 37

1934

After they moved into Bessie's apartment Hannah and the boys straightened out their things as well as they could in the spaces they were allotted. Hannah was surprised to find that the room layout of the apartment was originally a replica of a tenement railroad flat like where she had grown up on the Lower East Side. But this one had been completely refurbished and a full bathroom had been installed. Farthest from the entrance, Bessie had the only private room in the apartment. After passing the spaces occupied by Hannah on one side and the boys on the other, a door opened into Bessie's room. When the door was closed she and her friend Harry Zelinka, a fellow insurance agent could talk undisturbed.

But Hannah had no door to close off her space, nor did the boys. Their beds and hanging clothing were up for viewing to anyone walking through the hallway from the apartment entrance to Bessie's room.

Hannah gave the boys the larger of the two spaces her family occupied. But in her smaller space her double bed took up most of the area and made it difficult to get to her closet. She debated exchanging it for a twin bed, but the single bed would remind her that she was alone and would remain alone. With the double bed, even though the other side was empty, there was hope that some day Joe would be there to fill it. She decided to leave it and wrestle with it as is.

Living in Bessie's apartment Hannah felt torn up by the roots from what she once had. She also realized that she woke every day feeling further uncertain and edgy about what Bessie might ask her to change in her cleaning or cooking routines. *The apartment has to look as Bessie wants. The soup has to be spiced as Bessie likes.* And when Bessie's friend Harry joined them for dinner Bessie told Hannah not to use peppery spices because Harry had a delicate stomach.

This can't be a permanent arrangement for us, Hannah thought. *If not, what next?* Hannah worried what might happen to her if Joe continued to be unable to find work.

Even though communication was not Joe's chief asset, he phoned Hannah two months after she moved in with Bessie to see how things were going for her and the boys.

"It's all right, Joe. It's a place. It's not like having your own, but … it's a place."

After a moment Hannah asked, "And you, Joe, what did you find?"

"I hev a room mit da Svetloffs. He's from Kurland too. I met him in the synagogue. He's a *fromme* (a religious one). He goes every Saturday, winter and summer. They're nice. She invites me for dinner once in a while."

"You're working, Joe?"

"Yes, a day or two a week with Beulenberg."

"Every week?"

"No. For dat I need anodder flu epidemic."

"God forbid."

"I hev a liddle place. I make a few dollars."

"You have a shop?"

"It's not a shop … it's small. I hev a machine … I make a dollar here … a dollar dere.

And da boys?" Joe asked.

"They're fine, Joe. Daniel went to register again for college, and Seymour is still making $15 a week with Feigenbaum. He'll finish with his college soon."

"Good, good, Hannah." After a moment he added, "Ve're gonna be all right, Hannah, all right."

"If you say so, Joe." *But,* thought Hannah, *not if I have to stay at Bessie's.*

Joe repeated, "Yes, Hannah, it'll be all right."

"You have something in mind, Joe?"

"Alvays, alvays somet'ing, Hannah. Vat else? Nu, I'll call you again. Nice to talk mit you, Hannah."

"Good, Joe, I hope whatever it is, it works out. Nice to hear from you. Take care of yourself."

"I vill. You take care, too, Hannah."

"Thanks, Joe. 'Bye."

" 'Bye, Hannah."

They hung up.

CHAPTER 38

1934

Getting fired from the bank solved one problem for Daniel. He returned to Brooklyn College, took his finals, passed and was eligible to register for his second semester. Monday he stood in the long line at the registration office wondering whether he should have stayed with Phil Cohen to work on the liquor truck. *Twelve dollars in my hands every week,* he thought, *what a good feeling.*

The line was moving slowly. Daniel leaned out to check on how many students were before him. He counted 11 then realized that guy number six was Bernie Posner who had been in his graduating class at Lincoln High. "Hey, Bernie," he called softly.

Bernie didn't hear.

Daniel called his name more loudly.

Bernie turned toward the voice and saw Daniel waving to him. Bernie waved back and pantomimed "Hi." He looked ahead then looked at Daniel, trying to make a decision. He decided to give up the few places to talk to Daniel.

He came back to stand in line with his ex-classmate. They shook hands, talked about the courses they were taking, and bemoaned the lousy economics all around them. Daniel talked about how his family had been broken up because his father had lost his business and couldn't find other work, that his mother and brother and he were sharing an apartment with a friend.

Bernie said that his family had broken up too; his mother and father had divorced. His father had a button and buckle-making shop and was sending a monthly allotment check to the family, but wasn't home any more.

Daniel went on with his dissertation about going to college being foolish because there were no jobs at the end of it—or only crap jobs

213

like dishwashing at *Schrafft's Candies*. He'd rather be working instead of studying for the next three years. Money was what his family needed.

Bernie hadn't decided on a major yet, but had no conflict about schooling for the next three years to get a degree. Evidently his family was not in dire need.

Bernie suddenly lit up and said, "Hey Danny, my father is looking for a delivery boy. I think he'd hire you."

"Really?"

"Yeah. Do you want it?"

"Yeah, yeah."

"His shop is in Manhattan, on 30th Street."

"Can we go there after we register?"

"Sure."

It took them another half-hour to sign up for the next semester. They hurried to the subway and rode across the bridge into Manhattan. They entered one of the many factory buildings on 30th Street and stepped onto a freight elevator. Bernie pulled the cord to start it and grabbed it again when they reached the third floor. They walked through a narrow, dimly lit corridor until they butted up to a dirt-smudged door marked Posner Mfg. Co in dulled yellow paint. They heard voices inside.

Bernie knocked.

A man's voice said, "Come in,"

Bernie pushed the heavy door open and the boys went in.

To Bernie's surprise his mother was there, stylishly dressed, so out of place in the dirty shop. A triangle fluff of a hat tilted forward past her hairline to point to the center of her forehead. She was tightly wrapped in a sleek fur coat against the January cold. Obviously she didn't intend to stay. She and her ex stood facing each other across a scrap table that held broken and outdated parts of small machinery.

Apparently the boys had interrupted some unpleasant dialogue between the divorcees. Both their faces showed restrained anger.

Surprised to see her there, Bernie greeted his mother. "Hello, Mom."

"Hello, Bernie."

Bernie turned toward his father, a big man in both height and width, his dress as sloppy looking as the loose fat on his body. Unshaven, the blackness of the lower half of his face stood out. The ends of an opened dark vest swung loosely over his white shirt, his tie knot was pulled away from his neck, his shirt collar unbuttoned. He looked like he'd slept in his clothes and hadn't washed yet.

Behind Posner a man sat at a table working at a foot press device making covered buttons. Fascinated by the man's rhythmic movements Daniel wanted to continue watching him but had to pay attention to the Posners, especially the boss.

"Hello, Dad," Bernie said, "This is my friend, Danny. He's interested in the delivery boy job."

Posner turned to look at Daniel. "Are you strong?"

Daniel smiled shyly. "Yes."

Mrs. Posner spoke to her son. "Bernie, I have to do some shopping at Macy's then we can go home together."

"Okay, Mom."

"Did you register, Bernie?"

"Yeah, yeah, Mom."

Bernie turned toward Danny.

"Good luck, Danny."

"Thanks."

Bernie and his mother left.

While they were leaving Daniel turned to observe the man working at the table operating a foot press machine. Sitting, he handled a removable die in a smooth sequence of right arm, left arm, foot press, left hand, foot press, right hand, foot press, and out popped a finished covered button. The process continued seemingly non-stop. It was like the man's hands were dancing. Three other foot press devices on the long table sat idle. Danny wished he could work one of them.

Posner saw Danny's interest in the button-making operation. "When you can make a gross of eighteen-acorn, covered buttons in an hour you're a button-maker." He said it like it would be impossible for a kid like Danny to make the grade. He topped it with a cynical snicker.

Captivated by the man's synthesis of movement, Daniel wanted to continue watching but he had to pay attention to Posner.

"You ready to work?"

"Uh ... yeah."

"You get $12 a week "

Danny agreed without hesitation. "Okay, what do I do?" He always carried in his head the bare bones of how much he needed to make so the family could live in their own apartment again. *With Seymour's $60 a month,* he thought, *we only need my dinky $48 and we could afford our own apartment again, even if Beulenberg doesn't call Pa back. But it'll take a while to make sure our jobs are really there.* Daniel hated the thought of their being evicted again. He was willing that they should stay at Bessie's, until they knew that their income would again at least pay the rent.

"What do I have to do?" He repeated it more strongly to Posner's back because he had turned and started to walk toward his office. Daniel guessed that he was supposed to follow to get his instructions.

A desk, a chair and an eight-foot couch with an unusually high back, upholstered in heavy-looking brown and red tweed furnished the oddly shaped space that Posner used as an office. On the couch were two shoeboxes securely tied together with cord.

Posner gestured toward the couch. "You'll take the buttons to *Styline Dresses* on 33rd Street," Posner said. Suddenly he spoke angrily. "Don't give them to anyone but Lily Becker. I want her to know she got her goods on time."

Daniel nodded. "Okay."

Posner offered Daniel a sheet of paper. "The address is on the invoice. *Styline Dresses.* Don't lose it."

"Right." Daniel folded the paper and put it in his coat pocket. He pushed his fingers under the knotted cord in the center of the box and lifted it. The heavy weight of it surprised him. Daniel didn't yet know that each button was made of a metal shell covered in the dress material and there were 2,000 buttons in each box. The weight cut into his fingers. He had left his gloves home. He hadn't expected to find a job, only to register at school.

Out in the cold he shifted the load from one hand to the other. By the time he reached the address his hands were red and swollen. It was a fairly modern building with a push button elevator. Stepping out on the second floor he landed in front of *Styline's* reception desk. A steady, thrumming noise of many machines greeted him from the wall behind the desk.

Daniel spoke to the receptionist with the telephone apparatus around her head. "I have a delivery for Lily Becker."

The receptionist fingered some buttons and spoke into the small hornlike mouthpiece in front of her face. "Delivery for you, Ms. Becker." She listened a moment then said to Daniel. "She's not available now. Leave it and I'll sign for it."

"I was told to give it personally to her."

The secretary repeated Daniel's message into the mouthpiece, listened to Becker's annoyed response and relayed it to Daniel. "Is it from Posner?"

"Yes," said Daniel.

"Yes, it is," she said into her mouthpiece.

She flinched at Becker's angry response. She looked up at Daniel. "She ... she'll be out in a minute."

Lily Becker swung the factory door open and stepped into the reception area. Lips rouged and eyes shadowed she strode with a flaring energy. She took a pencil from her bushy brown hair as she approached Daniel. "Where's the invoice?"

Daniel held it toward her.

Becker snatched it, laid it on the reception desk, scribbled on it and offered it back to Daniel.

"Thank you m'am." He said it to her back because she was on her way toward the factory.

*   *   *

Joe called Hannah twice more at two-month intervals to see how she and the boys were doing. All were well and Hannah had nothing new to report except that Daniel had left college and was working as a delivery boy for a button and buckle maker. But Hannah sounded sad which caused Joe to ask, "It isn't any better, Hannah?"

"What can be better, Joe? It's still Bessie's house. I only work for her."

"At least it vas a bargain. You could save something from vat the boys make."

"Money isn't everything, Joe."

"Everyt'ing's gonna be all right, Hannah."

"You always say that, Joe. Are you Moses the Prophet? You know the country will change? Even Roosevelt after three years couldn't make it different."

Even though Hannah's bitterness bothered him Joe decided to keep his secret a little longer. "Take care, Hannah and don't feel bad. It vill change. T'ings vill change."

"You have the word from the Man up there?"

"Who else?"

"Call me and let me know what He says."

"I vill, Hannah, I vill. Be vell. *Zai gezundt.* (Be well)

"You too, Joe, and remember to send me the good news from above."

"Yes, Hannah. Goodbye."

" 'Bye, Joe."

CHAPTER 39

1935

Seymour finally got his two-year BA certificate in June. Giddy with relief, balancing shakily on his new emotional plateau he couldn't help spilling his great news to his boss and he got a surprising response.

"Hooray," yelled Dave and clapped his-soon-to-be executive assistant on the shoulder. "Sy, dat's what I was waiting to hear."

Seymour blanked. "You were?"

"Yes, have you decided about McKee's Rocks?"

Puzzled, Seymour stared. "McKee's Rocks?"

"Yes, we talked."

"Oh, oh, oh, yes, we talked."

"You run the McKee's Rocks operation for me and Ben. Are we a go?"

Seymour stammered, flustered by the dramatic 180 his life would take. "Well ... I'll have to move ... live there ... a room in an Orthodox family's house maybe."

"You're religious?"

"Yeah."

"That's easy. They've got as many kinds of Jews there as here. Jews argue with each other about God the same way all over.

"How far is it?"

"I'll pay your traveling expenses and you'll get a weekly salary of ..." Dave paused, smiling, waiting for Seymour to ask.

Seymour was silent, until he realized Dave was making a game of it. "How ... how much Dave?"

"Twenty-five dollars a week! All living expenses will be paid the first month to help you get settled.

Seymour had to get past the excitement of earning so much money before he could discuss it rationally. He juggled the ingredients mentally, decided, and talked to Dave as if he were thinking out loud. "Yes, even if I'm in McKee's Rocks I can still give Ma ten dollars a week. Yeah ... yeah, Dave, I ... can go for it. When...?"

"Whenever you can wrap up things here and be ready to go."

Seymour finished his workday and got into the subway to go home. The train had hardly started when Seymour realized he had gotten on the wrong train. Even though Hannah and the boys had moved into Bessie's Manhattan apartment almost a year ago Seymour had still taken the express to Brooklyn. He was so excited about Dave's offer that he forgot they were now living in Manhattan. He exited the train at the next station and waited for the local back to 23rd Street.

When he got home and told his mother about his new job offer, Hannah had mixed feelings about Seymour's good news. More of her world would be slipping away from her. Her older son would be moving to the western part of Pennsylvania—but a good job with good pay, how could she object? At least it wasn't going to happen tomorrow.

She wished Joe would call. He was the one who could still hold some of her world together.

Finally Joe had everything arranged. He called Hannah. "This Sunday, Hannah, you and da boys hev a good breakfast and be ready to take a ride."

Astonished, Hannah repeated, "Take a ride? You bought a car, Joe?"

"Don't ask qvestions yet, Hannah. Be ready Sunday, ten o'clock I'll pick you up."

"All right, Joe, I'll see that the boys are ready."

At supper Hannah told the boys and, of course Bessie, who was also at the table. The boys asked all the questions Hannah couldn't answer. She found herself repeating, "Wait for Sunday. Wait for Sunday."

Bessie ate silently, fearing that her arrangement with Hannah was in danger. Since they had put nothing in writing, Hannah was free to leave at any time, though it could make for hard feelings on Bessie's part. Hannah did her job well, and Bessie could trust her friend. Where could she find an honest, competent stranger to do the job as well? But the experienced businesswoman had to admit to herself that change is inevitable and one has to ride a falling or rising tide of events as best as one can. Bessie left the table abruptly, went to her room, closed the door and called Harry to talk about it.

Sunday morning at nine Harry picked up Bessie and they left for the day. Bessie had decided she didn't want to be there when Joe showed up. The Reinerman family celebrating their togetherness once again could be bad news for her.

Joe arrived at ten o'clock. After the Hello-Pa hugs the boys rushed down the stairs to see what kind of car he had bought. Joe and Hannah followed. Hannah was all questions but Joe was not a talker and he was hard put to explain it all. Before getting into the car the four stood around on the sidewalk to get the story from Joe:

Five months ago two of Beulenberg's boot makers of many years retired and Beulenberg took Joe on as a permanent worker. Joe saved most of his salary and his account became sizeable enough for him to develop a plan, about which he only barely hinted in his phone calls to Hannah.

Joe stopped talking to suddenly throw up his arms. "In da car, everybody, ve go for a ride."

Joe drove over the bridge to Brooklyn. He left the main road, turned onto a back street and parked at the curb of a red brick apartment house.

Hannah and the boys looked around. Two women were bouncing the handles of their baby carriages as they stood and talked in the small setback that led to the building's entrance. A couple came out of the building and headed for their car at the curb in front of the Reinermans.

Joe's puzzled passengers looked at him for an explanation.

"Everybody out," was his response. He walked them through the entrance into the small lobby to the elevator. When the car arrived and all were in Joe pressed number three. On the third floor Joe led them across the white tiled floor to a door with 307 painted on it. Underneath the number a card with the name Reinerman printed on it had been slipped into its metal frame.

Daniel pointed to the card. "Our name!"

The secret was out. Joe had rented an apartment for his family.

Hannah felt faint with excitement, more so when Joe handed her the key and said proudly, "Open it, Hannah."

Hannah excitedly fumbled with the key and the lock while Joe and the boys eagerly waited. Finally she unlocked the door. Dazed, his family entered disbelieving their good fortune. Their family had been blown in and out of apartments by one eviction and another, yet had landed, incredibly, safely in port. Standing inside the apartment they thought of Papa's steady job that would let them be able to relax here without further worry of eviction notices.

Joe couldn't help snickering and chuckling to himself as he watched Hannah, Danny and Seymour hurrying from one room to another to prove to themselves the apartment was real, and really theirs. Joe suddenly had a flashback of kicking violently to knock Vanya off him, running past the muscular Igor, out the attic door and down the stairs of Yarinevitch's house. He knew he wanted to go on, always go on. In America three bankruptcies had stopped him, but he continued to have faith in his skills and did find someone who wanted them. "Nu, Hannah," Joe said proudly, "Ve staht all over."

Daniel and Seymour grinned. The boys felt a new appreciation of their father's dogged determination to succeed despite the fact that the worst depression in American history had thrown twenty-five million workers from their jobs onto the streets, and still raged all around them.

Yes, Papa could do small but important things for them, like finding a way to make his hat fit Danny's head, or direct Seymour to look for a job with *Princess Shoes,* or finally agreeing with Hannah about moving to a five-room apartment when they had the money. But best of all, he gave his family a place to live despite the Depression, dictated by the beliefs engrained in him. He provided a comfort for his family that neither Hannah, Seymour, or Danny had felt during the last five years.

For the next twenty-nine years Joe Reinerman employed his shoemaking skills with Beulenberg until two weeks before his death from lung cancer at age seventy-five.